STRATEGIC

BOOK 5

MANEUVERS

ALASKAN SECURITY-TEAM ROGUE

Jemma WESTBROOK

Strategic Maneuvers, book 5 in the Alaskan
Security-Team Rogue series.
Copyright 2020 by Jemma Westbrook.
www.jemmawestbrook.com

First printing, 2020
Cover design by Robin Harper at Wicked by
Design

CHAPTER 1

THE ROOM WAS too cool.

"Where would I find the thermostat?" Pierce scanned the enclosed space from his spot in the corner, looking over the same four walls he'd been staring at for two hours.

The physician hovering over Zeke slowly turned his way, one brow lifting.

"It needs to be warmer in here." Pierce stood from the horribly uncomfortable chair he'd occupied since his arrival at GHOST headquarters.

The doctor turned away, going back to checking Zeke's blood pressure. "The temperature is just fine."

"He was submerged in freezing water." Pierce stepped toward the most current issue he was facing. "How do you expect to warm him in a room that's like a refrigerator?"

Zeke needed to wake up and he needed to wake up soon. There was too much on the line for him to continue lying there like he was.

The doctor turned to face him, not a hint of hesitation or uncertainty in his cool gaze as he repeated himself. "His temperature is just fine."

"Then why, might I ask, is he still unconscious?" Pierce tucked one hand into his pocket, running the pad of his thumb over the item inside it, reciting the lines he said to himself a hundred times a day now in an attempt to stop the past from returning.

And in an attempt to convince himself it hadn't already arrived.

One slow inhale.

A slow exhale to follow.

"He is still unconscious because we sedated him." The physician smirked. "Men like him don't appreciate being out of control."

Pierce scanned the physician from head to toe.

If he only knew.

"Be that as it may," Pierce turned from the doctor's cocky smile, taking slow steps across the small room to put a little distance between them, "there is information I need to ascertain from him, and in order to accomplish that, I need him to be awake."

It was the only reason he was willing to come here. He would get what he wanted.

And offer them what they asked in return.

Whatever that may be.

"He'll wake up when he wakes up. You can't control when that happens."

Pierce stopped, his gaze slowly leveling on where Zeke laid. His skin was pale, but the color was beginning to return to his cheeks. His breathing was slow and even. That of a man who slept well and deep.

Unfortunately for him, this was not the time for sleeping.

Pierce turned to fully face the man carrying more secrets than he cared to consider, staring down his unconscious face.

A few heartbeats later Zeke sucked in a deep breath, his eyes flying open as his entire body tensed.

Pierce turned toward the doctor, this time with a smirk of his own. "You may close the door on your way out."

Normally he would attempt to behave in a way that wouldn't risk severing the potential ties that could be formed today. He'd learned long ago connections were many times the only thing that saved you.

Normally he would be polite and appreciative and considerate.

He would be the man he worked so hard to show the people around him. The people who never knew the man he once was.

But he'd also learned that many times connections were the thing that ruined you.

Zeke held Pierce's gaze as the doctor left, the on-site physician for GHOST closing the door harder than necessary on his way out.

"I understand you saved Heidi."

Zeke didn't answer, but his stare didn't waver.

"As a thank you, I will respect your condition." Pierce's thumb warmed as it worked across the small bit of smooth surface on the item in his pocket, the drag creating more friction with each pass. "However…"

"What do you want from me, Pierce?"

"I want," keeping his words even and relaxed was almost painful at this point, "to know what the *fuck* is going on."

Zeke's brows barely lifted, the slow motion sending Pierce's hand to a fist in his pocket.

The urge to punish Zeke was strong. Show the lead of Shadow who was in charge.

Who made the decisions when Alaskan Security and all it protected were involved. "You took Heidi and Shawn from headquarters."

Zeke kidnapped them. Stole them in broad daylight.

"They almost died because you believe you can do anything you wish."

"They almost died because of *you*." Zeke's tone was so sure. So certain.

Pierce's breath stalled. "I'm to believe it's my fault you took them off-site to a supposedly non-existent location before driving them straight into the Chena River?"

"It's your fault I had to do it." Zeke glanced at the rails along the sides of his bed, reaching out to press one of the many buttons. The mechanical whir of a motor cut through the silence dragging out between them. The bed under his upper half began to angle up, raising Zeke to a sitting position. "They're after you."

His body stilled as every inch of him rejected the thought.

The potential truth it held.

"I'm the owner of Alaskan Security. Of course they're after me." His company was standing in the way of whatever goals the men attempting to take it down had. That was all.

Zeke eyed him. "You talked to Vincent yet?"

"Only to make the deal that brought me here." He was willing to do whatever it took to end this. Even find his way to beds he might never make it out of.

Zeke's eyes narrowed. "You made a deal with Vincent?"

"You left me no choice." Pierce pulled the hand from his pocket, forcing his fingers to lay loose at his side. "You put me in a position where I can't win."

"I don't think you understand the position you're actually in, Pierce."

"And *you* do?" It was easy to believe you understood things from the outside looking in. So easy to question a man's actions. To know you would do something differently.

Better.

It was clearly what Zeke believed and he'd acted on that belief, putting both Heidi and Shawn, along with Alaskan Security, in danger.

"I know enough to understand things aren't what they seem."

"Lovely." He didn't have time for this. Pierce turned for the door. "Best of luck with your future endeavors."

Zeke snorted behind him. "God you're a prick."

Piece paused at the door, staring ahead at the solid plane.

The color.

The texture.

Focusing on anything but the swell of rage tugging at the control he held so tightly.

He reached for the knob, the sound of the latch as it worked evidence of how far he'd come in his life.

It wasn't so long ago he wouldn't have walked away from the insult.

From the punishment that deserved to be doled out.

The hall was empty when he stepped into it.

Seemed empty.

Pierce glanced toward the camera tucked into one corner and waited.

"Get what you were hoping for?"

He didn't turn toward the voice at his back. "You know I didn't."

Vincent's steps were even and measured as they came closer. "I can't say I'm surprised." He didn't pause as he reached Pierce's side. "Come on."

The order grated on the deepest parts of him, digging into old wounds and buried bones. "And where is it you wish for me to go?"

Vincent stopped, turning toward where Pierce still stood. "If you want to have this conversation here we can." He looked up and down the hall. "But I assumed you wanted a little more privacy."

Vincent was older than Pierce. Mid-forties. Maybe fifty, but years of government work made it difficult to tell from mannerisms or speech.

Because they all acted the same. Cool. Calm.

Detached.

That was what made them different from him. The ability to separate their feelings from their actions.

Pierce eyed the camera in the corner, hiding it with the pass of a sweeping gaze and a sigh intended to project frustration. "Fine."

He allowed Vincent to lead him down the hall and through a set of double doors into another, more narrow hall. At the end they made another turn, one that put them at the back corner of the large hub disguised as a warehouse. The head of GHOST opened the final door on the left, standing to one side as Pierce went in.

The office was large enough that it should feel spacious.

It did not.

The walls were lined with monitors, each connected to a different feed. Some displayed city streets. Some showed vacant buildings.

One fed to a camera outside Alaskan Security.

"I wouldn't think you would need a camera there considering how many men you have inside." Betrayal made the words sharper than they should be. He was always aware Zeke and his men all had a foot on different soil.

He just believed their allegiance leaned a certain way.

"You wouldn't think." Vincent rounded the desk in the center of the room, dropping into the chair behind it before motioning to the single office chair on the opposite side. "Yet here we are."

The comment didn't sit right.

Pierce eased down into the chair, carefully positioning himself into the relaxed pose he wore like the skin it was. "What is it you want from me, Vincent?"

Vincent was as known of a figure as any member of GHOST could be. His name was whispered in theories and discussions. Suggested when no other options existed. Maybe not by name, but by reputation.

The Hunter.

He was exactly as he sounded.

A hunter.

Not the hunted.

Not if a person knew what was good for them.

"I want the same thing from you that you want from me." Vincent relaxed back in his chair only the way an untouchable man could. "Information."

"Then I believe you will be disappointed." Pierce glanced at the watch on his wrist. "Information is something I am significantly lacking right now."

Vincent didn't speak until Pierce's eyes lifted to his. "Am I keeping you from something?"

"I'm sure you know the demands of my situation." Coming to GHOST headquarters was imperative. The opportunity might not present itself again, and it was too big to waste.

But being away from headquarters and all he needed to monitor made him jumpy.

Agitated.

"Tell me what you know about your situation." Vincent rocked in his chair as if he had all the time in the world.

As if there wasn't someone breathing down both their backs.

"I believe we are in the same situation." Pierce lifted his brows at Vincent. "Are we not?"

Vincent's lips lifted in a little smirk. "We are not."

"You underestimate my team then." Vincent might believe the people hidden behind these walls were his key to survival, but Pierce would bet on Intel and their collective skills any day.

"You must be forgetting that I know your team, Pierce." Vincent tipped his head. "Tried to convince one of them to come join mine." He crossed his arms over his chest. "She declined."

Heidi.

It would be easy to let himself believe her rejection of Vincent's offer had something to do with what Pierce worked so hard to offer her and the women she worked with, but in the end Heidi's choice most likely started and ended with a different man.

"That is unfortunate for you."

"I don't disagree." Vincent smiled. "I should probably let you know I plan to continue trying to steal her from you."

"I would expect nothing less." Pierce resisted the frustration trying to ease under his skin. He didn't have time for this.

There were more important things to deal with.

"What exactly is it you wish you knew about the situation?"

"I think you're misunderstanding me." Vincent pointed around the room. "I don't *wish* to know anything. I already know what I need to know." He moved the pointing finger Pierce's way. "I'm asking what *you* know."

It was impossible to reach into his pocket, find the item he used to focus when the demons became too much. There was nowhere to walk. No distraction ready to occupy the spark of anger threatening to flame.

"I know you put two of my people in danger by bringing them here." Pierce crossed one leg over the other, reaching down to straighten the hem of his pants once he did. "In the hopes you could steal one of them away."

"They were already in danger." Vincent's gaze was sharp as it rested on him. "And if you don't realize that it's going to be a problem."

Of course he knew they were already in danger. Everyone at his company was in danger. Threatened by an unnamed source.

One the man across from him wished to know more about.

That made two of them.

"Unfortunately, knowing the scope of the danger does nothing to narrow down the source." Pierce held Vincent's eyes. "Unless you already know the source."

"I know you won't believe me when I tell you I don't."

"Why would you think I'd have difficulty believing you, Vincent?" Pierce dropped both feet to the floor. "It's not like you've been using my men against me and trying to steal my most valuable employees for yourself." He stood.

This was a waste of his time. Completely.

He was done with it.

The door was open before Vincent spoke again. "You can't handle this on your own. You don't have the resources."

Pierce turned. "And what are you suggesting? I'm not ignorant enough to believe you have any interest in working together."

"Honestly, I don't." Vincent looked him up and down. "I'd prefer to let this work itself out and deal with the fallout." He exhaled loud and long. "Unfortunately, that's not an option available to me."

"I'm not interested."

"I wasn't asking."

"I don't respond well to demands."

Vincent's lips curved in an amused smile. "Then consider this a friendly request."

Pierce turned from the room. Staying any longer would only make this worse.

And right now he couldn't handle anymore worse.

He made his way through the maze of halls to the door he first entered, pushing it open and stepping out into the freezing darkness. As he expected, a black SUV was parked right by the door, engine idling.

He went straight to the passenger's door, opening it and sitting inside.

The man in the driver's seat remained silent, never once glancing Pierce's way as they drove back to Alaskan Security. When they pulled up to the gate the driver from GHOST rolled down his window and punched in a code.

The gate slid open.

Son of a—

The second they were parked Pierce was out of the vehicle and headed to the front entry. He needed a drink. Something to take the edge off before old habits proved he was the one thing he couldn't afford to be ever again.

Out of control.

He didn't even bother watching to see where the man and the SUV from GHOST went. If they stayed, if they went. Didn't matter.

He went directly to his office, raking one hand through his hair as he walked down the silent halls. It was late enough no one was in the main building. Maybe a few of the cleaning staff passing through, but right now even they were most likely gone for the night.

Pierce walked into his office, bumping the door closed as the automatic lights—

They were already on. A fact he would have recognized earlier if not for the complete shit show his evening had been.

He stood perfectly still, back to the room and whoever was in it.

Whoever was here to see if it was possible to ruin his day a little more.

Even a deep breath couldn't settle the irritation this unwanted visitor caused.

Pierce turned, as ready as he could be to deal with whoever needed a piece of him next.

But the cool eyes that met his were like a bucket of ice, hitting him with a force little else could. "Mona."

There was nothing he wanted to deal with. Not a soul he desired to see.

Except her.

"How is he?"

He.

Zeke.

Of course she wanted to know Zeke's condition. It was fucking poetic justice.

And his own damn fault.

"He's fine."

Mona's chin barely dipped in a nod. "When will he be back?"

"He's not coming back."

Mona's eyes widened. "What? Why not?"

He should never have sent her to Zeke. He should have used the opportunity to train her in self-defense the way he wanted. Pulled her closer.

But restraint was not an easy thing for him. Never had been.

And nothing tested his limits the way she did.

"Zeke took two members of our team against their will. Led them straight into the line of fire." Pierce risked a step closer. "Heidi could have died because of what he did."

Mona's gaze sharpened. "Heidi survived because of what he did. He risked his life to save

17

her and Shawn both." She was the next one to close the gap between them. Stealing a little more of his sanity with each move of her feet. "You know better than anyone there are no sides right now, Pierce."

His eyes dipped to her lips, watched as his name slipped through them.

"There are always sides, Mona." Pulling his gaze from her mouth was agony. "Always."

She held his stare, chin lifted in glorious defiance.

It was something he'd waited so long to see from her, thinking it would mean the time had finally come.

That Mona was ready to see all he wanted to show her.

"You are not a side, Pierce." Her cool blue gaze raked down him. "No matter what you might think."

She slipped past him with silent steps, disappearing into the quiet hall, leaving him with nothing but regrets and the lingering scent of her skin.

At least he could take comfort in the fact that he'd been right.

Beneath Mona's soft and uncertain self was a strength even she hadn't known existed.

He'd meant to foster it. Nurture it. Help it to bloom and grow into something as beautiful as she was.

He succeeded.

Only the strength Mona possessed was a quiet calm he never saw coming. One that cut him off at the knees.

And now he was faced with the monster he created.

CHAPTER 2

"I WANT TO see Zeke."

Shawn stared back at her across his desk.

Mona lifted a brow in question. "Did you not hear me?"

He blinked. "I did. I'm just not sure I think that's a good idea."

Of course he didn't. "I don't remember asking how you felt about it."

She was tired of people thinking they knew what was good for her. It was something she'd allowed in her life for too long.

No more.

"I am concerned—"

"I don't need your concern, Shawn." Mona spoke a little louder. The way she heard Harlow and Heidi do when they needed to get their point across. "I need you to take me to where Zeke is."

Shawn leaned into his hands, rubbing them down his face. "You're not all I'm concerned about." He crossed his arms and fell against the back of his chair, face tilting toward the ceiling.

"Taking you off campus is a huge risk for everyone involved."

"Then give me the address. I'll drive myself."

"Not happening." Shawn shook his head. "Sorry to burst your bubble on that one, but there's no fucking way I'm letting you, or anyone else, leave here alone."

Mona tapped one foot on the floor, the slow beat helping her work through the situation. "I want to see him, Shawn. If you don't figure out how to make it happen then I will." Mona stood from the chair and silently opened the door, slipping out before pulling it closed behind her.

The hall was quiet as she went to the office she shared with the rest of Team Intel.

"What did he say?" Lennie was the only other member of Intel in the office. It was still early enough that most of the team was just getting up and going.

Especially since they'd had a late night last night.

"What I expected him to say." Mona eased into her chair.

Lennie lined up a set of picture frames across her desk, each depicting a different niece or nephew. "What about Heidi?"

"What about Heidi?" Heidi came into the room, a giant stainless steel cup in one hand and a container of fruit and yogurt in the other.

"Shawn won't take Mona to see Zeke." Lennie continued working on her desk, setting out a jar filled with an assortment of candy. "I thought maybe you could take her."

21

"She was just brainstorming with me. I don't expect you to take me to Zeke." Mona ran one hand over the arm of her sweater, smoothing it down the way she hoped to smooth this conversation over.

"I do know how to get there." Heidi lifted her brows Mona's way.

"You would need a car." Lennie stopped her organizing to look between Mona and Heidi. "And you'd have to figure out how to sneak it past Pierce. He doesn't seem to miss anything."

She wasn't wrong.

Heidi dropped into her new desk chair and flipped the lid off her breakfast. "Did he even come back last night?"

Lennie shrugged.

"I can check." Heidi flipped open her computer.

"He got back at midnight." Mona wasn't planning to tell anyone she'd all but accosted the owner of Alaskan Security last night, but having Heidi discover it on the security footage would make it seem like she was hiding something.

Which she was.

Her late night campout in his office might look different than it was, and the last thing she needed was for the rest of Intel to think she was trying to gain something from it.

Technically she was.

Just nothing for herself.

All she wanted was to see Zeke. Make sure he was okay. He would do the same for her.

"Midnight you say?" Heidi shoved her computer away, leaning forward as she dug a spoon into the container of yogurt. "Discuss."

"There's nothing to discuss." Mona resisted the urge to shrink down. Disappear a little. "I asked how Zeke was. Pierce said he was fine. That's it."

"So, you already know Zeke is fine?" Heidi's brows came together.

"I know Pierce claims Zeke is fine." Mona pushed her shoulders back a little, trying to appear more sure.

More confident.

"But I want to see it for myself." Among other things.

"I can hack into the security cameras at GHOST headquarters." Heidi scrunched her face up. "They'll know I did it though, so…"

"I'll figure something out." Mona glanced at the monitors. They had an enormous amount of footage of GHOST headquarters. She could probably figure out where the warehouse was on her own. Get the directions.

Take one of the SUVs.

"Good morning."

Two words sucked all the air from the room.

From her lungs.

She'd spent a lifetime being intimidated by people. Shrinking back from people with power.

Giving them more.

And none of those people were half as powerful or intimidating as the one standing in the doorway of Intel's office.

Pierce made her want to hide and throw up at the same time.

Especially when he was looking at her the way he was now.

"Sup, Pierce?" Heidi bounced back in her seat, kicking her feet up onto her desk. "We were just discussing your late night last night."

Pierce's gaze didn't budge from where it was fixed on her face. "Were you?"

Was he asking her? Mona glanced Heidi's way, hoping Pierce would follow suit.

He did not.

And no one else was answering him. The question hung in the air, eating at her nerves, feeding the fears that wanted her to stay silent.

Disappear.

"We were." Mona sat taller, swallowing the gag trying to strangle her. "I would like to see Zeke today."

"That's the reason I'm here."

"You're letting me go see him?" Last night Pierce seemed so averse to the idea. Now he was fine with it?

"I'm escorting you."

The gag was back with a vengeance.

Heidi snorted. "Imagine that."

Pierce finally tipped his head Heidi's way, eyes dragging along with it. "What was that?"

Heidi gave him a sweet smile. "I didn't say anything."

Pierce's gaze came back to Mona before Heidi finished her false claim. "Are you prepared to leave now?"

No. Definitely not. "That would be perfect." Mona stood, her legs somehow managing to support her weight. "I need to go get my coat from my room."

"No need." Pierce watched as she walked his way, waiting until she was past him before following behind her.

"It's well below zero out there. I'm quite sure I need a coat." It was nearly impossible to walk and talk at the same time. Each step felt like it might lead to a full-fledged face plant as she forced them out. Each word teased the tickle in her throat, threatening to send her retching.

"I don't disagree." Pierce paused at his office door, grabbing a heavy wool coat from the rack just inside. "But I have a small window in which to make this happen for you, and every minute spent finding your coat is another minute you won't be able to spend with Zeke."

His words were clipped and sharp.

Probably because he could think of a million things he'd rather be doing. "I'm sure someone else would be willing to take me."

Pierce's usually smooth steps barely lost their rhythm. "I've no doubt of that."

He was suddenly very close.

Mona almost jumped away. The only thing keeping her from showing her true colors was the shock of his nearness. "What are you doing?"

Pierce pulled the coat around her, wrapping the soft scarf paired with it over her neck. His hands worked the buttons down the front. "It's my responsibility to keep you safe, Mona. No one else's."

The coat was thick and heavy. Warm enough she was almost instantly hot, her cheeks flaming from the added insulation.

The coat was definitely the issue.

"Come." Pierce took her hand in his, leading her through the doors where a SUV was waiting, the tinted windows making it impossible to see who was inside.

The cold hit her instantly. She hadn't been outside since the night she, Harlow, and Eva were lured outside and taken by a team of men who didn't survive their kidnapping attempt. "Oh my God."

Her eyes burned as an icy breeze sucked the breath from her lungs.

"Inside." Pierce yanked open the back door to the SUV. "Get in the car, Mona."

Mona blinked at the watering of her eyes, the shock of the unbelievable cold stalling her feet.

Suddenly she was moving again.

Just not by foot.

Pierce hefted her body against his, easily lifting her up and onto the heated seats of the warmed vehicle. He was in right behind her, pulling the door closed before turning her way, tugging at the coat, working it tighter against her body. His sharp blue eyes snapped to the front seat. "Turn up the heat."

"Why in the hell do you live here?" It was an honest question, just not one she'd meant to ask.

His gaze came back to rest on her face, the edge there already gone. Pierce's lips barely lifted at the edges. "Should I remind you that you also live here?"

"Not by choice." Mona started to ease down, planning to burrow deeper into the coat that felt part cocoon, part fortress. A place where she could escape and hide from her immediate reality.

Instead she straightened, sitting a little taller beside the man who made her want to cower back into the woman she'd been. "I'm here because of you."

It was meant as an explanation. A way to prove her decision to be in Alaska was less insane than his.

But the change in his expression made it seem like Pierce didn't understand her attempted jab at his decision-making skills.

"That is good to know, Mona." His voice was softer, quieter.

Almost intimate.

Pierce was commanding. Controlling.

Dominating.

Everything that terrified her. Sent her stomach rolling and her heart racing.

He reached out, warm fingers brushing over her skin where her hair caught in the scarf he'd wrapped around her. "I wish I could apologize for bringing you here."

Her lungs were no longer working, which meant neither were her vocal cords.

He was so close. This man who more often than not set her on edge and made her insides threaten to revolt.

Whenever she thought she was turning a corner in this crazy journey to a new and better self, Pierce would show up, reminding her she was still the same woman.

Still just pretending to be something she would probably never be.

"Are you warm enough, Mona?" The low tone of his words snaked around her, slithering to that spot in her belly that twisted every time he walked into a room.

"I am. Thank you." She finally managed a full breath for the first time since Pierce arrived.

The blowing heat of the car warmed everything around her. The moving air carried the warm scent of spice and cedar wood. It was deep and rich and masculine.

Mona glanced down at the coat wrapped around her.

It was the coat she was smelling.

No. Not the coat.

The man who owned it.

"Is something wrong, Mona?"

Did he always call her Mona? "I'm fine."

Maybe saying it would make it true.

If she threw up on his coat it would never come out. There wasn't enough dry-cleaning in the world to remove barf from expensive wool and—

She reached up to run the tips of her fingers over the scarf.

Cashmere.

"Is the scarf too tight?" Pierce reached for her again, his touch solid and sure as it gently eased the ridiculously soft scarf away from her skin. "Is that better?"

"It's fine." As fine as it could be, all things considered.

She needed to find a way to survive this trip without passing out or vomiting, which meant she had to distract her brain and stomach. "Where are we going?"

"GHOST headquarters." His answer was immediate.

"Why is he there?"

Pierce's jaw barely tightened. "Because he is one of them."

"He is also part of Alaskan Security."

"Not any longer." Pierce turned his attention to the back window, his dark blue eyes slowly sweeping the span of roadway behind them.

"You can't just fire him." Concern for someone she thought of as a friend shoved all her nerves to the side, replacing her almost constant anxiety with something much easier to deal with.

Anger.

Pierce's eyes immediately came back to her. "I can."

She narrowed her eyes. "Just because you can, doesn't mean you should."

"And what would you have me do?" One dark brow lifted. "Bring him back? Give him the opportunity to betray us again?"

"How did he betray us?" Yes. Zeke took Heidi and Shawn off campus.

Technically against their will.

And while it was for a good reason, it didn't exactly forgive the poor decision.

He absolutely deserved a reprimand of some sort.

But to just fire him?

Pierce's nostrils flared. "Are you forgetting he took your friend? Put her in a situation that could have easily killed her?"

She had not forgotten that. It was one of the reasons she wanted to see Zeke. "And are you blatantly ignoring the opportunity it afforded you?"

Pierce's lips pressed together so she kept going. "GHOST wants Heidi and you have her. I can promise you she's not leaving, which means you have something they want." Mona tipped her chin. "Which also means *you* hold the power when it comes to GHOST."

Pierce stared at her as the seconds ticked by, the flare of anger keeping her nerves at bay waning with each passing breath.

Soon she would be back to potentially decorating his expensive coat with the remnants of her breakfast.

And that was without even considering what she planned to do when she saw Zeke.

Chances were good someone was going to need a wet wipe before she was done with them.

Finally Pierce shifted in his seat, angling his body toward the front seats. "I had not considered that."

Of course he hadn't. Because men were all about egos. Damage it and they went blind.

Pierce dipped his head. "Thank you."

"For what?"

His face turned toward her. "For showing me what I couldn't see on my own."

"Oh." His response sort of took the wind out of her sails.

Not that she had much to start with.

The SUV slowed, jostling as it went over a bump.

"We're here." The driver pulled into a spot along the side of a large nondescript building, parking right in front of a windowless steel door.

Movement caught Mona's attention.

A matching SUV pulled up on each side of them, along with one at the back, effectively blocking them in.

"It's just added protection." Pierce's door opened. "I won't risk your safety."

"Hey, Mona." Tyson gave her an easy smile from where he stood just outside Pierce's door.

Rogue was surrounding them, fully-geared and looking ready for anything that might come their way.

Pierce stepped out of the car, reaching one hand out. "This way."

The heavy coat was huge, and all the added bulk made it difficult to maneuver her way out of the car. Her hands kept slipping into the sleeves and the wool kept twisting and catching. Finally she reached out, taking Pierce's offered hand simply to speed the process up.

His grip was warm and tight as he pulled her free, his hold keeping her steady as the cold once again registered.

The only thing that got her inside was Pierce's hand, leading her along while her brain refused to consider anything but the bone-chilling air attacking her face.

A man was waiting, his black gear strikingly similar to what she'd seen on the men at Alaskan Security. "Nice to see you again, Pierce."

"Vincent." Pierce slid one hand into the pocket of his pants.

The man turned. "He's in a regular room now. I told him you were coming to talk to him again."

"I'm sure he's thrilled." Pierce's words were dry and flat.

Mona pressed two fingers to her lips, smothering out the laugh trying to sneak free at Pierce's words.

It was just nerves. She should be grateful it was a laugh attempting to escape instead of what usually wanted out.

Vincent turned and began to walk, leaving her and Pierce to follow behind him.

With every turn the likelihood of her breaking out into a fit of laughter went down.

And the odds of barfing went up.

She could do this.

Make sure Zeke was fine.

And then let him know how she felt about him.

Vincent paused outside a closed door, tipping his head toward it before immediately walking away.

Mona stared at the last thing keeping her from Zeke.

She took a deep breath, stopping once it was in to swallow down the panic clawing up her throat.

She'd come this far.

Just a little more.

"Are you ready for me to open the door, Mona?"

She didn't dare look at Pierce. Adding him into the mix would certainly prove catastrophic. "Open it."

He twisted the knob and pushed the door wide, stepping back.

His eyes were a weight she could feel. One she might struggle to ignore under other circumstances.

But the sight of Zeke in front of her stole all her attention away.

He was fine. Upright and looking none the worse for wear as he sat in a chair at a small table in the corner of the room.

She could do this.

She could do this.

Mona walked straight into the room. Right toward Zeke. The man she trusted.

The man who made her believe she could do all the things she wished she could.

"Mona." His brows went up as he started to stand.

He never made it.

Because she got to him first.

Mona stopped right in front of him.

Planted her feet.
And slapped him right across the face.

CHAPTER 3

PIERCE WASN'T SURE who was more shocked.

Zeke.

Or him.

Mona's pale blue eyes were narrowed and sharp. "She could have died."

Zeke stared up at her, gaping at the tiny woman as his cheek turned red and blotchy.

"How could you do that?" Mona pointed one finger right between Zeke's eyes, the sleeve of his coat slipping down to cover everything but the nude polish on her nail. "That was an awful thing to do." Her head barely shook, the white blonde of her hair skimming his scarf as she did. "I trusted you." Her head tipped back, chin lifting. "I defended you." She straightened. "And you almost killed my friend."

Zeke sat silently.

Mona sucked in a breath that was almost a sniff. "Fix it."

Zeke's eyes finally moved from her, shifting to where Pierce stood.

Mona spun to face him, her cool blue eyes leveling on his.

Pierce held her there, refusing to look away, hoping she would do the same.

She didn't disappoint him.

Finally he tore his eyes from hers, turning his attention to Zeke. "My office. Tomorrow morning at six."

Mona's shoulders relaxed, the bulk of his coat exaggerating the tiny change.

Pierce focused only on her. "Are you finished?"

"For now."

It took an enormous amount of restraint to hide his smile as he backed into the hall, expecting Mona to follow.

Instead she turned back to Zeke, scanning him from head to toe. "I'm glad you're okay."

Shadow's lead sat stoic and still as she turned and walked out of the room, chin high, steps sure.

Like a queen reigning over her court.

Pierce lifted his brows at Zeke before walking away, going after the woman who just faced down one of the most dangerous men in the world. He caught her just as she was about to take a wrong turn. "This way."

She continued on. "Where's that man who runs this place? I want to talk to him next."

"Probably not the best idea right now." Pierce snagged her arm. "I will make you an appointment."

Mona yanked her arm from his grip. "No. I have to do it now."

Her skin was a little pale except for the flaming pink of her cheeks. She appeared to be either a breath from passing out.

Or combusting.

And while the latter sounded highly appealing, it wasn't anything he was willing to allow. Not now.

Pierce stepped close to her, dropping his voice as he leaned into her ear. "This is a very delicate balance right now, Mona. You played your hand. Now you must wait for them to play theirs."

"This isn't a game." Her whisper was almost impossible for him to hear.

She was so damn smart.

Mona's eyes moved along the deserted hall, slowly scanning the bare walls until finally coming to rest on the camera tucked away in a corner. "Does he know what I did?"

"Absolutely he does. Vincent's probably looking you up as we speak." Pierce finally allowed the smile he'd been fighting. "Hoping to learn more about the vicious woman assaulting his men."

Her eyes snapped his way. "I'm not vicious."

"You just slapped a mercenary in the face, Love. If that's not vicious I don't know what is."

Mona's pale brows came together, her cornflower blue eyes quickly moving over his face. "He deserved it."

"I don't disagree." Pierce eased closer, taking advantage of the situation. "And yet you want me to bring him back to Alaskan Security."

Her narrow shoulders straightened under the bulky line of his coat. "I do."

"Then I am considering it." He barely shook his head. "But I won't make you any promises as far as Zeke's fate is concerned."

"Is that why you're meeting with him tomorrow?"

"*We* are meeting with him tomorrow." Pierce lifted his eyes at the nearly silent sound of steps. "It's time for us to go."

The last thing he wanted was anyone from GHOST getting close to Mona. They were the wild card he'd attempted to keep in his hand, hoping to use it to his own advantage in order to keep the sins of his past safely where they belonged.

Pierce pulled Mona close, taking her through the maze of halls to the door they'd come through less than fifteen minutes prior. He knocked twice.

Tyson opened it immediately, offering Mona another smile. "Have a nice visit?"

Mona nodded, tucking her head into the wrap of his scarf as the wind cut into the open door.

"Move quick, Love." Pierce tucked her into his side, hurrying her to the SUV. Reed held the door open as she climbed in, this time without any assistance from him.

Which was disappointing.

He'd thought maybe she had some sort of feelings for Zeke.

It was part of the reason he had no intention of allowing Shadow's former lead anywhere near Alaskan Security.

But now...

Mona sat very still beside him, chewing her lower lip as she stared straight ahead.

Pierce leaned into her ear, taking a guilty breath, letting the scent of her linger in his lungs.

He'd tried to pinpoint it. Attempted to narrow down what it was that tinted the air around her with a scent so soft and warm.

Unsuccessfully.

"Thank you for taking me to see him."

"You are welcome, Mona." He'd called her Ms. Ayers for so long. Should still be doing so.

But last night she was different.

And now.

Now he didn't want to take her back to headquarters. Not after seeing how far she'd come.

Far enough to test the restraint he learned to have.

"Why do you want me to meet with you tomorrow?" Her eyes came his way for a second before quickly snapping back to the windshield.

"You are his champion." The fact didn't grate as much as it did this morning.

All night.

Her desire to see Zeke kept him awake. Restless and agitated.

And he still couldn't deny her what she wished.

"I just think you are looking at this wrong."

Very few people told him when they believed he was wrong. He was surrounded by grown men who hesitated to disagree with anything he said.

It was how he liked it. He was the only one who knew the full story of what all Alaskan Security protected, which meant he was the only one capable of making the decisions involving it.

But Mona was different.

"Tell me why you think that."

"You're being difficult because he hurt your feelings."

"Most people don't believe I have feelings."

"Most people don't believe you sleep either." Her eyes moved his way, cautious as they held his. "Or eat."

He was surprised by that one. "Why wouldn't I eat?"

"No one ever sees you eat."

"No one ever sees me shower either. Doesn't mean I don't do it."

A light flush crept across her cheeks, spreading down the smooth skin of her neck that wasn't hidden by his scarf. Mona grabbed at the cashmere. "Can he turn down the heat? This coat is hot."

Pierce couldn't pull his gaze from the pink of her skin. "Luca, can you lower the vents?"

It wouldn't help. The heat of the car had nothing to do with her sudden warmth. "I can assure you, I eat." He leaned a little closer. "And I shower. And I sleep. Just like everyone else."

Mona huffed out a little laugh. "You're nothing like everyone else."

The SUV came to a stop.

A second later his door opened, ripping away the bit of her time he'd managed to claim for himself.

It wasn't enough.

"I will prove I am." He was a little desperate. A little frantic.

Mona's brows lifted. "You want to prove to me you're like everyone else?"

He wanted to prove to her he was like no one else, but admitting that wouldn't give him what he wanted. "I do."

"Why?" She seemed genuinely confused.

"It's important that Intel and I can work together." His mind was grasping at straws, trying to find the one that would bring her close again. "I need to close the divide between us."

"Then you should talk to Harlow." She was so smart. So good at identifying the way things should be. Any other time he would marvel at the ability.

Right now it was fucking up his plans.

"You know everyone. Harlow has just met most of the team. You are the logical choice."

Tyson cleared his throat.

Pierce ignored him. No one was leaving this car until he knew when she would be his again.

Mona pulled his coat closer. "Fine."

She didn't sound convinced, but at least she'd agreed.

"Okay. Good then." Pierce stepped out of the SUV. This time Mona was immediately behind him, stealing the chance to help her out.

To hold her hand in his.

She was so cautious. It was one of the many things that drew him to her.

But it made luring her in a delicate balance. One he still wasn't exactly sure how to accomplish.

Mona went straight for the glass doors leading inside, her feet almost at a run along the sidewalk.

41

"Doesn't seem like she likes the cold." Tyson closed the door to the SUV.

"It doesn't, does it?" Pierce watched through the glass as Mona hurried through the entry and disappeared down the hall.

"She really smack him?"

He glanced at Tyson. "How do you know that?"

Tyson grinned. "Heidi hacked into the security system at GHOST."

Of course she did.

"Who all knows?" Pierce walked to the front of the main building.

"Pretty much all of Rogue." Tyson stayed right beside him.

Pierce pulled the door open, holding it wide so Tyson could go in first. "What about Luca?"

"Nobody's telling Shadow shit right now." Tyson kept his eyes in front of them instead of turning back toward the front of the building and the single member of Shadow he included in the excursion. "You couldn't find anyone else to drive you?"

"Luca's the best defensive driver here."

It was a fact no one would argue. Even then it was a decision Pierce wavered on right up to the last possible moment. "And he had all of Rogue to keep him in line." While his trust of Zeke and Shadow in general was on unsteady ground, the full truth of the matter was not that Shadow lacked the ability or desire to do what was needed of them at Alaskan Security.

The issue was where their ultimate allegiance laid when the waters got muddy.

Pierce came to a stop at the door to his office.

The bulk of Intel was scattered around the space.

Lovely. Just what he wanted to deal with right now. "Good morning."

"It is, isn't it?" Heidi grinned at him from where she sat in one of the chairs across from his desk.

"Is there something I can do for you?" He crossed the room, moving toward the window that overlooked the back training yards.

"We're more worried about what we're supposed to be doing for you." Harlow skimmed the tips of her fingers across the spines of the books lining the shelves along the walls. She tipped one out. "Why do you have a copy of The Secret Garden?"

"Why wouldn't I have a copy of The Secret Garden?" Pierce lifted a leaf from the plant sitting in front of the large window. The edges were brown and dry.

Harlow pulled the worn book free of its spot. "Have you actually read it?"

"I've read all the books in here." He moved to another leaf, inspecting it.

"You're shitting me."

He turned toward Harlow. "I am not." Pierce tipped his head toward the shelf sitting just to one side of his desk. "Not those of course."

Harlow's lips lifted in a little smile. She was one of the few people at Alaskan Security who knew of the hidden passage leading to his office from the tunnels below. "Of course."

"So what are we supposed to be doing?" Heidi slouched down, letting her head rest against the back of the chair where she sat. "Because I'm getting bored."

"And a bored Heidi isn't anything you want to have on your hands." One of the new arrivals sat in the chair next to Heidi. "She'll end up trying to break into government security systems just to see if she can."

"I believe that's already been accomplished today." He lifted his brows at Heidi. "Correct?"

Heidi's lips pulled into a slow smile. "I recorded it if you want to watch it again."

"Maybe another time." Pierce strode to his desk. "For now I think it's best we continue as we have gone. It is most important that we find a way to identify the man at the top. Without him we will never be able to end this."

Harlow scoffed. "Why does it have to be a man?"

The uneasiness he'd been fighting for weeks lodged deeper, trying to dig into a possibility he'd rejected time and time again. "We should all hope it's a man." Pierce scanned the faces glaring back at him. "Because I've recently discovered women are much more dangerous."

Heidi glanced Harlow's way before her eyes returned to meet his. "It's a man."

He couldn't hide his surprise at the certainty in her tone. "You know this?"

"Define *know*." Harlow came to stand beside Lennie, one of the women who worked for Mona and Eva at Investigative Resources.

"I would call it an educated guess." Heidi lifted her brows in a questioning way as she turned to Lennie. "Right?"

Lennie nodded. "I'd call it that."

Heidi turned back his way. "It's an educated guess."

He waited for one of them to elaborate.

They just stared back at him.

"Could you tell me *why* you believe it's a man?"

"Mona figured it out." Heidi's lips moved into a little smile. "Which I'm sure won't surprise you."

"Ms. Ayers is quite an intelligent woman." The formality of her surname was a necessary evil. One he wished to dispose of as soon as possible. "I will be happy to discuss her thoughts privately."

Heidi eyed him. "How considerate of you."

Pierce paused, his gaze lingering on Heidi. "Actually, I believe I do have something I would like for you to do."

"Thank God." Heidi straightened. "You want me to spy on GHOST?"

Her immediate correct assumption was more surprising than it should be. "I do."

Heidi's smile was wide and immediate. "We can totally do that." She stood and made it to the door before turning back. "You know they're probably going to know I'm doing it, right?"

"Feel free to be as obvious as you wish."

Heidi's smile turned to a wicked grin. "I knew you had some balls in those fancy pants."

"What is that supposed to mean?"

Heidi gave him a little shrug. "You're just normally so," she pointed one finger his way, wiggling it around, "proper."

"And that made you assume I had no balls?"

"I wouldn't say *no* balls." Heidi wiggled her brows. "Just maybe not enough to take on GHOST."

Her assessment calmed the unrest he'd been fighting longer than anyone would believe. "In that case I'm happy to surprise you."

The rest of the women followed her out.

"Wait." Pierce caught Harlow just before she left. "Where's Alec?"

He was easy enough to remember, even in all the current chaos muddling his brain. There was a single man from Investigative Resources who chose to make the move to Alaska.

"He's been spending time with Dutch." Harlow smirked. "I think he's in need of a little testosterone time."

"I see." That was most definitely not the case. Being surrounded by brilliant, strong-willed women was not something a man tired of.

Not a man he'd keep on staff anyway.

Pierce picked up his phone as soon as Harlow was gone, punching the button that would connect him with—

"How can I help you Mr. Barrick?"

Pierce looked down at the phone on his desk. He'd pushed the correct line. "I'm sorry. Who is this?"

"This is Elise. Your office manager."

"Did you rearrange the autodial buttons on my phone?"

"They were disorganized."

"The buttons on my phone were disorganized." Pierce rubbed his eyes. "How is that possible?"

"They were not in alphabetical order."

"And now they are?"

"Now they are."

He disconnected the line and punched the first button.

Dutch picked up on the second ring. "I'm surprised you found me."

"Would that have anything to do with the new office manager rearranging the autodial on my phone?"

"First of all, it's called speed dial."

"And second?" Pierce tucked one hand in his pocket, working his finger over the item tucked inside.

"Second, Elise came and asked if it would be helpful for her to reprogram it."

"And you told her it would?" He pulled a notepad from the drawer and scrawled out the names he'd set up, numbering them in alphabetical order. "I don't know who in the hell I'm calling now."

"Heidi told her to do it. Said you'd love it."

Of course she did.

"Where are you?"

"Depends. How was your meeting with Vincent?"

Pierce closed his eyes.

He's started this company from the ground up. Filled it with men he knew and men he'd come to know.

And now they were all turning on him.

"Never mind." Pierce hung up the phone.

Whatever they were doing was fine. He would deal with it one way or another.

But for now he had better things to occupy his mind.

And his evening.

CHAPTER 4

"I DON'T KNOW where he went." Heidi walked through the doorway of Intel's office, her brows drawn together. "He's been gone for hours."

"Probably need a break." Lennie's eyes stayed on her computer screen, fingers moving gracefully across the keyboard as she worked her way through the list of possible names they'd come up with connected to GHOST.

Heidi snorted. "Pierce? No way." She walked to her desk, falling into her seat as she grabbed the large mug always close by and took a long sip through the wide plastic straw. "That guy doesn't shut off. He's wound tighter than a clam's ass at high tide."

Eva glanced Heidi's way. "How long did it take you to think that up?"

"I Googled it." Heidi's grin was wide and filled with obvious amusement.

"You Googled a way to insult Pierce?" Mona tried to wrap her brain around the concept. It would never occur to her to look up creative ways to put someone down. "Why?"

Heidi's eyes went wide. "Who says it's an insult?" She lifted one shoulder. "Working hard is a good thing."

"You didn't say he was a hard worker. You said he was uptight." It was a ridiculous thing to argue about, but for some reason it bothered her that Heidi would be so dedicated to creative ways to say Pierce was lacking.

"He *is* uptight." Heidi's grin from earlier slowly reappeared. "But I bet it's fun as hell to see him when he snaps."

Mona turned away, forcing her eyes back to her own computer screen. "I doubt it."

Her eyes looked at the monitor but her mind refused to consider anything besides Heidi's words.

I bet it's fun to see him when he snaps.

It didn't sound like fun at all actually.

For some reason it sounded a little sad.

"You're going to need Botox before the week's out if you keep frowning like that." Heidi wiggled a bag of Swedish Fish at her. "Want some candy?"

Mona held her hand out in Heidi's direction. "You know I do."

Heidi stretched behind Eva's desk, depositing the entire bag in Mona's hand. "Take the rest. Shawn's making dinner and if I don't eat it all he gets his feelings hurt."

"How long are you going to keep pretending to like plain chicken and vegetables?" Eva scribbled across a Post-It and smacked it onto her desk next to the collection of other papers lined across it.

"Relationships are all about sacrifice." Heidi's eyes rolled a little. "Apparently I'm sacrificing flavor."

"At least he can cook." Harlow turned to stare at the monitors across the front of the room. "Mine has to mooch off Brock."

"He likes it." Eva rearranged a few of the notes forming a timeline of events. "He'd cook for everyone here if he could."

"Don't tell Dutch that. He'll be at your door three times a day." Harlow's head tilted as she scanned the video playing across the screen. "I just pulled the feed from the post office and it looks like Chandler hasn't been there yet this week."

"Really?" Mona watched the feed along with Harlow. They'd almost been able to set their clocks by Chandler's arrival at the Post Office. "You think the money stopped coming?"

Harlow shrugged. "Or he's dead."

She'd known Chandler since college. His arrival in her life was something she could now pinpoint as the single worst thing to happen to her.

Not that there was much competition. She'd led a charmed life with the exception of one cheating ex-fiancé.

And the sociopathic narcissist she never saw coming.

"We should go see if there's anything in the PO Box." It would narrow down the possibilities. If there was no money then Chandler had no reason to be there, which meant he was still alive.

Maybe.

If there was money then he was most likely dead.

Harlow turned Mona's way. "The PO Box *is* in your name."

"Pierce will never let her do that." Heidi's eyes narrowed at her computer. "I'll see if I can change the information. Put it in someone else's name."

"No." Mona didn't mean to say it so loud. She cleared her throat. "No. I can go."

She'd let Chandler manipulate her into someone she didn't recognize. Over the years he'd fed on her anxiety. Her natural tendency to apologize for everything.

She allowed him to make her weak.

"I'll go." Mona tried to swallow at the nervous closing of her throat and nearly choked on her own saliva.

Some days undoing years of damage to her self-confidence felt impossible. It was another by-product of her 'friendship' with Chandler. He slowly broke her down until she was no threat to his agenda.

If anything she helped his case. Made it seem like he had her in his corner.

"Alright then." Heidi rubbed her hands together. "Who gets to tell Pierce?"

"I do." Mona almost gagged. "I'll do it tomorrow."

Heidi leaned to peer down the hall toward Pierce's office. "Unless he's dead too."

"He's not dead." The words snapped out, an involuntary reaction to the suggestion.

Heidi didn't seem to notice. "Probably not. He'd have to be human to die."

Harlow's head fell back. "I've told you a million times. He's not a freaking robot."

"Have you even seen the shit the government is capable of doing?" Heidi looked around the room. "Cause I have." Her gaze landed on Mona. "And if they were going to make a robot then it would probably look just like Pierce."

"He is a little too good looking to be real, isn't he?" Lennie crossed her arms and leaned back in her chair. "And didn't he get shot or something?"

The memory of that night sent a flood of heat through Mona's limbs. "He was wearing a vest."

Not that it would have helped if the bullet was a few inches higher. And still he jumped in front of her, using his body as a shield to protect hers as he took her to the ground in a way that she barely even felt the impact.

"Still." Lennie looked toward Harlow. "Do we have footage of that?"

Harlow lifted a brow. "You want to watch Pierce get shot?"

"I mean, if I'm going to decide whose team I'm on then I think it only makes sense." She pointed to Mona. "Right now I'm leaning toward Team Mona."

"Give it time." Heidi twisted in her seat to look Lennie's way. "You'll come to my side eventually."

"What are you picking sides over now?" Shawn strode into the room. His hair was damp and the veins in his forearms were more pronounced than normal.

Heidi's eyes dragged down him from head to toe. "Been working out?"

Shawn's gaze came to Mona for a second before going back to Heidi. "Had someone who needed to work some steam off."

"Not you though." Heidi gave him a little smile. "I'm sure you were perfectly fine."

"I'm always fine, Kitten." He held one hand Heidi's way. "You ready to call it for the night?"

Heidi let out a long, loud sigh. "I guess." She snapped her laptop closed before tucking it into her bag. Shawn picked it up as soon as it was zipped, hooking it over one arm before wrapping the other around Heidi.

He shot one last look into the room on their way out. "Night, ladies."

Eva rubbed her eyes. "I don't think I can look at this anymore." She'd spent the day working out the multiple and intersecting timelines they were dealing with. "Maybe I'll be able to wrap my brain around it better tomorrow."

"Take a break if you need it." Harlow still stared at the screens. "Fresh eyes make a difference sometimes."

"You should probably take your own advice." Eva stood from her desk. "You've been watching that footage all day."

"The more we know about what they're doing, the better our chances of figuring out what they know."

"Why won't they just tell us what they know?"

"Not sure you can just walk into GHOST and demand they tell you what they know." Harlow fell into her chair. "The government only likes to offer information when they have to."

But wasn't that the case? GHOST was in this for a reason. If they had the ability to end it on their own, wouldn't they have done it already?

"That makes sense." Mona chewed her lip for a minute, mulling over whether or not to share her suspicions with the rest of the women.

But suspicions alone weren't really helpful, and it could take them down a rabbit hole they didn't have time to explore.

But she did. Especially now that all her friends were paired off, happily spending their evenings snuggled up with the men who snatched them away.

Mona forced out a yawn, doing her best to make it seem authentic. "I think I might head out for the night too." She gently closed her laptop and tucked it into her leather bag. "It's been a long day."

"Yeah it has." Harlow grinned at her. "Wanna watch it one more time before you go?"

"I do not." If she'd known everyone would witness her meeting with Zeke she might have done things differently.

Or not.

Lennie raised her hand. "I do."

"He's going to die when he finds out we all know you slapped him." Harlow's smile widened. "I think that's my favorite part."

She wasn't wrong. Zeke would most likely never hear the end of it from the ladies of Intel. "I guess we'll find out." Mona grabbed her bag. "See you in the morning."

The halls were oddly quiet as she made her way toward the front of the building. It felt later than it was, the darkness making it seem like it should almost be time to go to bed even though it was barely after seven.

To be fair, she'd been up since five, so bed probably wouldn't be far off if there wasn't something important to be accomplished.

Mona passed a few of the men temporarily camped out at headquarters. The place was packed to the gills with teams that were normally spread across the states, and it was all but impossible to find the kitchen in the rooming house unoccupied.

Currently, there were five men digging through the freshly-stocked fridge, putting together whatever they decided to eat for dinner.

Mona bypassed the kitchen and went straight to her room even though she was starving. Hopefully later it would be less populated and she could find something to eat in peace.

She needed to remember to give Elise a list of items to keep in her own kitchen. Unfortunately, her brain power was being used by about a million other things, and that list usually ended up being put off.

And it would probably happen again tonight.

After swiping her badge across the digital lock on the door to her room Mona went in, dropping her bag on the loveseat before kicking off her shoes as she headed to the small bedroom. After putting the shoes in their place, she dug out a set of thermal lounge pants and an oversized brushed-jersey sweater, along with a long-sleeved thermal t-shirt. She shivered as she stripped down and layered everything on, the chill of the room stealing the heat from her body. It was nearly impossible to get warm here.

Apparently unless she was wrapped in Pierce's coat. The thing must be made of some sort of self-heating lining, because it kept her reasonably warm in spite of the blisteringly cold air outside. She'd almost hated to return it to his office on her way in this morning.

But only almost.

She'd just finished changing when someone knocked on her door.

Probably Eva. Her best friend saved Mona the trip to the kitchen more times than not, bringing over a plate of whatever amazing thing Brock made for dinner that night.

Mona hopped toward the door, pulling on a pair of thick socks as she went, her stomach growling at the prospect of delivered dinner.

"I am so glad you're he—" The words died in her throat as she pulled open the door.

"I'm happy to hear that." Pierce's dark eyes skimmed down her in a slow sweep. "I wasn't expecting this to be such a casual event."

What in the hell was he talking about? "I'm sorry?"

"Our dinner plans." Pierce stepped into her room, his overwhelming presence immediately sending her two steps back to clear his path. "Are you ready?"

Pierce was in her room.

Claiming they had dinner plans.

Mona shook her head, trying to clear it of the thoughts running around her brain like there was a fire. "We don't have dinner plans."

"We do." Pierce turned toward her, his body much nearer than it usually was. "We made them this morning on our way home from visiting Zeke."

"I—" There was nothing to string together. No thoughts. No words. Not even a few syllables to line up.

"Dinner is ready whenever you are, Mona." Pierce's tone was soft. "Did you not wish to see that I do, in fact, eat?"

That's how this happened.

Part of her brain picked up the conversation from this morning, waving it around to taunt her with it. Remind her of the terrible thing she'd agreed to.

"I'm already in my pajamas." It was a weak argument at best, but it was all she had.

His deep blue gaze drifted. "I did notice that."

Her stomach growled. Whether it was in protest or from emptiness was anyone's guess.

Pierce's lips lifted at the edges, not quite to a smile, but into a hint of the shape. "Shall we go?"

If her hunch about GHOST and Alaskan Security was right, then Pierce might hold the key to finding the truth.

And getting some answers.

"Let me change."

"No need." Pierce opened the door and waited.

"How is there no need? I can't go out like this."

"We are not going out. We are staying in." Pierce tipped his head toward the hall outside. "Come on. Before something terrible happens."

"Terrible?" That got her feet moving. Mona hurried out to the hall. "What's wrong?"

"Beef Wellington doesn't stay in the oven forever, Mona." Pierce pressed one hand to the small of her back. "This way." He urged her to the door leading to the underground tunnels. He opened it, the weight of his hand propelling her into the silent space.

"Where are we going?" Mona followed him down the stairs toward the maze that ran under Alaskan Security.

"We are going to my rooms." Pierce led her around a corner to where another steel door was tucked into a short hall. Pierce swiped his badge and the heavy lock clicked open. He waited for her to go through before following behind.

Another set of stairs was just on the other side of the door. Mona craned her neck to look up the open well. The industrial treads spanned up three floors. "I'm guessing this is how you get your exercise."

"It's one way." Pierce's hand once again came to her back. "Would you rather take the elevator?"

Of course there would be an elevator. "I'm fine. I lived on the third floor before coming here."

"In Cincinnati." Pierce's steps fell in time with hers, his shoes making soft sounds as they hit the cement. "Was there a reason you chose the third floor?"

"The view was nice. It looked over the river." Mona took the stairs a little faster as her stomach finally started to realize what was happening.

"I'm sorry you don't currently have a view like that here."

Her heart was pounding, but it had nothing to do with the exertion of the stairs.

This was a bad idea.

Puking on Pierce's coat was one thing.

Barfing all over his room was another.

When they reached the top step Pierce swiped his badge once more, unlocking the next door.

No.

The final door.

"Is something wrong, Mona?"

She stared through the open door. "No."

There was a lot wrong, actually.

Any thoughts she had that Pierce was like everyone else evaporated like water in a hot skillet at the sight of his space at Alaskan Security.

This wasn't a room. This was a home.

One nicer than any she'd ever set foot in. A large kitchen stared back at her. A center island topped with a butcher block counter stood between her and an industrial range and hood. The floor was marble tile and a matching mosaic covered the back splash. Sleek black counters sat atop richly-stained cabinets.

It was exactly what she should have expected if it occurred to her Pierce had a home.

Which it hadn't.

Imagining Pierce doing anything but running Alaskan Security was nearly impossible.

A digital bell chimed.

"As much as I hate to rush you, our dinner is most definitely done." Pierce's hand pushed against her back, propelling her a few steps into the room. He left her where she was, going straight to the oven. He opened the door and used a towel to pull out the tray inside. "Do you drink wine, Mona?"

She was staring at the ceiling now where the interior workings of the building were exposed and painted matte black, giving the space a lofty feel, if the unreal could feel like a loft.

She might as well be in Oz at this point because nothing made sense anymore.

Pierce had a beautiful home where he cooked beef wellington and wore jeans and fitted thermal shirts.

And for some reason she was stuck in the middle of it.

Mona forced a breath into her lungs.

Tonight was not a night for wine.

"Got any gin?"

CHAPTER 5

MONA WAS FULL of surprises.

"I do have gin, as a matter of fact." Pierce opened the door to the space under the island that served as his liquor cabinet. "Any particular kind you prefer?"

Her eyes finally came his way instead of roaming the kitchen. "I don't think it matters at this point."

Interesting.

"I will surprise you then." Hopefully the drink would be the least of what surprised her tonight. He'd spent an hour beside Shawn on the treadmill, trying to burn off as much energy as he could, hoping it would help him keep the calm he needed to offer this evening.

"Do you drink gin often?" Pierce pulled out one of his favorite options, and went to fill a tall glass with ice.

"Only when I'm stressed." Mona took a few more steps, her eyes going to the beef wellington he'd spent the afternoon assembling.

"So I can assume you're stressed?" He pulled a can of ginger ale from the fridge before going back to the island. He poured in the gin and a bit of framboise then reached for a lime from the basket of fruit in the center of the island.

"That's a safe assumption." Mona leaned closer, peering at the array of fruit he always kept on hand.

"I hope you're hungry." Pierce cut the lime, squeezing half over the cocktail before topping it off with a healthy pour of the ginger ale. He picked up the filled glass, keeping it close as he rounded the island. "I don't often get the chance to cook anymore so I took full advantage."

Mona's gaze lingered on the wellington before coming to the drink he held between them. "*You* cooked dinner?"

"This may come as a surprise to you, but Brock isn't the best cook at Alaskan Security." He lifted the drink closer to Mona. "We won't tell him that, though."

It was the first of many secrets he wanted to share with her. The first of many glimpses he wanted to offer her into his life.

Into himself.

Mona took the glass. "Thank you." She tipped it back and swallowed down a few healthy gulps that must have had her throat burning from the cold.

She was nervous. He expected it.

Tonight was about showing her there was no reason to feel that way around him.

"Do you enjoy sweet potatoes?" Pierce pulled himself from her side, going to the other oven where the rest of the food he'd prepared was holding its warmth.

Mona didn't respond. He removed the covered bowl of mashed sweet potatoes and the tray of roasted asparagus, setting both on top of the range before turning to face her. Her eyes were wide where they fixed on his chest. "Mona?"

Her cool blue gaze immediately bounced to his face. "What?"

"Is there something wrong?" He leaned back, relaxing against the warm front of the stove, trying to look as calm as he wanted to be.

"Um." She blinked a few times, shaking her head a little. "It's just strange to see you not wearing a suit."

He wanted her to see him as something besides what she clearly did.

He wanted her to see him as a man. Flesh and bone.

Not the untouchable false front he created out of necessity. "It happens on occasion."

"I guess I never really thought about it." Her eyes started to dip again. They only made it to the line of his shoulders before coming back up and widening even more.

"Well I certainly can't sleep in a suit." He straightened, slowly moving her way. "Or shower in one."

The same flush from this morning rewarded his gamble. She may not want to consider it, but

Mona definitely thought of him in ways other than the role he took in the outside world.

It was time to foster their private world. Show her the role he planned to take there.

"Where would you like to eat?"

Mona rolled her lips inward, pressing them together for a second before releasing them. "What are my options?"

Pierce rested one hand on the large kitchen island. "We can eat in here." He slowly eased closer. "But I usually eat on the sofa."

Her pale brows came together. "Really?"

"Really."

Since his last risk paid off so well, he decided to take another.

Pierce caught her hand with his, sliding his fingers between hers. "Since you came dressed to relax I think the sofa is the most logical option."

She was off-balance around him and it worked in his favor. Made it easy to lead her along the path he'd designed to help her find her bearings with him.

The living room was just off the kitchen. He took her there, directing her to the large, well-stuffed sofa he'd had custom-made for the space. It was covered in soft leather that always felt warm.

Pierce snagged the white chenille blanket from the arm, shaking it out. "Sit."

Mona didn't make a move. She eyed the couch. "We're going to eat on this?"

"We are." He held the blanket up. "Sit."

Her head tipped a little as her eyes slowly came back his way. "Do you always just tell people what to do?"

He froze. "I—"

Mona rounded the glass-topped coffee table instead of walking past him. "I think I'd rather eat in the kitchen." She took a few steps before doubling back, leaning in and snagging away the blanket. "I will take this though." She wrapped it around her shoulders as she walked back to the kitchen, leaving him staring after her, a smile working across his lips.

He followed slowly, watching as she worked her way onto one of the high-backed stools around the island, the chenille blanket impeding her process. Once she was finally situated, Mona tipped back the rest of her drink.

"Would you care for another?"

She pursed her lips, blue eyes working over the empty glass. "Probably." She reached across the island, holding the glass his way.

He took his time, letting his fingers drag over hers as he slipped the glass free. This was a dance like none other he'd attempted and it was exhilarating.

Watching her. Knowing what to expect.

Then being wrong.

Mona surprised him at almost every turn. She was the unexpected element his life had been missing for so long.

She was a breath of fresh air in a room that was stuffy and stale.

Pierce went to work on her second drink, the feel of her gaze a comfortable weight that kept him grounded and focused.

"Do you drink a lot?"

"Some." Pierce repeated the process, building the cocktail in her glass before offering it to her. "You?"

"Not as much as I probably should given the circumstances." Mona took it and immediately sipped, her full lips pressing against the clear rim in a way he couldn't ignore.

"And those are?" Pierce pulled two plates from the cabinet.

"Hmm?" Mona's eyes watched him over the drink, lips parted as the cool liquid flowed between them.

It was more than enough to make him instantly hard.

Which was the exact reason he called Shawn this afternoon. He'd hoped to exhaust his body enough it would struggle to react to her.

Clearly that would not be the case this evening.

"The circumstances." Pierce turned to the stove, trying to block out the image of Mona with parted lips and wide eyes that fixed to his as she drank.

"Oh." Mona cleared her throat. "Everything that's happening here. It's stressful."

Pierce filled her plate first. "Do you regret coming here?"

It was a fear he harbored.

That Mona might choose to return to Cincinnati when this was all over. Leave him here, alone with the past he would always have to face.

Steal the air she brought into his suffocating life.

"No." Her answer was quick and confident. "Will I regret *staying* here?"

He turned at that.

She huffed out a little laugh. "Ask me in the spring."

He let out the breath caught in his lungs. "I will remember to do that." Pierce set her plate on the butcher block and turned back to plate his own dinner.

He hadn't eaten with another person in years. In spite of the fact that many of the friends from his younger days were around him, there was a distinct line between them. One that formed before they ever met.

In a moment that brought him unbelievable pain.

And unbelievable responsibility.

Every decision he made was his alone to make, and it set up a barrier that couldn't be crossed.

When Pierce turned back Mona's plate was untouched. "Are you not hungry?"

"I was waiting for you." She frowned. "It would be rude to just start eating."

"It would make me happy if you were so impressed by what was in front of you that waiting to taste it was impossible."

"I can't imagine that would ever be impossible."

"I disagree." Pierce slid onto the stool across from her, reaching across the space to pass her a fork and knife. "I would imagine there are many times when waiting to taste something seems quite impossible."

The tint of pink he was quickly becoming addicted to seeing crept across her skin.

Mona's eyes went to her drink. She immediately tipped it back for another swallow. "I will take your word for it."

Pierce cut into the slice of beef wellington on his plate. It was the most impressive, yet relatively normal, thing he could think of to make for her. "What's your favorite food?"

Mona's eyes widened as her lips closed around her fork, a bite of the wellington disappearing into her mouth.

Pierce shifted in his seat, straightening out one leg in an attempt to find a little more space in his jeans.

Mona held one hand over her mouth, blessedly blocking his view of her lips. "I think this might be my favorite food."

"Good. I'm glad I've satisfied you."

The flush of her cheeks deepened.

It was a dangerous game to play. One that tested him as much as her.

Mona swallowed her bite of food, immediately washing it down with the rest of her drink.

Two cocktails in less than fifteen minutes.

Not a good start.

Pierce went to the fridge, retrieving two bottles of water. He cracked the seal on the first and set it in front of Mona before opening his own. He had to find a way to calm her without the aid of alcohol. "I would like to discuss our meeting with Zeke tomorrow."

The pink of her cheeks disappeared almost immediately. A fact that settled him immensely. "Are you going to let him come back?"

"I am open to the option." He studied her as she continued to eat. "But I'm apprehensive about it."

Mona nodded a little. "I understand."

"Do you?"

"I mean, I try." Mona took a drink of the water he gave her. "There's a certain amount of trust you all have to have in each other, right?" She poked at her potatoes. "Otherwise everyone is at risk."

"I have to keep everyone here safe. I can't do that when one of my men is trying to fulfill two separate agendas."

"Are there two separate agendas?"

If anyone else asked him the question there would have been no hesitation in his reply.

But this was Mona.

She deserved his consideration.

"I'm not sure how we could share an agenda with GHOST." He wanted her to elaborate. Share her thoughts with him.

Share more than that. "Tell me what you think."

Mona's eyes slowly lifted to his. "If GHOST didn't have to be involved in this they wouldn't be, right?"

70

"That's right." Pierce rested his forearms on the edge of the counter, leaning close, waiting for her to continue.

"So they're in this because for some reason they have to be." Mona's voice was a little stronger. "It's possible they are simply concerned about their own security. Whoever we're dealing with is clearly capable of getting into places they shouldn't."

"Okay."

"But I don't think that's it." Mona caught the left inside edge of her lower lip between her teeth.

"What do you think it is?"

"I think for some reason they need us." The words tumbled out and her lips pressed together.

Pierce let the idea settle for a second, studying the woman across from him as he did.

"Vincent wanted to make a deal with me."

Mona's brows lifted. "The man from GHOST?"

Pierce nodded.

"What was the deal?"

"I don't know. I walked out."

"That's unfortunate." Mona went back to her dinner. "I'd be interested to know what it was."

"We should go ask him." The offer was out before he could think it through.

Not that it would have changed anything.

"*You* should go ask him. You're the owner of the company."

"And we've discovered I'm useless on my own." Pierce smiled, knowing he found his next foothold in the wall he was scaling. "I need a handler."

"I'm sure Heidi or Harlow would be better suited for that job."

"I disagree." Pierce wiped his mouth with the napkin draped across one thigh. "Heidi and Harlow would only make things worse."

A sharp knock came from the living room. Mona jumped, her eyes snapping in that direction. "What's that?"

Damn it.

He pushed from his chair. "It's the main door. I'll be right back."

The person on the other side was knocking again by the time he got there, the sound getting louder with each rap. Pierce pulled open the door.

Dutch stood on the other side. "Vincent's here."

"He's here?" Of all the poorly timed— "Why?"

"He's got a team of ten guys with him. Wants to talk to you now."

The alarm on the back door started to wail, the sound shrill and loud.

"I'll be down in a minute." Pierce started to close the door.

Dutch blocked the door with his foot. "Is there something wrong with that door? You need me to reset it?"

"I'm sure it's just a glitch. I'll see you in a moment." Pierce fought the door closed, immediately turning to go to the kitchen where Mona was fighting with the door there.

"Is the building on fire?" He went to the alarm, punching in the code to reset the system. The piercing noise immediately cut off.

"Why is this door locked?" Mona yanked on the handle, shoving at the lever like it might suddenly free her.

"The doors here are self-locking. The only way out is to know the pass code."

"Well you should probably put it on a sticky note or something in case someone needs to escape." She huffed out a breath, releasing the handle and turning his way. She gasped a little, stepping back, putting as much distance as possible between them.

Which wasn't much, considering her back was now pressed against the door.

"Is that what you need to do, Mona? Escape?" He couldn't help but ease a little closer.

Her eyes dipped, hanging on his mouth long enough to make her thoughts clear. "I don't want Dutch to get the wrong idea."

"And what would the wrong idea be?" Pierce shifted his weight, managing to steal a little more ground.

"That we're—" She swallowed, her throat working as her eyes came to his. "That we're—"

"Lovers?"

The barely-there flush he'd enjoyed seeing on her skin was nothing to the full-fledged flame tinting her skin now. "That's not what I was going to say."

"What were you going to say?" He took advantage of her distraction, inching even closer.

"I was going to say involved."

"Is that not the same thing?"

"No." It was a whisper as her eyes again fell to his mouth.

"Tell me the difference." He wanted to know how she saw things.

What she wanted.

"One is more." The tip of her tongue skimmed across her lower lip in a way that almost made him groan. Those lips had been torturing him all night. If she made a habit of adding her tongue to the mix he would be as good as ruined. "One is just sex."

Three little letters. One little word.

But coming from her mouth it was so much more. A sin and a prayer riding the same wave.

"I have no interest in being your lover then, Mona." He hadn't intended to be so forward with her. Not yet.

His phone started to ring from where it was tucked into his back pocket.

"Fuck." He should have stayed and talked to Vincent if for no other reason than to avoid this damned interruption. He slid his phone out, ignoring the call from Dutch.

"Who was that?"

Pierce punched the code into the keypad, unlocking the door. "Dutch." He took her hand in his, pulling her from the door so he could open it.

"Where are we going?" Mona's steps were silent as she followed him down the steps.

Pierce glanced at her. "Remember when you said you wanted to meet with Vincent?"

CHAPTER 6

"NOW?" MONA HAD to rush to keep up with Pierce's steps. "I'm in my pajamas."

He paused, turning to rake his deep blue eyes down her body. "Good point."

At the landing to the second floor they stopped. Pierce pulled open the door and tugged her through it, taking her straight to the door to her room. He swiped his badge and the lock clicked open.

"Did you just unlock my door with your badge?"

He held it open. "Can we talk about this while you get changed?"

"You can't be in here while I get changed." Her skin was hot again.

She glanced down. The blanket from Pierce's sofa was still wrapped around her. No wonder she was hot.

"I promise to close my eyes."

"No." It wasn't that she thought Pierce would try to peek at her. The thought of him being interested in seeing anything she might have was ridiculous.

It's not like he wanted to—

The sound of voices carried up the stairs leading from downstairs.

Pierce wrapped one arm around her waist, pulling her body tight to his as he swung them both inside and closed the door behind them.

The long line of his frame pressed to hers, strong and solid and—

Oh God.

She didn't mean to look down.

It was just so shocking. So baffling.

Maybe it was the jeans. Just the added bulk of the fly.

A lot of added bulk.

That had to be it.

Certainly Pierce would not be—

He released her. "Go. Get dressed before they hunt us down and you lose the opportunity."

Her head was spinning, tripping around in a cyclical stupor. "How could they find us?"

"I don't know if you're aware, but there are cameras everywhere, Love."

Did he just try to make a joke?

And what was that he said at the end?

"Go." Pierce pointed to her room. "Hurry."

Mona took a few steps backward before turning and rushing to her room in the small suite where she'd been staying. There wasn't enough time to do much more than pull on a pair of pants and shove on some shoes.

The shirt would just have to be what it was. At least she kept her bra on earlier. Less than two minutes later she had on a pair of jeans and flats and was back out into the small living room area.

Pierce held his hand out her way. "Come on. My phone's ringing again." He snagged her hand as she came close, opening the door a bit and peeking out.

"Does it matter if they find us now?" She was no longer in Pierce's room. She had actual clothes on. No one would ever realize—

Mona glanced down where his hand held hers. "Why do you keep holding my hand?" Her brain finally seemed to work its way through the evening's events, lining them up in a way that seemed...

"And did you call me Love?"

Pierce's body went still.

He released the handle of the door, letting it close, once again shutting them in her room.

He turned to face her, standing silently as his gaze held hers.

Like he wasn't currently being hunted by half the building.

Like a powerful man wasn't waiting for his presence.

He took her to see Zeke. Risked the safety of many men to make it happen.

Made her dinner.

"Oh." The whisper slipped free as her stomach dropped to her toes.

The door behind her vibrated as a fist banged against the other side. "If you don't want the whole building to know you're in there you need to get your asses out right now." Brock sounded a little panicked.

Pierce didn't move. Didn't flinch.

Just watched her.

Mona dropped her eyes to the floor between them, pulling her hand from his and crossing her arms over her chest. "We should go."

She turned and opened the door, refusing to look at Brock as she slipped past him, hurrying down the hall toward the main building. The connecting tunnel was still covered, making it impossible for anyone outside to see her as she passed through the space. Mona stared at the spot where a bullet came through the glass.

The same bullet Pierce stepped in front of to protect her.

She pressed one hand to the side of her face, fingertips pushing into her temple as she walked faster.

It was a crazy thing to consider. It's why she hadn't.

In spite of what now seemed to be overwhelming evidence.

Mona's other hand went to her belly as it squeezed in a way that wasn't as uncomfortable as she expected.

Normally the thought of Pierce made her nerves clench and her throat tight. He was intimidating as hell.

But now…

"Ms. Ayers." Vincent stood in the entry, men lined around him. He tipped his head her way. "It's nice to see you again."

Maybe it was the recent revelation occupying her brain.

Or maybe it was mental exhaustion.

Or maybe all her efforts to find her way back in time were finally paying off. Bringing her closer to the woman she was before Chandler broke her down one tiny chip at a time.

Mona stopped, facing him down. "I'm not sure I share that sentiment."

Vincent's mouth softened in what was probably as close to a smile as the man could accomplish. "Where's Pierce?"

"Pierce is right here." A second later he was at her side, tall and broad and relaxed. "I apologize for the delay. I was meeting with an important individual."

Vincent's brow lifted. "More important than me?"

"Absolutely." The answer came immediately.

"Huh." Vincent turned to look toward Pierce's office. "I'd be interested to know who that is."

"I'm sure you would." Pierce held his arm out, gesturing down the hall. "Shall we?"

Vincent eyed Pierce a second longer before turning and walking toward Pierce's office, five of his men following behind him while the other five stayed at the front of the building.

Pierce shot Brock a glance.

Brock's head dipped in a barely perceptible nod.

Pierce's eyes came to hers. "Are you ready?"

"I'm not sure I should—"

"I am." He said it like that was all that should matter.

"I am no one." Mona shook her head, keeping her voice low. "There's no reason for me to be in there."

"This morning you asked for a meeting with him."

"That's when I was mad." This morning she was considering laying into the man in charge of GHOST for his part in almost killing her friend.

"I'm sure it'll happen again." Pierce's lips lifted in a smile. "Vincent has a way of bringing it out."

Mona glanced to where the men from GHOST flanked the entrance to Pierce's office. "He's used to getting his way, isn't he?"

"Absolutely he is." Pierce backed toward his office. "Would you enjoy helping me burst his bubble?"

"How are you going to do that?" Mona took a tiny step his way, the offer making her more interested than she was a second ago.

"A brilliant woman told me I have the power in this situation." His smile turned to something she'd never seen on him before.

The devilish grin Pierce wore transformed his whole face, taking the almost regal lines of his jaw and nose and making them seem almost boyish.

And it made her do something she normally didn't. "She does sound smart."

Confidence wasn't anything she owned. It was something she tried to fake, learning from the new friends around her.

But right now she felt a little confident. A little sure she might be able to hold her own.

Mona started walking, following Pierce like a rat in Hamelin.

Hopefully she didn't go over a cliff.

Vincent was standing at the window, staring down at the random plant in front of Pierce's window. "Your plant needs water."

"Thank you for the observation." Pierce closed the door and strode straight to his desk, leaning against it instead of going to sit. "What can I do for you, Vincent?"

"You're sounding more accommodating than I remember." Vincent turned to face Pierce. "I'm happy you're coming around."

"I don't know that I'd call my revelation coming around." Pierce was back to the man she knew. The one who always appeared in control. Always seemed to recognize he was the most powerful man in any room.

The same one who usually made her want to throw up.

Vincent's face carried a hint of amusement. "What would you call it then?"

"Understanding." Pierce held Vincent's gaze. "I'd been looking at our relationship entirely wrong."

"Had you." Vincent crossed his arms. "And how was that?"

"I assumed you were in the position of power." Pierce's smirk sent a shiver down her spine.

But fear was not what it carried. When he wasn't terrifying her, Pierce was causing equally debilitating emotions to wreak havoc on her insides.

"I'm always in the position of power, Pierce."

"This isn't a friendly visit. You didn't come to make sure we were all safe and happy." Pierce's tone was cool and controlled. "You need something from me. Otherwise you wouldn't be here."

The head of GHOST stared Pierce down, one eye squinting more than the other.

"What is it I can help you with, Vincent?"

Vincent stood a little straighter. "I'm not so sure I'd be celebrating a win just yet." His hard eyes moved to Mona. "Could you open that door, Ms. Ayers?"

Mona glanced to Pierce.

He gave her a nod.

She slowly opened the door to Pierce's office.

One of the men from GHOST stood just on the other side, a computer in his hands. He held it out to her.

She took it since there wasn't really another option. "Thank you." Mona turned to the men at her back.

"We discovered a listing an hour ago." Vincent came over, carefully taking the laptop from her hands. He walked to Pierce's desk and set it down, flipping it open and resting his fingers across the print pad in a specific succession.

"A listing?" Mona stepped in behind him, curiosity pulling her toward the laptop. "For what?"

"A hit man."

"What?" She bumped Vincent, knocking a little more space to see the computer screen. "For who?"

The head of GHOST tapped the pad, pulling up a photo.

Her whole body went cold.

She started to tip back.

An arm banded around her waist, tight and solid, supporting her weight as her knees buckled.

"That's unfortunate." Pierce's tone was dry as he stared at the screen over her head, the hard line of his body pinned tight to her back.

"A few weeks ago we heard some rumblings that suggested you were the actual target of all this." Vincent eased his large frame into one of the chairs across from Pierce's desk. "I was hoping to get things handled before it came to this, but you didn't seem too interested in discussing it."

Was he trying to put all this on Pierce?

Mona turned from the grainy photo of Pierce holding her hand as he led her from GHOST headquarters this morning. She sized up the smug man acting like he had no skin in this game. "If you think you're going to make us believe that you're here out of the kindness of your heart then—"

"It's awfully nice of you to think I have a heart." Vincent's gaze was cool and disconnected.

"I think you're here because you have to be. You're in this and you want out and you can't do it alone."

Vincent smirked. "I figured you were the one who talked some sense into Pierce." He glanced Pierce's way. "If we can keep her from getting killed you should give her a raise."

Mona's head bumped back a little. "Why would I be killed?"

"Didn't you read the listing, Ms. Ayers?" Vincent tipped his head toward the computer. "It's not Pierce they're after." He paused. "Technically."

Mona spun back to the screen.

SINGLE TARGET. FEMALE. PROOF OF DEATH REQUIRED.

"It's Chandler." He was the only person she could imagine that might want her hurt.

"According to one of my contacts Chandler Larson is dead." Vincent leaned back in his seat like he was discussing the weather.

It wasn't a complete shock. Chandler being dead was one of the options she and the rest of Intel were considering. "Then there's money in the PO Box."

"The PO Box?" Vincent was suddenly not so relaxed. He leaned forward, his eyes sharpening immediately. "What PO box?"

"There's a PO Box in my name. He was going to it every week. We think Tod was mailing him money." Mona frowned. "But maybe it wasn't Tod who the money was coming from."

Tod had been dead and Chandler was still going to the PO Box. Still retrieving envelopes.

Maybe not still.

"What else?" Vincent's whole body was very still, his eyes completely focused on her.

"That depends." Giving him their information prematurely wasn't something she was willing to do. "Why are you here?"

Vincent's eyes lifted to Pierce. "I might try to steal more than just one of your employees, Pierce." His gaze leveled on Mona. "I'm here because the same men who are hunting your boss are causing a shit storm for me."

"I thought they wanted to kill me?" Good God it sounded insane coming out of her mouth. Never in a million years would she have imagined anyone would attempt to outsource her killing.

The complete bizarreness of it had to be the only reason she wasn't passed out on the floor.

Or chucking on Vincent's boots.

Vincent took a deep breath, his eyes on her as he let it back out in a slow, controlled exhale.

He was silent for a minute.

Long enough the urge to vomit was starting to brew in her belly.

"We have reason to believe you are simply a way to get at Pierce." He tipped his head. "That's where the technically comes in. Pierce is the ultimate target, but not the immediate one."

"I thought this was about the cartel? I thought they were trying to find a path to start smuggling drugs into Canada?" That was the most likely scenario they'd come up with. The only one that made any sense at all.

The money. The location. The brutality. Drugs were the most likely reason for all of it.

"I think that's just a bonus." Vincent's focus went to Pierce. "Taking him down seems to be the primary objective."

"Taking him down." Mona glanced to Pierce. "What exactly does that mean?"

"It means it seems like your boss pissed someone off at some point in his life and they're ready to even up." Vincent continued to watch Pierce. "Sound familiar?"

Pierce's jaw was tight, the muscles there flexing under the pressure.

"Pierce?" Was it possible he knew who this might be?

Pierce wiped one hand down his face, scrubbing over his eyes as he went.

"Do you know who it is?" Her stomach squeezed with both fear and anticipation.

If Pierce knew who this was then they could just find them and finish this.

Whatever that might entail. At this point whatever it was would be more than fine.

She'd killed someone.

And now someone was trying to kill her.

The rules in life were blurred into nothing now.

Pierce's deep blue eyes found hers.

"I believe the name you are looking for is Anthony Sanders."

CHAPTER 7

AS MUCH AS he tried to pretend otherwise, he always knew this day would come.

Knew the past he fought so hard to keep at bay would eventually connect to the unraveling of his present. The potential demise of his future.

Unfortunately it might not only be his future at stake.

"Who is he?" Mona sat in the chair across from his desk.

Vincent left the second he had the name, leaving Pierce alone to face down the woman he dragged deep into the darkest part of his history.

She deserved the answers she wanted, but there were only so many he could give her. "He is someone I used to know."

One brow lifted. "Just someone you used to know?" She huffed out an unamused laugh. "That explains why he wants to ruin you. Former acquaintances do things like that all the time."

"His brother was married to my sister."

Mona's mouth opened. Then it closed.

Then it opened again. "So he was your in-law."

"I'm not sure either of us would claim that." Pierce rounded his desk, pulling open the drawer on the left and lifting out the bottle of scotch he tucked there when all this started. He poured a couple fingers into one of the tumblers hidden in the same spot.

Then he added a little more.

"His brother was abusive to my sister. Mentally." Pierce tipped back the glass, swallowing everything down. "Physically." He rocked the tumbler in a circle, rolling it against the edge of the base as he stared at the cut glass. "I tried to end it."

"What does that mean?" Her voice was so soft. Each word careful and quiet as it passed through her lips.

"It means I found him." Pierce lifted his eyes to hers. "Made it clear what would happen to him if he hurt her again."

He'd put Rafferty in the hospital that night. Part of him wanted the man to die then and there.

If only he had. So many things would be different.

"Did he?"

Pierce focused on Mona's face as he tried to pull from the past. "Did he what?"

"Did he hurt her again?" The hesitation was there.

Because she already knew the answer. It was there in her eyes.

"Yes." Pierce poured another fill of scotch, swallowing it like the last. "He killed her."

Mona's gasp was barely audible but it hit him like a wave. "Then why is Anthony trying to hurt you?"

Pierce tapped his fingers against the smooth surface of the desk. "Because I did what I said I would."

"You killed his brother." She didn't ask.

"I did." Pierce capped the scotch.

"But his brother killed your sister." Mona was pleading a case that was long decided by money instead of courts.

"And he suffered the consequences for it." Pierce set the liquor back in place, closing the drawer. "I did not."

"So he wants to kill you." She shook her head. "That doesn't make any sense."

"His brother paid a price for what he did. Anthony believes I should pay that same price." It was a partial explanation, but more than he'd ever given anyone.

"By that logic someone will have to kill him for killing you." Mona scoffed. "This is insane."

"This is the way it goes when people are raised without limits." Pierce stood from his chair. "They believe they can do whatever they want without repercussions."

Mona stayed seated. "So what do we do?"

He smiled in spite of everything. "We figure out how to do what needs to be done."

"I should go get Heidi." Mona finally stood. "She'll be able to find him."

"It can wait until the morning."

Mona turned to him. "How can this possibly wait until morning?"

"GHOST will work through the night on it. You were correct in your belief that they want out of this. In order to get out of this they will do what it takes to find Anthony and clean up the mess he's made." Pierce stepped closer. "The best thing we can do is stay safe until they figure out how to accomplish that."

"I'm not sure that's possible." Mona glanced toward the door of his office. "We went through this before." Her fair skin paled a little. "There might be someone else here who—"

"You should stay with me." It was a perfectly simple solution. One that would ensure her safety and his sanity.

Mona shook her head. "No. That's not a good idea."

"You were curious about my showering habits, were you not?"

The paleness of her skin was gone in an instant, replaced by the flush he should feel bad for causing. He'd done it on purpose. With complete and total intent.

A reminder that Mona most definitely considered things she might not be willing to admit.

Yet.

"No." She shoved a finger his way. "You were the one who brought up the showering. You're the one focused on showering habits."

His eyes dipped. "That is absolutely true."

The flame of her cheeks deepened. "I can't stay with you. It just can't happen."

It definitely could. And should.

And would.

It was decided the minute he thought of it.

"There are only a handful of men I would trust with your life, Mona. There simply aren't enough to protect two locations." Pierce walked to the bookcase just behind his desk, releasing the hidden latch before swinging it open. "We have to stay in the same place."

To be honest there was only one person he trusted completely with Mona's safety, but that admission wouldn't make her any more willing to agree to his terms.

Mona's eyes widened as the shelf twisted on its axis to reveal the opening behind it. "Of course you have a hidden passage."

"And that means?" He loved hearing her assessment of everything. The way she analyzed with both concrete information and the abstract.

Mona waved one hand his way. "It means you're exactly the kind of person who has something like this."

"Based on what?" He was ready to get her moving, but first she had to work her way to the only logical conclusion. That meant he had to be patient. Give her the time she needed.

"Based on how you dress." Her eyes went to his jeans and thermal shirt. "How you normally dress. How you speak. How you act. All of it."

"Noted." He held one hand toward the opening. "Shall we?"

Mona huffed out a sigh, her head tipping back to the ceiling. "This is insane."

"Insane or not, we have to keep the company in mind. The more men we require to guard us, the less men are available to protect everyone else."

"Damn it." Mona huffed out another sigh, this one significantly more aggravated sounding. "Fine." She marched past him.

"The code is 9741." Pierce twisted the shelf back into place and reengaged the latch.

"You probably shouldn't give out the code to your secret doors." Mona punched the numbers into the pad, each glowing button giving off a soft beep when she pressed it.

"I don't." He pulled the door open as soon as the lock clicked open. "After you."

Mona glared at him a second before stomping her way down the stairs. She stopped at the next steel door.

"5428."

This time she hit the pad harder, stabbing the small buttons with the tip of her finger as she entered the code he gave.

"Make sure you remember these." Pierce caught the door as she started to open it, knocking it closed. "And I will be the one to go first this time, Love."

Her eyes widened a little. "Stop."

He shook his head a single time, leaning closer to her in the small space. "No."

He'd waited years for someone like her. Someone soft and calm but strong and defiant. He saw it in her from the very first.

92

Knew he could help her see it too.

"You have to." Mona's blue eyes dipped to his lips. "I can't—"

"What is it you believe you can't do, Love? Because I can promise you there is nothing you can't do."

Mona's eyes squeezed shut. "This is not what I thought it was." Her hands came up to rest at the sides of her face. "This is not—"

"Stop saying what it's not." Pierce edged in a little more. "Tell me what it is."

Her eyes snapped open, narrowing a little as they focused on his face. "This is insane."

He laughed a little. "I can promise you I'm quite sane, Love."

"I don't think I believe you."

"And why is that?" He liked when she bantered with him.

No one else would.

"Because we just found out someone is trying to ruin your entire life before he kills you and you seem fine."

"It's my job to seem fine, Love." He should never have started calling her that. It was impossible to stop. "It's my job to be calm when no one else is."

She scoffed. "Are you trying to say I'm not calm, because I feel like I'm handling finding out there's a hit on me pretty well."

The reminder of all that was at stake sobered him immediately. "No one will hurt you, Mona. I can promise you that."

She shook her head. "You can't."

It was the part of all this he was working hard to avoid focusing on.

Because Mona was right, and if he acknowledged the danger she was in he might lose his mind. He couldn't handle the weight of one more head on his shoulders.

"I can do anything."

Her eyes locked his. "Does that mean you were raised without limits too?"

God she was brilliant. So quick. She could have figured all this out ages ago if she'd known everything. He reached up, tracing the line of her face with the tip of his finger. "No, Love. I was not."

Her skin was as soft as he knew it would be. Smooth and warm. Like velvet.

He pressed the pad of his finger against her chin, lifting it higher. "I was the exception."

She was inches from him. Her small frame pressed to the door he held shut. "You are always the exception, Pierce."

It could have been an insult.

Maybe a compliment.

Didn't matter.

"I plan to prove that to you."

She inhaled. A soft sound that would be lost if they weren't locked in the silence of the stairwell leading from his office.

The breath held as she stared up at him. "I don't need you to prove anything to me."

"The proof isn't for you." He leaned in a little more. "It's for me."

"What proof do you need?"

"I need proof I'm deserving of you." Her soft scent was everywhere now. He no longer had to chase it like a drug. "That I can provide what you need."

"I don't need anything."

He smiled. "Then there is something I need to prove to you." Pierce tipped her chin higher. "Because I'm quite sure you have needs, Love."

Her lips barely parted and her jaw went soft.

This woman definitely had needs, and now he couldn't help but wonder if anyone ever met them.

Mona's chest lifted and fell a little faster but everything else about her was completely still.

"And I'm quite sure I am capable of satisfying any and all of them."

Her lips clamped shut.

Pierce ran his finger up the center of her chin, stopping once he reached her lips. "What do you think, Love? Do you think I'm capable of giving you anything you need?" He made a slow swipe across her lower lip. "Anything you want?"

As soft as Mona's skin was, her lips were infinitely softer. It pushed him to the edge he always kept firmly in the distance.

And as much as he knew he should, walking away from it was impossible.

She didn't answer. At this point it was difficult to tell if she was even breathing.

Her skin suddenly went pale.

Very pale.

The finger at her lips stalled. "What's wrong, Love?"

Her hand came between them, shoving his out of the way as it covered the mouth he'd been so ready to feel under his.

"I think I'm going to throw up."

****

"HOW ARE YOU feeling?" Pierce walked into his living room with a cup of tea.

Mona stared at him over the edge of the blanket covering nearly all of her body. She was tucked into the corner of his sofa, feet pulled up under her, looking only slightly less green than she had in the tunnels. "I'm okay."

"Good." He held the tea out.

She took it, her fingers carefully avoiding his.

He'd pushed too hard. Tried to take too much too soon.

And his ego had taken a hit because of it.

Mona's reaction was understandable, one he might have seen coming if he had maintained the control she deserved from him.

She sipped at the tea, her eyes staying on him as she swallowed.

The silence dragged between them, unsaid words hanging heavy in the air.

"I supposed I should have made my intentions with you clear from the start."

Mona's eyes widened as she pressed the cup to her lips, this time not actually drinking.

"I have been by myself a very long time, Mona. I've had many nights alone to think about what I want. What I have to offer." A bit of blonde hair fell free from behind the curve of her ear and his fingers itched to put it back in place.

To use it as an excuse to touch her again.

But he'd been greedy before and now he was back behind the starting line because of it.

"And what I want offered to me."

The cup finally lifted from her lips. "I think that's the part that's tripping me up." She took a slow breath, her eyes falling closed for a few seconds. "I'm confused about what you believe I have to offer you."

"Aside from companionship?"

"Yes." Her expression was unamused. "Aside from that."

He'd never had a woman ask why he chose them. Most were more than happy to enjoy the perks he had to offer without question.

That was the first of what she had to offer.

"You are intelligent. You offer insight I miss."

"So is every other woman in Intel."

"You are calm."

"I just almost threw up on you because you tried to kiss me."

"I didn't actually try."

"You were working up to it."

"Those are two totally different things, Love." Pierce relaxed a little. She was talking to him now. He could work with that. "And I can promise you that when I kiss you there will be more than trying involved."

Her jaw shifted a little and her shoulders squared. "Who says you'll ever get to kiss me?"

"I do."

Her eyes narrowed a little. "You don't get to decide that."

"You'd be surprised what I get to decide." He worked to hide a smile. "I can accomplish many things, Love."

"Not this." Mona sat a little taller on the sofa.

There she was. The woman he saw beneath the layers of uncertainty and hesitation.

She was fucking stunning.

"I am quite confident in my abilities." He let his eyes drop to her mouth. "And I'm certain you will regret your decision to avoid them."

Her skin flushed but she didn't back down. "I doubt it."

As much as he loved her soft side, this part of her was like a drug to him. The fight he saw in her eyes. The defiance in the tip of her chin.

Mona was all he needed. The calm to his storm. The peace to his turmoil. The center to his chaos.

And he could be all she needed. He would prove it. Whatever it took.

"Would you care to wager on it?"

She blinked, his offer clearly catching her by surprise. "You want to bet that I'll let you kiss me?"

"Absolutely I do."

"That seems counterintuitive."

"I don't intend to lose."

Her nostrils flared a little. "Neither do I."

He did smile at that. "Good."

He wanted her to know she could fight him. Tell him he was wrong.

That he would welcome it.

"Prepare yourself." Pierce stood. "Because tomorrow I plan to be completely irresistible." He held his hand out to her. "Come. It's time for bed."

She scoffed. "If I'm not kissing you then I'm definitely not sleeping with you."

Pierce bent down, bracing one hand on the arm of the sofa and the other against the back, caging her in as he moved close. "I will be kissing you, Love." He inched closer. "And I can promise once that happens you will most certainly want more from me." Pierce leaned into her ear. "And I will give you all of it."

CHAPTER 8

GOD HELP HER.

Because he wasn't completely wrong.

If her stomach would cooperate she might have let him kiss her. Might have happily let him do just about anything.

And right now it was impossible to tell whether that was a good idea or a bad one.

As Pierce straightened, the smell of him pulling away, her lungs finally allowed in a little air.

"The second door on the right is your room for the night, Love." He tipped his head toward the hall off the living room. "Go. Get some sleep."

She didn't want to sleep in Pierce's home.

She also didn't want to sit here with him looking at her the way he was.

Like a predator sizing up his next meal.

Mona jumped up from the sofa and hustled across the room, refusing to turn around even though she felt the weight of his stare as Pierce watched her go.

The second door on the right turned out to also be the last door on the right. The first seemed to be a half-bath based on the limited peek she managed while running past.

Mona darted into the door, closing it behind her and leaning against the solid pane. She hadn't even bothered to turn on the light, but the reflection of the outside lights against the snow illuminated it with a soft glow.

She let out a huff of air, whispering under the breath. "You've got to be kidding me."

The switch was on the wall just beside the door. It was a slide-style dimmer. As she lifted it, a solid band of light edging the ceiling brightened, bathing the room in warmth. The actual fixture was hidden behind trim, making it seem almost as if it was the sun peeking over a continuous horizon.

Because of course the sun would have to rise and set in Pierce's bedroom.

And this was most certainly his bedroom.

A king-sized bed was centered along the wall opposite the door. The headboard was covered in tufted leather the same shade of deep tan as the sofa in the living room. The mattress was wrapped in white sheets and piled with blankets in varying shades of grey. Armed lamps were mounted to the wall at each side, situated perfectly for late night reading.

Which made sense.

Pierce's office was lined in bookshelves, but for some reason it never occurred to her that he might actually read those books. A sizable stack on one of the nightstands made it seem like the books were for more than show. She strained to read the lettering across the spines, but it was impossible to read the titles from where she was still pressed to the door. It shouldn't matter what they were anyway.

She should just go lay on top of the covers and try to sleep. Ignore everything around her. Pretend she was in her own bed.

But she had to pee.

Mona crept to one of the other two doors leading from the room and quietly twisted the knob.

It was not the bathroom.

She should just back away and try door number two. Stop taking peeks into the private life of a man she was only just beginning to know.

Instead she flipped the switch, lighting up a large walk-in closet filled with expensive suits and gleaming dress shoes. An island of drawers stood in the center. A tray sat on top of the smooth surface. Cuff links of different styles were lined in a separated section of the tray. The other side of the tray held a selection of watches and a single bottle of cologne.

Mona turned to look out the open door and into the empty bedroom before glancing back to the bottle of cologne sitting on the tray.

Smelling it wouldn't tell her anything she needed to know.

Especially considering she already knew exactly how the man smelled.

One more peek out the door and the bottle was in her hand, heavy and smooth as she uncapped it and lifted it to her nose, closing her eyes as she took an indulgent breath.

The deep scent of bergamot and cedar sent her stomach flipping and her cheeks heating.

She could almost pretend he was there. That she could be close to him. That she could let him close to her.

"Would you like something to sleep in?"

Mona jumped, quickly setting the bottle down as the familiar bite of panic took the excited twist of her stomach and wrenched it to something else.

Something she didn't know how to control.

She swallowed hard, turning to face him. "I was looking for the bathroom."

"You may go anywhere in my home you wish, Mona. I want you to feel comfortable here."

"You mean since I have to stay here until they catch Anthony." That's all. She would stay until they found him and then she could go back to the comfort of her own space.

Pierce's eyes eased over her face, the side of his lips barely lifting. "Something like that." He came close, moving in right at her side to open one of the drawers on the island. He pulled out a pair of black sweatpants and held them out to her. "Here. Take these. You'll be more comfortable."

Literally nothing was going to make her comfortable at this point.

"Thank you." She took the pants. Arguing about them would only keep him here longer.

"I promised I would provide all you need, Mona. I meant it."

Sweet baby Jesus.

It was getting nearly impossible to decide which was a more likely outcome to his nearness.

Vomit.

Or unconsciousness.

Pierce pulled a second pair of pants from the drawer before closing it. Mona held the pants he'd offered tight to her chest, waiting for him to leave.

Instead Pierce gripped the fabric of his navy thermal shirt and tugged it free of the jeans slung low on his hips. In an easy move he peeled it up his body and over his head.

Mona took a step back. Then another, managing to spin around just as his thumb flipped the button of his pants loose.

"In the morning we can have breakfast and discuss our next move." His voice was low and deep behind her.

But it barely registered.

All she could hear was the sound of fabric against skin as Pierce changed less than three feet from her.

This was not going to be the solution Pierce thought it would be. No way could she stay here with him like this.

Even if his chest was just as impeccable as everything else about him.

"Sounds good." Mona side stepped out of the closet and darted around the bed, rushing for the other door. She closed it behind her and let out a breath.

She wasn't supposed to be running from things that scared her anymore.

She was supposed to be standing up for herself.

Taking charge.

But taking charge when Pierce was concerned was impossible.

Which meant she had to get away from him.

Mona set the pants he gave her on the counter and pressed her ear to the door. When the door to his room opened and closed she waited a minute longer before peeking out.

The blankets were folded down on one side of the large bed, turned down and ready for someone to climb in.

And that's exactly what she was going to do.

Mona fell to the mattress, fully clothed, yanked the covers over her head and closed her eyes.

Pretended she was anywhere but there. Hiding in a Pierce-scented cocoon.

****

EVA SAT AT her desk when Mona walked into Intel's office. "Good morning."

"Not really." Mona flopped down in her seat, letting her head fall to her desk.

"Seems like it should be considering you didn't sleep in your own bed last night."

"I don't want to talk about it." She didn't want to even think about it.

"Yeah. That's not an option." Eva scooted her chair across the floor using her feet to pull and her hips to thrust it forward. "I'm going to need details." She rested her arms on Mona's desk, dropping her chin on top of them. "Lots of them."

Mona straightened. Maybe she could deflect. "Chandler's dead."

"What?" Eva shot up. "How do you know?"

The clutch of her insides relaxed a little. "The guy from GHOST came to see Pierce last night."

Eva's lips twitched. "So then how did you come to know this information?"

Shit. "Some guy named Anthony Sanders put a hit out on me."

Eva's eyes narrowed. "Anthony Sanders?"

Mona opened her mouth to explain.

Except that explanation led right to the one thing she was doing her best to distract Eva from.

Pierce.

"We should probably look into him. Find out all we can." At best she was on borrowed time.

But it was still time.

"What do we need to find out?" Heidi strode into the room, her arms loaded with computer bags, beverages, and the breakfast Shawn sent her with each morning.

"GHOST found a lead for us to follow." Mona kept it as generic as possible. "A man named Anthony Sanders."

Heidi snorted. "He sounds fancy." She set her container of eggs on the desk before dropping everything else around it.

Eva opened the top drawer to her desk and started rifling through the contents. "He hired a hit man to kill Mona."

"I'm not sure that he's actually hired anyone." It was one of many things she neglected to find out last night.

Too much happened too fast and it shorted out her brain.

And her guts.

"Where did GHOST find this?" Heidi flipped open her computer as she settled into her seat. "Oh my gosh. I can't get over how much I love this fucking chair."

"I am happy to hear that." Pierce walked into the room, a smooth wooden tray held in his hands.

"What are you doing?" Mona was already on her feet. Maybe to stand up to him.

Maybe to run.

It was anyone's guess at this point.

Pierce hit her with a dazzling smile. "I brought you breakfast." He set the tray on her desk. "Since you left without eating this morning."

She'd snuck out the kitchen door with the aid of the passcode Pierce gave her. Unfortunately Abe was camped out on the other side, so her walk of shame wasn't witnessless.

Not that it was a true walk of shame.

Yes, she slept in Pierce's bed, but it was all by herself. Even then there was way more tossing and turning than there was sleeping.

"I'm not hungry." Mona backed away from her desk, trying to put a little more distance between them.

Not that it was going to help. She was stuck being close to him around the clock for the foreseeable future.

"I think you'll change your mind." Pierce opened a small cardboard container of orange juice and poured it into a glass filled with crushed ice.

"Is that fucking quiche?" Heidi stood from her chair, leaning to get a better peek at the food on Mona's desk. "And fried potatoes?" She looked down at her own container of eggs before turning back toward Mona. "If you don't want it I do."

"It's ham and asparagus quiche with rosemary hash browns." Pierce took a step back. "I figured you'd be hungry after last night."

Mona picked up the knife situated on the tray. Technically it was made for cutting butter.

She eyed Pierce.

But it would probably cut him too if she jabbed hard enough.

One dark brow lifted and he smirked at her. "I'll see you at lunch, Love."

Oh God.

She was definitely going to have to shank him.

It was the only way to recover from this.

The whole room was silent as Pierce left. She didn't have to look to know Heidi and Eva were both staring at her.

She could feel it.

"What the fuck is with all the plants in here?" Harlow stopped just inside the door, one side of her nose scrunched up as she looked around the room.

Mona glanced toward the line of windows.

She hadn't even noticed the plants. There were at least ten of them. All different sizes and types. Everything from broad-leaved tree-ish plants to spindly spikes with dangling vines dripping with miniature versions of the mother plant. "Those weren't there yesterday."

"No shit." Harlow went straight for them, grabbing a few leaves and rubbing them between her fingers. "They're freaking real." Her head snapped toward where Mona, Heidi, and Eva sat. "I hope he doesn't expect us to take care of these things."

"Mona fucked Pierce." Heidi shoved in a bite of her eggs, grimacing as she chewed. "Are you really not gonna eat what he brought you, Monster?"

"Bout time." Harlow went to her desk. "He any good?"

"I didn't sleep with Pierce."

"I didn't say you *slept* with him." Heidi edged behind Eva, bringing her fork along as she came Mona's way. "I said you *fucked* him. Two totally different things."

"She didn't fuck him or sleep with him." Eva's lips spread into a sly smile. "But he definitely wants her to." She twisted her chair Mona's way. "Am I right?"

"I did not sleep with or fu—" Hell she couldn't even say it without nearly choking. "I didn't have any sort of relations with him."

Heidi stuck her fork in the quiche and worked a chunk loose. Her eyes widened as she chewed. "You probably should. This is freaking amazing."

Mona dropped into her seat, head falling to the back of her chair. "I'm not doing any of those things with Pierce."

Outside of the fact that it was a terrible idea to sleep with your boss in general, sleeping with Pierce was a doubly bad idea.

She'd never survive it.

He could manage to make her hot and nauseated at the same time.

However that was possible.

Which was why he could never win this bet he thought up. Letting Pierce kiss her would end one of two ways.

She would either barf down the front of one of his expensive suits...

Or she would end up having sex with him, and sex with Pierce would probably ruin a woman for life.

Hell, she was half ruined by him already.

"Why not?" Heidi stabbed a few potatoes onto her fork. "I bet he's real good at it." She eyed Mona as she ate. "Definitely better than twat face's stupid ass."

"Everyone is better than he was." Mona's stomach growled a little as the scent of the food worked its way into her nostrils.

"How did he find another woman to sex him?" Heidi shoved the plate Mona's way. "Try the quiche first."

She did not want to eat the food.

But she also wanted to eat the food.

Dinner last night was fantastic. What she got to eat of it.

And this appeared to be no different.

Who would have thought Pierce could cook?

Mona picked up the fork and cut a little off the slice of egg pie. She glanced Heidi's way. "Pierce is trying to convince me to let him kiss me."

She and Eva had been friends forever, but talking about things like this with her best friend always felt awkward.

It still did, but somehow Heidi made it less so.

"Holy shit." Heidi turned to Eva then back to her. "You haven't even let him kiss you yet?" She shook her head at the breakfast. "I shoulda played harder to get. Maybe I'd at least get more cheese on my damn eggs."

Harlow edged out from behind her desk. She peeked at the plate. "Damn, Mona. I might have to make Dutch start mooching off Pierce instead of Brock. That's fancy as shit."

She wasn't wrong. In addition to the quiche and potatoes, there was a bowl of cut fruit topped with a spoonful of yogurt that was drizzled with honey and sprinkled with sliced almonds.

Mona reached for the spoon. "What in the hell am I going to do?"

"You're going to ride this out." Heidi rested one cheek of her ass on the edge of Mona's desk. "That's what you're going to do."

"I'm not doing that." She didn't have a clue what to do in this situation, but riding it out was not an option. She couldn't handle the constant upset.

Always wondering what might happen next.

"You could just rip the band aid right off." Eva wiggled her brows. "Let him kiss you. See what happens."

Mona rested one hand on her belly as it flipped. "I'm not doing that either."

"Then you kiss him." Heidi pointed at the center of Mona's face. "Do it when he's not expecting it and then just walk away."

Mona tried to imagine having the balls to do something like that. "What would that accomplish?"

Heidi grinned at her. "Then he'll be as miserable as you are."

And it would be over.

Bet finished and won on a technicality.

"Oh yeah." Heidi picked up a slice of banana and popped it into her mouth as she turned Harlow's way. "And some guy wants to kill Mona."

Harlow held up one finger. "I'm going to need you to take a couple steps back."

"Technically it's not about me." Mona grabbed the glass of juice as she fell against the back of her chair. "He just wants to get to Pierce."

Harlow's brows slowly lifted up her forehead. "And he knows that killing you would get to Pierce how?"

Damn it.

This was a fricking vicious cycle.

Mona sipped at the icy juice, shrugging her shoulders as she slouched down in her seat.

Heidi snagged one more bite of banana before turning to go to her desk. "I can find out."

This was the main problem with what she did for a living.

There was no way to keep a secret. Somehow, some way it would be found out.

Like when your boyfriend cheats on you.

There's no way to ignore it and move on when the women around you declare war.

And little did Anthony Sanders realize that was what was about to happen to him.

But he wasn't going to lose something as trivial as his gym membership and the password to his Amazon account.

It wasn't just a team of women he'd pissed off. It was a team of women who ran a pile of men who solved their problems in a completely different sort of way.

Which meant Anthony Sanders was probably going   to   end   up   dead.

CHAPTER 9

"MR. BARRICK?" ELISE stood in the open door to his office. "There's a delivery here."

"Excellent." Pierce stood from the chair where he'd been waiting.

Expecting Mona to come through his door instead of the new office manager.

He followed Elise to the front entry where Brock, Wade, and Rico stood in the center of his late night purchases.

Rico lifted a brow. "Have you lost your fuckin' mind?"

"We are all stuck in a single location, living on top of each other. I thought we could use something to make the atmosphere a little more tolerable."

Wade lifted a fiddle leaf fig. "So you bought five hundred plants?"

"Fifty. I bought fifty plants." He scanned them. "It appears they're all here."

"Where in the hell are you going to put all these?" Brock shoved at a crate of smaller philodendrons.

Pierce turned to Elise. "I suppose that's up to you."

He'd hoped Mona would be the one to choose where the plants went. She was the reason they were here.

He heard her tell Eva how upset she was to give away her houseplants before her final move here.

He would have flown them to Alaska if he'd known.

So this was his second best option.

To provide her with replacements.

He'd started with the one in his office, hoping it might draw her in.

Then the ones that went into her office last night.

Now these that would go anywhere else she might decide to visit.

"I would like one of each in my private rooms." Pierce glanced down the main hall. "Some in the recreation room. Some in the common area of the rooming building. And anywhere else you think could use some greenery."

Elise looked out the glass doors. "We're in Alaska. Everywhere could use some greenery."

"What is this?" Lennie, one of the women who came from Investigative Resources stopped as she came through the door of the walkway leading to the rooming building.

"Plants." Elise went to stand at Lennie's side. "You want one in your room?"

"Really?" Lennie looked from Elise to Pierce. "Can I?"

"Of course." He tipped his head toward the array. "Choose whatever you want."

Lennie carefully worked her way around the boxes and pots, pausing to stroke her fingers down a broad leaf on one of the fiddle leaf figs before moving on. Finally she chose one of the smaller spider plants. "This one is nice."

"What about this one?" Rico tugged the pot of the fiddle leaf fig Lennie showed attention, pulling it away from the rest. "Didn't you like this one?"

Lennie gave him a soft smile. "I don't want to take one of the big ones."

"It's gotta go somewhere, mi vida ." Rico hefted the pot off the ground.

Lenni gave him a look from the corners of her eyes, one dark brow lifting. "Seriously?"

Rico's easy grin faltered.

Pierce couldn't help but smirk. At least he wasn't the only one struggling with the women from Ohio.

Rico's smile was completely gone now, replaced with a familiar intensity. "I'm very serious, mi amor."

Lennie rolled her eyes. She grabbed the potted plant, jerking it away from Rico. "You're going to have to do way better than that, Romeo." She wrestled it onto one hip, the height of the tree towering over her head as she walked back toward the door to the walkway.

"I'll keep that in mind, Loba."

Lennie's steps slowed, her face tipping Rico's way a tiny bit before she took off again, this time faster.

"I think she might chew you up and spit you out, man." Brock started pulling out the smaller plants and lining them down the desk.

Rico leaned to watch as Lennie disappeared down the newly-enclosed walkway. "I sure as hell hope so."

The speaker on Brock's shoulder barked to life. "We got someone coming up to the gate."

Brock leaned into the mic. "Any idea who it is?"

Pierce checked his watch.

Damn. The morning had not at all gone how he expected. "It's Zeke." He pointed to the plants as he caught Elise's attention. "Take care of those."

She lifted a brow.

"Please." The addition wasn't something he was yet used to. "And thank you." He turned to Brock. "Send Zeke to my office."

"I don't get a please and thank you?" Brock yelled down the hall after him as he hurried to Intel's office.

He'd hoped Mona would come to him. Be intrigued by his offering this morning.

It appeared he was, once again, incorrect.

"Mona." Pierce stopped at the door. "I am in need of your assistance."

Heidi grinned at him. "Yeah you are."

Pierce scanned the room. "Where's Mona?"

Heidi's eyes dropped to her computer screen. "Maybe you shoulda checked your office as you passed."

He started to turn.

"Hey." Heidi's tone was a little sharp.

He glanced her way over one shoulder.

"If she gets hurt because of you I'll stab your eyeballs out with a spork." She popped a chunk of cheese from a plastic baggie into her mouth. "And then I'll make you eat them."

"Noted." Pierce didn't wait for her response.

Mona wasn't getting hurt.

Heidi's threat didn't matter.

Pierce walked into his office. Mona stood at the window next to the plant he foolishly thought would be enough to show her he listened to what she said. "You're here."

She turned. "Is our meeting with Zeke canceled?"

His excitement at her presence dampened. "He is pulling in now."

"Good." Mona turned from the window, not even glancing at the plant at her side as she walked past it to the chairs in front of his desk. She sat in one, spine straight, chin lifted.

Prepared to take on a man who killed people as easily as he protected them. The same man she slapped across the face with a fierceness Pierce longed to see in his own presence.

"Zeke!" Heidi's howl carried down the hall. A second later a blonde flash flew past the open door.

Pierce backed out of his office, ready to run interference if Shawn caught sight of his lady chasing down another man.

Heidi skidded to a stop in front of an uncertain-looking Zeke. "How are you feeling?"

Zeke's eyes went to the door of Shawn's office as the team lead for Rogue stepped out, leaning one shoulder against the door jam. He took a step back. "I'm fine." He edged back a little more. "How are you?"

"Pshh." Heidi waved one hand at him. "I'm fine." She grinned. "Are you back now?"

Zeke's eyes lifted to Pierce. "That's not up to me."

Heidi turned to Pierce, one side of her nose lifting. "Are you kidding me right now?"

"It's not up to me if Zeke comes back either." Pierce tucked one hand in his pocket, trying to appear at ease. "I'm not the only one he's betrayed."

Heidi crossed her arms. "It was for a good reason."

"That's a matter of opinion." Pierce ran his thumb over the bullet he kept close, a reminder of the lengths he was willing to go to in order to keep all under his watch safe. "Do you believe I should be allowing everyone to act based on their own thoughts and agendas?"

Heidi's lips pursed.

At least one of them wasn't arguing with him.

"That's a lot of plants, Pierce." Vincent appeared at the end of the hallway. "You starting a greenhouse?"

He should have anticipated Vincent would accompany Zeke. "Good morning, Vincent. Can I get you something to drink?"

"No thanks." Vincent passed Zeke and walked straight into Pierce's office. He tipped his head Mona's way. "Ms. Ayers."

"Good morning, Vincent." She eyed the head of GHOST. "I wish I could say it's nice to see you again."

And now she wasn't fucking scared of the man in charge of one of the most dangerous government organizations in the world?

"Please sit." Pierce rounded his desk, leaving Zeke to find his way in. He lowered into his own chair.

"How are you holding up?" Vincent spoke to Mona, basically ignoring Pierce.

"Believe it or not this isn't the first time my life has been threatened." Mona lifted a shoulder. "I think I'm getting used to it."

"I want to come back." Zeke's tone was sharp as he walked through the door. He tipped his head Mona's way. "Shadow is the team most qualified to keep her safe."

"I'm sure Rogue would disagree with you." Pierce leaned back in his seat. "And so far they haven't attempted to kidnap anyone, so I would have to agree with them."

"You know damn well I had to do it. You would never have let her off the premises." Zeke shoved one hand toward the door across the hall. "And I took Shawn too."

"I should be appreciative that you chose to kidnap two of my employees instead of one?"

"He took two employees against orders." Vincent turned to face Pierce, straightening in the chair. "He risked his position at GHOST by taking your man."

"In that case I should be offering him a medal." Pierce turned his gaze on Zeke. "For being so honorable in his deceit."

Zeke took a step forward. "We had to be sure Heidi was all we thought. There was no other option."

"Besides kidnapping her?" Mona's words were soft but solid. "You are arguing that your only option was to kidnap her? Risk her life simply so you could see if she was all you thought?"

Mona wasn't talking to Zeke. Her cool blue eyes were fixed on the man in the chair at her side, narrowing as he stared her down.

"There's a lot you don't know Ms. Ayers."

"Then enlighten me." Mona turned in her chair, hooking one arm over the back. "I had a big breakfast so I'm good for a few hours."

Pierce hid his smile behind his steepled fingers as he watched, unable to look away from her as she found her footing.

Her voice.

"We were concerned Ms. Rucker could be part of the group trying to take down Alaskan Security."

Mona didn't bat an eye. "That's a lie. You never thought that."

"Are you forgetting that two of your own employees were part of it?"

"They were not both my employees. We fired Howard—"

"And the other one was your business partner." Vincent's expression was smug. "It's not a far jump to consider Ms. Rucker could be involved as well."

"She's not." Mona's chin lifted.

"I agree, but I wasn't willing to put my men's lives on the line until I was sure of her alliances."

Mona glared at Vincent a second longer. Finally she crossed her arms. "So what now? We just wait?"

"Not much for waiting, Ms. Ayers." Vincent's gaze turned to Pierce. "I'm sure Pierce isn't interested in waiting either."

Vincent wasn't wrong. "How do you propose we end this?"

"We've got to flush him out."

"No." Zeke said it the same time Pierce did.

Pierce shook his head. "Absolutely not."

Mona looked from Vincent to Pierce to Zeke. "How do we flush him out?"

"It doesn't matter. It's not happening." Pierce stood up, ready to do whatever it took to get Vincent away from her.

He wasn't fast enough.

Vincent focused on Mona. "With you, Ms. Ayers."

****

"ABSOLUTELY NOT." PIERCE glared at Vincent across his desk. "It won't happen."

Zeke stood at the door they'd just whisked Mona out through. "It'll happen over my dead body."

Vincent turned to face Zeke, his brows lifting. "Is that right?"

Zeke gave a slow nod. "That's right."

Zeke's sudden shift chafed for more reasons than one. "Now you decide you're on my side?"

"This wasn't about sides, Pierce. This was about doing what needed to be done."

"And this is what needs to be done." Vincent stood. "Ms. Ayers is our best bet. Between your men and mine she will have the best possible protection."

"It's not enough." Pierce would put just about anything on the line to stop this before there were more lives at risk.

Anything but her.

"We found another listing this morning." Vincent pressed the tips of his fingers together as he watched Pierce. "Traced it back to a PC here in Fairbanks. I've got eyes on the location now."

"Then there's no reason to use her." Pierce grabbed a pen. "What's the address?"

Vincent was silent.

Pierce dropped the pen, leaning back in his seat. "So what you want is for us to work with you." He met Vincent's stare. "But you have no intention of working with us." He shook his head. "You can't have it both ways."

Vincent stood. "I'm not sure you have any choice in the matter, Pierce." He turned to the door, pulling it open. "Let's go."

Zeke stayed put.

Vincent looked him up and down. "Let's go, Reaper."

Zeke shook his head. "No."

Vincent scoffed. "Are you kidding me?"

"Pierce is right. I can't have it both ways." Zeke crossed his arms over his chest. "Especially if you're gonna start putting down lines."

Vincent worked his jaw from side to side, holding Zeke's gaze a second longer before walking from the room.

Zeke stared at the spot Vincent vacated.

"He'll be back." Pierce stood from his seat, needing to work off the pent-up aggression brought on by Vincent's suggestion. "He doesn't have a choice or he wouldn't have been here in the first place."

"He's wasting fucking time." Zeke moved deeper into the room. "The longer this listing is out there the more danger she's in."

"Not if she doesn't leave the premises." They'd learned from their mistakes. They were on lock down with every man assigned a shift, utilizing all hands in order to patrol the entire property. "She's safe here."

"Did you fucking forget they almost shot her here?"

Pierce tucked one hand into his pocket, running the tip of one finger over the damaged bullet stowed there. "I have most definitely not forgotten." He took a slow breath, weighing his options.

He'd planned to sit on his decision about Zeke for a while longer. Use it as a reason to speak with Mona this afternoon.

"Collect Shadow. Brief them on the situation and meet me in conference room A in two hours."

Zeke didn't hesitate. He was gone immediately.

His concern for Mona should be more upsetting than it was, but right now Zeke's clear affection for her would only solidify his commitment to her safety.

And that was what mattered most.

Shawn ducked his head out of his office, watching as Zeke passed.

Pierce lifted one hand, waving the lead of Rogue in.

Shawn stared down the hall as he crossed, his eyes hard when they finally landed on Pierce. "So he's back just like that?"

"Vincent forced him to choose sides." Pierce walked to the window, staring out as he always did when he needed to focus.

To collect. To conquer.

"He chose us then?"

Technically Zeke chose Mona. "Something like that."

"What's this I hear about a hit on Mona?" Shawn came to stand at his side. "Heidi's freaking out."

"Apparently there's two." Pierce rolled the distorted bullet between his fingers. "I need her to find the listing. Vincent said they were able to trace it back to an address in Fairbanks."

"What's the address?"

"Unfortunately, Vincent believes he can use us without having to offer his assistance in return."

125

Pierce turned to Shawn. "Until he's willing to admit that's not possible then we are on our own."

He didn't entirely believe that to be the truth. Vincent may say GHOST wasn't willing to work with Alaskan Security, but his actions said otherwise. His team had been the first there when Zeke, Shawn, and Heidi went into the water. There was no way an Alaskan Security Team would have made it to the location in time and Vincent knew it.

And he'd stepped in.

"Heidi will find it." Shawn held complete faith in the woman he loved.

He wasn't the only one. "I know."

"I'm meeting with Shadow in two hours. I plan to send them to the location she finds."

"So you're sending Shadow to the same place GHOST is?" Shawn smirked.

It would be amusing if Mona wasn't the one in danger. "I am doing whatever it takes to keep Mona safe."

"We will all do whatever it takes to keep her safe." Shawn didn't need to say what was the blatant truth.

He was not the only one who saw how special Mona was. She'd managed to find her way into the hardest of hearts, burrowing under skin thickened by seeing the worst the world had to offer.

A movement caught their attention, sending them both turning toward the open door.

Mona's cool blue eyes rested on Shawn. She pointed to the door. "Out. I need to talk to him."

CHAPTER 10

MONA SAT AT her desk. Arms crossed. Foot tapping the floor.

Eva sat beside her. "They just kicked you out?"

That's exactly what they did. The second Vincent said he wanted to dangle her like bait Zeke was at the door, pulling it open as Pierce all but lifted her from her chair and dragged her out of the room.

Dumping her out in the hall like she couldn't handle what Vincent was suggesting.

So she wanted to puke when she got nervous.

Occasionally almost passed out when dealing with men like Vincent.

But didn't it show something that she still powered through? Still held her ground when he stared at her with his air of authority and danger?

And she'd slapped Zeke for Christ's sake.

What else did they want from her?

Mona turned to where Heidi sat. "Can you get in touch with Vincent without anyone else knowing?"

Heidi hesitated.

"Not you too." Mona held her arms out. "I've worked so hard." She pointed to the door. "I practically yelled at Vincent in there without gagging once."

"It's not you." Heidi shook her head a little. "I don't know these men from GHOST, Monster. I don't trust that they can keep you safe."

Mona caught her head in her hands.

She had to do something.

This could end. They could get Anthony to show his hand and take him down.

Then she could finally be free of the mess she'd made.

The real monster she'd created by allowing others to make her something she was ashamed to be.

And there was only one person who could help her.

Unfortunately, it was the same person she seemed to struggle with the most.

But that's what this was about. Overcoming. Walking away from the woman she intended to put behind her.

Mona stood up, smoothing one hand down the front of her sweater. She took a deep breath and started walking. "I'll be back."

"Oh shit." Heidi's words followed her through the door.

They echoed in her head.

Hell yeah, oh shit.

It was do or die time.

She did or someone else might die.

And that someone might be Pierce.

An uncomfortable sensation fisted her stomach. It wasn't the normal bite of the nerves she fought so hard to overpower.

It was something else.

Something different.

Something she didn't want to name. Definitely not now. Not when she was just finding her momentum.

Mona marched straight into Pierce's office, ready to do what had to be done for the good of everyone.

She'd had a hand in where they were now.

If she hadn't been such a pushover.

Such a wet damn rag.

This might have all been avoided.

Shawn was in Pierce's office. Both men stood near the window she'd looked out earlier as she waited for him.

The second she walked in they both turned her way, as if they could sense her presence.

Good. Maybe they should. Maybe she was a presence.

Mona stabbed one finger toward the door, locking eyes with Shawn. "Out. I need to talk to him."

Pierce's gaze stayed on her as Shawn glanced his way. Pierce tipped his head toward the hall. "Go. I'll come find you when we're done."

Mona stood tall as Shawn walked past her.

She refused to drop Pierce's heavy stare. She'd dealt with tougher men than him.

Today even.

The door clicked shut and they were alone.

It could have sent her crumbling.

But there was too much on the line.

Her friends.

Her new home.

Maybe even the man in front of her.

That meant she had to pick up her skirt, grab her balls, and act like she knew how to use them.

Mona set her shoulders and went straight for him. Confusion flashed across Pierce's gaze the second before she grabbed his face with her hands.

She closed her eyes, scared of what she might see next, and pulled his lips to hers.

If she'd surprised him it didn't show.

There was no hesitation. No pause before understanding dawned.

It was always there.

One of his hands immediately went to her hair.

The other went to her ass, pulling her tight to him, taking what she intended to be a simple victory kiss and sending it somewhere completely different. Somewhere she might not have ever been before.

His skin was warm under her palms. His body was solid and strong where it held her, pressing the scent of him into every breath she fought to take.

This was supposed to just be about winning. Earning the leverage she needed from a man who sent her heart racing and her head spinning just by walking in the room.

She thought it was because of what he was. Who he was.

And maybe that wasn't entirely incorrect.

Because this man kissing her now was most definitely someone she should be scared of.

His mouth slanted over hers, deepening the kiss. The faint tingle of mint cooled her tongue as his stroked against it, making her already swimmy head spin at a rate she might never be able to stop.

Might never want to.

His taste. His smell. His warmth. All of it was an addiction she didn't know was hers.

Not until this very moment.

Pierce's hand in her hair fisted tight, holding her in place as his lips left hers.

Mona's lids were heavy as she lifted them, barely managing to get them open halfway before giving up.

The blue of his eyes was penetrating.

Consuming.

The hand in her hair immediately released, his fingers sliding free to curve against the side of her face as his mouth came to hers again. The hand on her body slid to the back of her waist.

Now his lips were different. Softer.

Less demanding.

Less what she knew him to be.

And in an instant she snapped out of the haze Pierce's kiss dropped her into. The fog of desire and realization split, revealing a moment that now felt artificial.

Fake.

Mona pulled away, her eyes easily opening to meet his.

What she saw there bolstered her, dug up a power she'd struggled to find.

She dropped her hands from his face but didn't step away. "I win."

Victory thrummed through her veins, chasing the thrill she'd felt seconds before.

Pierce's brows came together in confusion. "I'm sorry?"

He had no idea how sorry he was about to be.

"The bet you made last night." Mona smiled. "I win."

Pierce blinked, his lack of understanding making her feel taller.

Stronger.

This man who controlled everything and everyone around him no longer controlled her.

Her stomach no longer clenched at the thought of his presence.

Her throat no longer went tight at the smell of his skin.

The sound of his voice.

All because she knew the truth.

Pierce was scared of her.

****

"I KNEW YOU could do it." Heidi sat in one of the chairs in Eva's room, legs tucked up under her. "Is he going to let you go out?"

Mona shrugged. "Don't know."

She didn't care either. "I just told him I won and then walked out."

It was the first time she hadn't wanted to shrink down under the weight of his gaze. In fact, the feel of it on her back as she walked away fed her newfound sense of power.

Lodged it deeper.

"Did you hear from Vincent?" Mona leaned to peek at the array of snacks spread across the coffee table. Brock was on night duty tonight so they were all collected in Eva's suite, celebrating a productive day.

"You know I did." Heidi grinned over her wine glass. "I wish I could of been there to see his face when he realized we know everything he knows."

They'd discovered the address GHOST found and passed it along to Shawn so he could figure out the logistics of keeping an eye on the townhouse in downtown Fairbanks.

They wouldn't find anything there. It was one more recently-vacated spot they'd been two seconds too late on, but at least it would make them feel like they were doing something.

"You think Vincent knows we found the address?" Eva plopped onto the couch next to Mona.

Heidi shrugged. "It doesn't seem like it."

"We'll find out soon because I guarantee they're trying to figure out where in the hell I've been." Heidi hunkered lower in her seat.

"Will they be able to figure it out?" Mona picked out a slice of French bread and smeared on some warm Brie before relaxing back.

She hadn't felt relaxed in forever. So long it felt almost foreign to be able to eat easily without the twisting of her belly reminding her of all the things she needed to worry about.

To feel guilty about.

"For sure they'll be able to figure it out, but it might take them a day or two. I was real careful." Heidi sipped at her wine, watching Mona over the glass. "So how was it?"

"How was what?" She knew damn well what Heidi was asking about.

Heidi scoffed, immediately seeing through the false confusion. "You know exactly what I mean."

"It was fine." It was more than fine.

Until it wasn't.

But even then it was something.

Something important.

"Fine? You're trying to convince me kissing Pierce was just fine?" Heidi pointed at her. "You're a liar and a thief of joy."

"How am I a thief of joy?" Mona looked to Eva for help, but her friend shrugged.

"I've been waiting forever for Pierce to finally do something and now you won't even tell me if his tongue was in your mouth."

"You haven't been here forever." Mona started to drink her own wine but stopped. "And what do you mean you've been waiting?"

"The chairs. The peacocking. The way he always sits on your desk when he comes into our office." Heidi shook her head as she emptied her glass. "And don't get me started on him taking a bullet for you."

"He would have done that for anyone." There wasn't a doubt in her mind Pierce would have stepped in front of literally anyone at Alaskan Security under the circumstances.

"Maybe that was a bad example." Heidi poured a little more wine into her glass. "But he's still been into you at least since I showed up."

Mona turned to Eva.

Eva winced, her face scrunching as she gave Mona a tight smile.

"You knew too?"

"I was pretty sure if you realized he liked you it would only freak you out."

She wasn't wrong.

"He tried to kiss me in the tunnels." The admission jumped out. "I almost threw up on him."

Eva let out a breath. "Thank God. I was starting to worry that I was wrong."

"I'm glad my anxiety helped ease your conscience." Mona grabbed a small bunch of grapes from the fruit tray. "But maybe I would have handled it better if I had more time to get used to the idea."

She wouldn't have handled it better. Knowing earlier might have actually made it all worse. At least she'd been able to power through it only being intimidated by Pierce in general.

Not Pierce who was interested in more from her.

"So are you sticking with 'kissing Pierce was just fine'?" Heidi wiggled her brows.

"I think he didn't know how to react." At first he definitely did. There was no mistaking that the man who held her so tight owned the act in less than a heartbeat.

Owned her.

But then he changed in the blink of an eye, and it was like she was kissing someone else.

And it turned out she didn't like kissing that guy.

But she did like kissing Pierce.

Mona tipped back her glass, draining the rest of her wine. "I'm tired. I was up late last night."

She'd been expecting Pierce to come to collect her at the end of the day, insisting she stay at his place again.

Weren't they supposed to be sticking together? Didn't he say there were only so many men to go around and it would stretch them thin to guard two locations?

He did say that.

"I'll see you girls in the morning." Mona stood up and walked to the door. She opened it to find Abe standing outside. She eyed him. "What are you doing here?"

"You know what I'm doing here, Monster." He tipped his head toward the ceiling separating them from the rooms above. "I got orders."

She pursed her lips, the evening's wine relaxing her even more. "Go tell Pierce that if he was really worried about me he wouldn't send someone else."

Abe's brows lifted. "You really want me to tell him that?"

She mulled over the possible ramifications for a few seconds before straightening a little. "Yup."

Mona walked past Abe. "Have a nice night." The sound of Shawn's voice carried over Abe's shoulder speaker as she opened her door.

"He's going to lose it if she starts acting like that."

Mona smiled as her door clicked shut.

Good.

Pierce made her so crazy she almost barfed every single day.

Now it was his turn to feel a little uncomfortable.

Mona brushed her teeth and swished some mouthwash before layering on a swipe of deodorant and spritzing both the perfumes she mixed on the ultra soft pajama set she changed into before going to Eva's room.

It was time to go to battle, and now that things felt more evenly matched the prospect was less daunting.

Maybe a little exciting.

She'd lived a sheltered life of private schools and coordinated friendships. It set her up perfectly to land where she did, the tool of a manipulative asshole.

If she was going to be a tool it was going to be on her own terms.

She was going to be the one deciding how she was used.

Mona walked out of the bathroom, scanning the space as she decided where to wait.

The door to her room unlocked, shoving open to reveal a slightly rumpled Pierce.

That didn't take long.

She crossed her arms and lifted her brows. "Can I help you?"

It seemed like Pierce suddenly realized what he'd done. He straightened, tugging at the hem of his jacket. "I just came to make sure you were okay."

"And that necessitated barging into my room uninvited?"

He glanced back to the door as it clicked closed.

"Pierce?"

His attention slowly came back her way.

"Why are you here?" His normally perfect hair was loose, falling to one side in a way that made him look less polished. Less buttoned-up.

And more real.

"I just told you. To make sure you were okay."

"You knew I was fine." She smirked at him. "You sent Abe to be sure of it."

His nostrils barely flared. "There is a hired hit on your head." Pierce took a step toward her. "Or have you forgotten?"

Pierce used to intimidate the hell out of her. It was primarily due to his constant ability to be in complete control of everything when she couldn't even control her own insides. How could she hold her own next to someone like that?

Someone who never felt powerless.

Someone who owned every emotion. Every reaction.

But now she knew the truth.

Peirce was just a better actor than she was.

"Is that something a person forgets easily?" Mona stood still as he continued to advance on her, looking more like a predator than the sleek, sophisticated businessman who used to make her shake in her shoes.

Luckily she was no longer prey.

"I would think not." Pierce tucked one hand into the pocket of his pants.

It was something he did regularly.

Maybe it was part of the act. The same one that stole the kiss she was so lost in earlier today.

"Then you can safely assume I have not forgotten there's a price on my head." She smiled a little, holding up her pointer and middle fingers. "Two prices actually."

Pierce stopped, his whole body going still. A wildness flashed in his eyes and it sent a thrill through her.

This was the real Pierce. The one he put in a suit every morning. Hid under perfect words and muted responses.

"You found the second listing." He wasn't asking.

He also didn't appear to be amused.

"Heidi found it this afternoon." They weren't going to tell him, but right now the information served a valuable purpose.

The girls would understand.

Pierce's eyes narrowed. "And you chose not to share that with me?"

"I did."

"How am I to keep you safe if you withhold valuable information?" His words were tight as they slid through clenched teeth.

"Now *you* want to keep me safe?" Mona glanced to the door as she lowered her brows in false confusion. "I thought Abe was in charge of protecting me?"

"You know damn well I sent him—"

"That's right." Mona bobbed her head in a nod of agreement. "You sent Abe to be my protector because he's the most qualified for the job."

She'd never in her life purposely tried to make someone mad. Quite the opposite actually.

She never wanted to rock the boat. Never wanted to live with the fear that someone was angry with her. Might confront her about it.

And look where that got her.

Definitely nowhere as nice as this.

Pierce's left eye twitched, and the muscles of his jaw looked tight enough to crush the teeth he was clenching. "You believe Abe is the man most qualified to protect you?"

"It would seem so since he's the one standing outside my room."

Pierce's chin dipped, the change in angle casting a shadow across his face.

"But who's the man standing inside your room, Love?"

CHAPTER 11

HE NEVER MEANT to come here tonight.

They needed space.

He needed space. Time to get himself back together after what happened.

What he did.

And this was proof he should have stayed away.

Mona hadn't moved since he walked in. She simply stood there like she was expecting him, no hint of surprise on her face as he walked right into her room.

Her private space.

Pierce raked one hand through his hair like he had a hundred times already. "I should go."

"Whatever you think is best." Mona took a deep breath. "I'm sure Abe and I will be just fine."

He caught the barest twitch of her lips.

Was it possible she was doing this on purpose? Taunting him?

No. Definitely not.

"Goodnight, Pierce." Her chin lifted. "Tell Abe he's more than welcome to come in and sleep on the sofa if—"

The rest didn't make it through her lips.

Pierce caught Mona's body with his, the thought of Abe sleeping so close to her making him act without thinking. He pressed her tight to the bit of wall separating her bedroom and bathroom doors. "He will sleep on your sofa over my dead body."

Her breath caught. It wasn't a gasp of surprise. Not even close.

Which made it so much worse.

Mona's eyes held his. "You're the one who sent him."

"I sent him because I can't be around you right now." Pierce closed his eyes, trying to work up the fight it would take to walk out of her room.

Leave her to a man she was safe with in this moment.

"Yet here you are."

He opened his eyes against his better judgment. "You questioned my concern for you."

"And you came to prove you were worried about me? Is that it?" Her eyes dipped to where his body met hers. "Because it looks like something else brought you here."

He'd meant to lift her up. Show Mona all she was capable of being.

The power she held.

But this.

This might be a problem.

"You brought me here." His attention fell to her lips. The same lips he'd tasted not so long ago. "You did this on purpose."

"I don't like when you try to lie about who you are."

"Who is it you think I am, Love?"

Her gaze lifted to his. "You are the man here with me now." Her hands came to rest on his chest in a touch so light he could barely feel it. "The man who kissed me first today."

His whole body buzzed as his vision narrowed. "Who the fuck else kissed you today?"

Mona's fingers did a slow crawl along his chest, following the line of his lapels, before stalling out on the button placket of his shirt.

Her calm usually spread, blanketing him with one of the many things he didn't naturally possess, but right now it was maddening. "Who fucking put their mouth on you, Mona?"

Her skin instantly flushed and her pupils dilated. Her tongue slid across the inside of her lower lip. "No one put their mouth on me." She rubbed her lips together. "I put my mouth on you." Her eyes dropped his, falling to his chest.

Then dipping lower.

This was supposed to be slow. Carefully calculated steps to ease her into all he wanted.

Strategically maneuvering her life closer to his until there was nothing keeping one from the other.

Her fingers flicked the top-most done button on his shirt, sliding it free. The pad of her pointer slid into the opening to skim over his skin.

He caught her wrist. "What are you doing?"

143

Mona's lips rolled together again, torturing him. "I'm not completely sure."

"Certainty is an important thing, Love." He lifted her wrist to his lips and brushed a kiss across her pulse point, expecting to feel her heart racing.

She wasn't comfortable around him which actually made things significantly easier. It gave him a purpose.

A need to fulfill. One that made his own needs easy to control.

But while the beat of her heart was steadily fast, it was by no means racing out of control.

"Certainty isn't the issue." Mona's other hand moved down the center of his chest. "It's more an issue of what to do first." Her hand reached his waistband.

Letting her continue with whatever terrible plan she had was not an option.

Pierce snagged her other wrist and brought it to his mouth, delivering a matching kiss, this time lingering a little longer against her soft skin. He breathed deep, hoping her closeness would help him the way it always did.

Her small frame moved against his, sliding in a way that would bring most men to their knees.

Leave them begging for the chance to serve her.

And he was no exception.

Pierce tightened his hold on her wrists, pulling them high and holding them to the wall over her head. "You'll do nothing first." He leaned into her, gritting his teeth against the feel of her against him.

The scent of her around him.

"I am the one who goes first."

Mona scoffed. "Typical man." There was a bitterness in her tone as she worked against his grip. "In that case you can go back to wherever you came from."

And it brought him no small amount of joy. "I don't believe you understand what I mean." Pierce held both her hands with one of his. He slid his free palm down her arm and along the curve of her jaw bracing it there to force her eyes to his. "He who goes first brings the first pleasure." Pierce shook his head. "Not receives."

"Oh." The single word rushed out with an exhale. "Well that's different."

"Very different." He nosed along her neck, breathing deep. "Is that something you want from me, Mona? Pleasure?"

Her body went still. "Honestly, I don't know what I want from you." Her head tipped to one side as his lips found her skin. "Maybe I need a little more clarification on what exactly you're proposing."

He shouldn't be proposing anything. He should be walking right back out of this place. Banning himself to his rooms until he could rein this poor behavior back in.

But that would mean walking away from her. Leaving this moment.

"I want to touch you. Show you what I have to offer."

"I thought that's why you made me dinner." She wasn't giving in as easily as he expected and it made it easier to keep going.

"Dinner is the least of what I can give you, Mona." He could give her anything.

Everything.

But he had to do it carefully. Slowly.

She was just finding her feet and he couldn't rip them out from under her.

Mona needed him to keep his head.

His control.

"Dinner was pretty good." She arched her back, body pressing to his. "I'm not sure you can offer me anything better."

If he didn't know better he'd think Mona was doing this on purpose. Trying to goad him into something she most certainly wasn't equipped to deal with.

Shouldn't have to.

"You would be surprised what I'm capable of, Love." He lowered the hand at her neck, forcing it away and to a more respectable location. One that gave her more freedom.

More control.

The one thing most valuable to him.

"Stop it." Her voice was sharp and strong. Mona ripped her hands free of his, pushing between them to shove at his chest. "Stop changing."

In the blink of an eye she was behind him. "Go." She pointed to the door. "Just go if that's how you're going to be."

Rarely was he speechless.

"I mean it." She said each word slowly, breaking them apart with long pauses between.

"I don't think I understand what the problem is." He'd done nothing wrong.

He was being so careful. So cautious to make this comfortable for her.

The finger pointing to the door swung his way. "You. You're the problem." She snorted out a scoff. "Who even are you?"

"You know who I am."

It was more true than it should have been. He'd given her a glimpse of what he was today. It was something he'd regret forever.

Now she was confused. Scared of what she saw in him.

He couldn't blame her.

Mona shook her head. "I *don't* know who you are." Her chin lifted. "You won't show me." Her eyes skimmed down him. "Because you're afraid."

"I'm not." It came out sharp and fast. An immediate response to a cut that still bled.

He was not afraid. Not ever.

But Mona didn't understand. Didn't know the truth of how dark his past really was.

"Prove it."

"No." He wouldn't. Not to her. Not ever.

"Fine." She once again pointed to the door. "Then go."

This was not how he intended things to go. Not how he imagined their time together would unfold.

He planned to help her navigate the shift she was experiencing. Show her how to be careful.

How to avoid going too far.

"As you wish." Pierce turned for the door.

"Don't pull that Princess Bride bullshit on me."

He pressed the fingers of one hand to his eyes, trying to rub away the exhaustion there. "Nothing I give you is bullshit, Mona."

"Liar."

He slowly turned her way. "What did you call me?"

"I called you a liar." She walked toward him. "You hand out bullshit like candy." She waved her hand around him. "All of it's bullshit. The clothes. The way you act. The way you talk. All of it."

"You don't know what you're talking about."

He hoped to God she didn't.

Because if Mona knew all she claimed then there was no way they could be together. Not ever.

"You pretend to be this man you show everyone." She shook her head. "But that's not who you are. Not really."

Fuck. "Stop."

"No." Mona kept coming toward him. "Everyone else might be fine with it but I'm not." Her pale blue eyes were narrow as they stared into his soul. "I can't be around people who aren't real, Pierce. I won't do it anymore."

Couldn't she see he was protecting her? Giving her the best of what he could be?

"I am real. I promise you." He might not be willing to show her all he was, but every bit of what he'd given her was real.

Was him.

Her eyes moved over his face. "You hide."

Her ability to see through him was devastating. "Doesn't everyone?"

Her gaze held his as her shoulders lifted and fell with a deep breath he could feel in his own lungs. "What do you want from me, Pierce?"

It was an answer he thought he knew. Had spent hours working out.

But this was changing everything.

All of it.

"I don't want anything from you." The answer was outdated, but it was all he had.

Mona's eyes dropped. "Then there's no reason for you to be here, is there?" She turned and walked toward her room.

"So it's fine that you don't know what you want from me, but I should know what I want from you?"

She stopped, her body very still.

He hadn't meant to speak to her that way. Shouldn't have done it.

Mona turned. "Fair enough." She sucked in a breath. "What I want from you is honesty." Her gaze raked down the front of him. "I want the real you."

"That's not an option."

"And why is that?"

"The real me is not fit to breathe the air around you, Love. Take the man you see and be happy."

"Don't tell me what to do."

The immediate retort took him back. "I'm sorry?"

"You heard me. We're the only two here." Mona shook her head. "I spent too long entertaining men pretending to be something they're not. I'm not doing it anymore."

"Those men did it for themselves."

"And you're doing it for who?"

"I'm doing it for you."

Mona crossed her arms. "And I've told you I don't want it."

Pierce raked one hand through his hair. At this point the pomade from the morning was useless, working away over an evening of frustration.

And it just kept going.

"You don't understand what you're asking for." How could he make her understand this was the best thing? The only way this could be.

They could be.

A bitter laugh slipped free on her next exhale, soft and low. "Fine." She walked to the door, pulled it open.

Abe was still outside and now Tyson joined him. She gave them one of the soft smiles he used to crave before turning to him, the smile immediately disappearing. "Goodnight, Pierce."

He dipped his head.

How had this unraveled so quickly? Gone so wrong so fast?

He walked past her. It took all he had not to stop and grab her. Slam the door and lock everyone out.

Show her just what she wanted to see.

But that would be a mistake. One significantly larger than walking out of her room right now felt to be.

Tyson started to follow him.

"Stay with her." It was his fault they were apart. His inability to control himself is what landed them in this spot.

Made her believe he lied.

Made him consider telling her she was right.

****

"MR. BARRICK?" ELISE poked her head into Pierce's office. "The man from yesterday is back."

"Vincent?" He stood from his desk. "Send him in."

Elise leaned to peer down the hall before stepping into his office. "I'm not sure it's you he's here to see."

He paused at the side of his desk. "Is he asking for Zeke?" If Vincent was here to cause problems for Zeke then it would end quickly. He was ready for a fight, and there was no one he'd like to take his frustration out on more than the head of GHOST.

"No." Elise's answer was hesitant.

"Then who in the hell is he asking for?" Pierce strode across his office, ready to find the outlet he was itching for.

"Mona."

He stopped, head snapping toward the new office manager. "Absolutely not. He cannot see her."

"It's too late." Elise gave him a little shrug. "She was waiting for him at the front doors."

"You're fucking kidding me." Pierce went straight across the hall to Shawn's door and banged his fist against it before turning to Elise. "Is Heidi in there?"

Elise pressed her lips together as she shook her head.

"Thank God." Pierce banged again. This time Shawn pulled it open.

"What in the hell is wrong?" Dutch, Seth, Gentry, and Zeke were packed inside the small room.

"Vincent came to meet with Mona."

Zeke immediately stood. "Over my dead body."

"Technically he's not just meeting with Mona."

Pierce turned to Elise. "What in the hell does that mean?"

Elise's eyes slid to the end of the hall.

"Damn it." Shawn was past Pierce and running down the hall. He grabbed the frame of the door as he reached Intel's office. "It's fucking empty."

Pierce stepped closer to Elise. "Where are they?"

She glanced toward the hall leading to the conference rooms.

Pierce started to head that direction. Elise grabbed his arm. "You can't let her do it."

"Damn it." Pierce went straight to the hall, the leads for each team at his back.

Only one door was closed, making it easy to find the location of the unapproved meeting. He scanned his badge and flung the door open.

Mona glared at him. "Can I help you?"

"What in the hell do you think you're doing?" All he saw was red. There was no chance to filter what came out of his mouth. No ability to temper his reaction to the situation.

"I am doing what needs to be done." Mona leaned back in her chair, crossing her arms over her chest as she continued to stare him down with a defiance that made everything worse.

"Get out here." Pierce stepped back, making room for her.

"No." She turned away from him, all her focus going to where Vincent sat. "Now. As you were saying."

"No fucking way." Pierce stormed into the room, knocking over empty chairs as he went. "Whatever she's trying to negotiate is not an option." He grabbed Mona's arm, pulling her from the chair and hauling her away from Vincent.

The man who wanted to use her just like the man who came before him.

Mona didn't fight him. "It's my life. It can be an option if I want it to be."

"You. Are. Wrong." He dragged her toward the door. "Risking your life will never be a fucking option."

"You're using that word an awful lot right now, Pierce." Heidi spun in her chair, watching as he managed to get Mona out the door. "It's almost like you don't want to let Mona help us find Anthony."

"She's not getting any-fucking-where near him." He motioned to the room as he shot a look at the men in the hall. "Deal with that."

Mona's feet kept pace with his as he all but carried her to an empty room, shoving her in and slamming the door behind him.

He spun to face her, but her expression stopped him short.

Her cheeks were flushed and her lips lifted in a single-sided smirk.

"There you are."

CHAPTER 12

WHY HAD SHE worried for so many years about people being upset with her?

Pierce was definitely pissed as hell at her right now and there was nothing scary about it.

"What in the hell were you thinking?" He was already raking his hands through his hair, messing it up, loosening the perfect confines he combed it into every morning.

"What are *you* thinking?" She held her ground. "We can stop this now before anyone else gets hurt."

She didn't just invite Vincent here to piss Pierce off, she legitimately wanted to be used as bait.

And prove she could make the choice herself.

That she was finally in control of her life.

Of herself.

"I will not allow–"

"Then I quit."

Pierce looked like she slapped him. "You can't quit."

"Of course I can." Mona crossed her arms. "If you're not my boss then you have no say-so in what I do or don't do."

"If you for one second think this has anything to do with me being your boss then–"

"I would hope that's what it has to do with, otherwise it means that you believe you should be able to tell me what to do."

"Maybe someone does need to tell you what to do." Pierce moved into the room, slowly circling his way toward her. "Because you're going to get yourself killed."

"No one's managed to kill me yet." It was a fact she leaned on almost every day. She'd been kidnapped. Dragged through the freezing air and snow by men who definitely had bad intentions.

She'd been shot at.

She'd killed a man to protect her friend.

She was not what the men she once knew tried to convince her she was.

And she definitely was not what Pierce thought she was.

"I have no intention of tempting fate, Mona. Not when it's you on the line." His steps were slow and even, but there was something different about them. They were still careful. Still perfectly spaced.

Calculated.

Like he was hunting her.

"It's not your choice to make." Mona stood straighter as he continued to come closer. "It's mine."

"I will go to lengths you can't begin to imagine to keep you safe, Mona. You don't want to force my hand on this."

She laughed.

Because the whole situation was so insane it had to be funny. "I'll take my chances." She started to edge around him, planning to carefully make her exit.

Because old habits died hard.

Instead she stood tall as she walked right past where Pierce stood, seeming to take up so much more space than he actually did.

Her hand made it to the door, managing to get it open.

But that was it.

A second later she was up off the ground, head down, ass up.

Pierce strode past where Dutch, Shawn, Seth, and Gentry stood, arguing with the rest of Intel.

"Put me down." Mona gave him one chance.

Pierce ignored her and kept walking.

Zeke taught her more than how to shoot a gun. After the night she, Harlow, and Eva were taken she'd struggled to sleep. To eat.

To function.

Zeke helped her through it. He taught her how to feel strong. In control.

Capable of handling anything that came her way.

Even bull-headed rich men who were used to getting their way.

Mona let Pierce take a few more steps, waiting until they were in a spot where she could hit the ground running.

Then she lifted her upper body hard and fast, straightening high over Pierce's head, using her weight and momentum to throw his balance off and loosen his hold on her.

Only it didn't happen.

Pierce's arms held her tighter. "Watch your head." He yanked open the door to the walkway leading to the rooming house. "Not that a concussion wouldn't work in my favor."

Mona dropped down as he walked straight through the door. "For someone who's worried about my safety you're awfully fine with decapitating me."

"Not decapitating. Just concussing." Pierce went through the door at the other end before heading directly up the stairs.

"Change the codes on my doors."

"What?" Mona craned her neck, trying to get a look at what in the hell he was talking about. "You can't just lock me in my room, Pierce."

"I have no intention of locking you in your room." He didn't stop at the second floor. Instead Pierce kept going up the stairs like he wasn't hauling an extra person along with him. "I'm locking you in my rooms."

"You can't just lock me up." Mona tried to wiggle free, attempting to work her legs loose. "It's against the law to hold someone against their will."

"Sue me." He reached the third floor. "I'll give you Charles' number. I'm sure he'll be thrilled."

158

Pierce managed to swipe his badge and open the door with one hand. The hall he walked into was silent. A single door stood at the center.

He dropped her to her feet right in front of it before tapping his ear. "What's the new front door code?"

Dutch. Damn it.

"Tell Dutch when I see him again–"

"Thank you." Pierce ignored her threat as his hand went to the keypad.

She held her breath as his finger hovered over the numbers.

He tipped his head her way. "Close your eyes."

"No way."

Pierce's arm looped around her waist, pulling her close. "I didn't expect you to be so difficult."

He didn't sound completely upset about the revelation.

"I didn't expect you to be such a pain in the ass."

Pierce's lips curved into a small smile. "Surprise."

And then his body was pressing her to the door as those same lips came to hers in a kiss that stole her thoughts. His mouth was hot and hard, demanding as it claimed hers. Owning every breath she managed to take.

This was the man she wanted to know. The man she was willing to do insane things to force from hiding.

Mona shoved her fingers into Pierce's hair. He'd already had his hands in it. What would a couple more hurt?

The dark strands were surprisingly soft. Longer than they seemed when they were slicked into place. She fisted his hair a little tighter, using it to pull him closer.

He made her so damn mad.

But he made her other things too. Especially when he wasn't trying to treat her like one wrong move would break her to pieces.

Pierce growled into her mouth, his frame pushing harder into hers, pinning her to the door as his hand went to her ass, pulling her closer, making it impossible to ignore the rigid line of his dick.

She'd spent a lifetime being too scared to take chances. Too worried to even consider if a risk was worth the reward.

It was a lifetime too long.

Before she could decide against it, Mona dropped one hand from his hair, moving it directly to the solid jut of his cock.

Pierce's lips dropped hers as he sucked a breath through clenched teeth.

It emboldened her. Fueled the sense of power she was only just beginning to recognize might be hers.

She stroked along his length, rubbing her hand over the fabric of his pants.

Pierce's lips caught hers as her second hand worked the button of his pants free and dipped inside.

His groan was like the air she used to fight to find in his presence. It fed her. Nourished the tiny bit of her just beginning to bloom.

His body was hot and hard everywhere. It made her want to see all of it. Touch all of it.

Taste all of it.

See just how out of control she could make this man be.

Because that's what this was about. All of it.

Control.

Who had it.

Who needed it.

Suddenly Pierce's fist hit the door, making it vibrate against her back. His arm went tight around her waist as he dragged her from the door.

Five beeps came in rapid succession.

It took her a second to realize where they came from.

"Damn it, Pierce." She wrestled against him. "Let me go."

He managed to get her through the door before doing exactly as she asked, releasing her immediately.

"Did you just do that to distract me?"

"You should believe what I say, Mona." He raked one hand through the hair she'd managed to completely work loose. "I will do anything to keep you safe." His gaze was dark as it held hers. "Even from yourself."

"Is that really how you want it to be?" He was setting up parameters she couldn't have even considered until a day ago.

Until she realized they weren't so different.

Until she realized he was as human as everyone else.

Just a man.

A man that might still be above almost all others, but a man no less.

"That is how it has to be." Even with his suit undone and his hair unkempt Pierce still carried an air of power.

Of control.

But this was war. A war he started. One built on misconceptions. Both hers.

And his.

"So you're just going to leave me here all day?" Mona swept her eyes around the room. "Alone."

"I would hope you're not considering burning the building down."

She was not, actually. "Is that something you think I would do?"

"At this point I believe you could be capable of anything."

Why did that make her warm inside?

"I guess you'll find out." They both would, because right now she wasn't sure how exactly she was going to handle this.

"I think we both know this is temporary at best." Pierce tugged at the lapels of his jacket. "It's only a matter of time before your army comes to set you free."

Her eyes dipped to his hands as they worked the waistband of his pants back together, fingers gracefully restoring the polish he worked so hard to present. "Then what?"

"Then I suppose I will have to come up with something else." Pierce tucked one hand into the pocket of his pants. "He will kill you, Mona. Don't doubt that for a minute."

She shook her head. "It won't happen."

Pierce came toward her. "Why can you not understand the very real danger this man presents?"

"I do understand he's a danger." She watched Pierce's eyes, unable to look away from them, from all they told her. "Which is why I want to do this. I can't let him ruin Alaskan Security." Mona swallowed down the tinge of fear trying to clog her last words. "Ruin you."

Pierce froze.

Maybe that was too much. Maybe she should have held that bit back. Kept it close for a while longer.

"There's only one person in this world that could ruin me, Love." Pierce stepped in close enough his front almost touched hers. "And that's you."

And then he had her again. Arms pinning her body to his, mouth hot on hers.

It was as if a part of him came unleashed, springing free from the restraints he used to bind it.

And the first thing it wanted was her.

Mona wrapped her arms around his neck, holding on as Pierce walked her across the room and down the short hall.

"You ruined my bed." He pushed her into his room, backing her toward the center where his bed was stripped, the sheets and blankets piled on the floor. All that covered the mattress was a fitted sheet and a single blanket. "All I could smell on it was you."

"You shouldn't have made me sleep in it." It was almost impossible to keep her spine with him under normal circumstances, but now that he was here, the Pierce she wanted, it took everything she had.

But it was the only way to keep him here. The only way to keep him from remembering he was supposed to be something else.

Someone else.

"I will do it again." He took her down, arms holding her as they dropped to the mattress. "Only this time I intend to be right beside you." His lips skimmed down her neck. "Under you." His teeth caught the lobe of her ear. "Over you." The tip of his tongue flicked across her skin. "Inside you."

Sweet mother of God.

Her thighs clenched at the thought, pressing at the ache between them.

"What's wrong, Love?" His tone carried a smile. "Is it something I can help you with?"

"Now you want to help me?" She gasped as he gripped her tight, dragging them both over the smooth sheet. "Because it seems like that's the opposite of what you've been trying to do."

"Keeping you alive isn't being helpful?" His lips locked onto the spot just under her ear as one hand gripped her leg behind the knee, pulling it away from the other, stealing the friction that was keeping her sane.

"Keeping me alive at the cost of everyone else isn't helpful."

"I disagree." Pierce's hips wedged between her thighs. "I think keeping you alive at any cost is helpful." He pushed against her, dragging the length of his hard cock along the line of her pussy.

Her eyes rolled closed and her head fell back. "That's because you like me."

"I would say I do much more than like you." Pierce's hand came to her neck, fingers and thumb against her jaw as his mouth once again owned hers.

His leg shoved hers, pushing it to one side, making more room for where he continued to rub against her, the stiff line of his dick giving her so much more than she was able to accomplish on her own.

The thin fabric of her pants did little to buffer each rake of his body against hers. Every part of her was on fire, burning with a heat she used to dread.

Used to fear.

Not anymore.

Because now she knew fire was fuel. A heat that fed the fight she didn't know she could possess.

Mona gripped the lapels of his suit, pulling him closer, using the fight she found to force him where she wanted him.

"That's right." Pierce's lips left hers to slide across her jaw. "Take what you want."

The low hum of his voice, the perfect way he said each word. It was as if the two parts of him came together. The perfect polish of his outside and the darkly-demanding half he tried to hide from everyone.

Both were with her in that moment.

Offering to give her all she wanted.

Maybe not all.

Some.

Every move he made pushed her higher to the point she wanted to reach, but never quite took her to the peak.

His hand went to her ass. Gripping tight as he pushed her hips into his, changing the angle just enough to—

"Oh my God." Her hands fisted the fabric of his jacket, holding on as she came.

Because Pierce rubbed his dick on her.

His completely-clothed dick.

He leaned into her ear. "Now imagine what will happen when I touch you."

She should not try to imagine that.

"Imagine what will happen when I put my mouth on you."

A little gasp formed all on its own and her thighs clenched at his hips.

Pierce chuckled, low and deep. "Was that not enough for you, Love?" His hand slid to the hem of her sweater, fingers teasing the skin of her belly. "Do you need more?"

Did she?

She did.

Mona forced her fingers to drop his very rumpled jacket so they could work on the buttons of his shirt. She managed to get a few undone before Pierce's demeanor changed in an instant.

She felt it.

The air around him seemed to shift. Everything about him seemed to come into focus.

"What's wrong?"

Pierce touched his ear. "I'm here."

Her stomach dropped.

She forgot he'd been talking to Dutch earlier.

He touched the earpiece again, his eyes immediately coming to hers. "I would never share this part of you with anyone." His deep blue eyes skimmed lower. "This is only for me. Understand?"

She swallowed at the sharpness of his tone.

Not because it made her nervous like it might have not so long ago.

Nope. The idea of Pierce wanting her all to himself did something very different to her insides.

He tapped the earpiece again. "I'll be there shortly."

One more tap then his forehead dropped to hers. "I have to go."

"You're going to leave me here?"

One dark brow lifted. "The only other option is to go everywhere I go."

It wasn't an unappealing thought.

"I'm not done discussing the option of using me to lure Anthony out."

Pierce's eyes closed and for the first time she noticed something.

He looked tired.

Worn down by all of this.

"But I can wait."

His lids slowly lifted. "I just want you safe, Mona. That's all."

They had similar goals.

Unfortunately they worked against each other.

"I know." She reached out to smooth down the creases her hands pressed into his suit. "You should probably   change   before   we   go."

CHAPTER 13

OF ALL THE poorly timed—

"Pierce. I need an ETA."

He should have taken the damn thing out of his ear.

But they would have still come for him.

"I need ten minutes." It took everything he had to get off the bed. The same bed that tormented him all night. Teasing him with fleeting hints of her scent until he couldn't stand it any longer and ripped every blanket off.

Even then sleep didn't come.

"Come on." He held his hand out. "We need to get moving."

We. How long had he been on his own? No one to share the burdens he worked so hard not to struggle under.

Mona's hand immediately went into his. "What's wrong?"

"Vincent's back." Pierce pulled her up from the bed before going straight to his closet, unbuttoning his shirt as he walked. "He brought someone with him."

"Someone?" Mona followed behind him, her presence bringing him an odd peace. Especially given she was one of the things causing him the most unrest.

He shucked his jacket, tossing it across the rickety chair tucked into one corner. "Based on Dutch's extreme desire for me to be downstairs I would say Vincent's found someone interesting for us to talk to."

His shirt was the next to go, joining the jacket as he searched for their replacements.

"I like the blue ones."

He glanced Mona's way.

"They match your eyes."

He pulled a white shirt with blue pinstripes free of its hanger. "That is good to know." He pulled the shirt on, finding no small amount of satisfaction in the way her eyes followed his every move, lingering in some places longer than others. "Although I was under the impression your interest in me was only recently realized."

Mona's eyes snapped to his. "I don't remember saying I was interested in you."

"I will remind you of that this evening when you are begging me to give you all the things I've promised."

Her skin immediately flushed. It was a reaction he wasn't even sure she realized she had. It was the only hint he'd initially had that his desire for her might actually be reciprocated.

"I guess we'll see about that."

170

She was beginning to surprise him almost constantly. "We will most definitely see."

Mona pointed to his lower half. "Don't forget your pants."

"Is that your way of telling me you'd like to see all I have to offer you?" He loved the pink of her skin. The drop of her lids. The quickening of her breath. It made it impossible for him to focus on anything other than bringing it back.

"I plan to do more than see it."

He missed a button, his fingers fumbling as his brain latched onto her words.

She smirked at him, crossing her arms over her chest. "But it seems like that will have to wait for tonight." Her eyes dropped to where his dick throbbed. The tip of her tongue skimmed over her lower lip a second before she caught it between her teeth, gaze filled with an almost palpable hunger. His cock strained against the confines of his pants, the temptation of her mouth making him ache.

"Got an updated ETA for me?"

Fucking Dutch.

He tapped his ear, activating the mic attached to his piece. "Five minutes."

Mona's smirk was back. "Better hurry then." She turned away to saunter back into his room, leaving him to finish dressing alone, stiff and fantastically frustrated.

Pierce quickly finished pulling on a navy suit. He was just tying his shoes when Dutch was back. "You're killing me right now."

"We're walking out the door." Pierce strode into the bedroom, expecting to find Mona waiting there, but the room was empty except for the pile of bedding on the floor.

"Mona?" Had she already found the new codes to his doors? It wouldn't surprise him if she had. The women of Intel were dedicated to each other. There was no doubt in his mind if Mona wanted out there would be no shortage of women ready to do whatever it took to set her free.

A sound in the kitchen caught his attention.

Mona stood at the island, perusing the bowl of fruit there.

"Take anything you want. It's yours." He buttoned the front of his jacket as she ran her fingers over a few options.

Finally she selected something and pulled it free.

"Not that. You can't have that." He pointed to the bowl. "For the love of God pick something else."

Her brows came together as her eyes dipped to the banana in her hand.

He saw it the second it happened. Her lips curved. "You said I could have anything I wanted. That it was mine."

"Not that." He pointed to the bowl. "Put the damn thing back."

"No." She peeled back the outside, revealing the fruit. Her eyes held his as she slid it between her lips, cheeks hollowing as those same lips wrapped tight.

"Pierce!"

"Come on." He gritted his teeth as he grabbed her by the arm, pulling her toward the back door. "You better finish that before we get to my office. I won't have Vincent imagining all the things I am right now."

He probably already did.

There was something about Mona that a man couldn't help but notice. She might not be the woman they noticed first, but she was definitely the one they couldn't look away from once they found her, and it had as much to do with her coolly classic beauty as it did the way she carried herself. The way she treated the people around her.

The way she fought for her friends. Held them accountable when they were wrong.

Even if that friend was a man who killed for a living.

"Are you planning to continue training with Zeke?" Pierce opted for the elevator, not wanting to drag Mona down three flights of stairs then back up one.

"I need him to teach me how to get out of a single-shoulder carry." She broke off a chunk of banana and popped it in her mouth.

Thank God.

"He taught you correctly." He'd been happy to see she learned more than simply how to handle a firearm from Zeke. "But it's best used on someone who doesn't know the extent of your training."

"Zeke told you what he taught me?"

"Should I warn him to be expecting another assault?" Shadow's lead might deserve another, but not for this reason. "He did not inform me of the exact specifics of your time together."

"Our time together?" Mona ate the last of the banana as the elevator reached its destination. "You make it sound like we had a relationship."

To be fair, he'd considered that it might have been a possibility. "If you did then that's your business."

"Really?" She eyed him. "So you wouldn't have a problem if I had something with Zeke?"

She'd slapped Zeke out of anger for what he'd done to her friend.

Not something he'd done to her.

He was sure of it.

Almost.

Mona's brows lifted. "That doesn't look like you wouldn't have a problem." She pointed in his direction. "You look like real Pierce right now."

"Real Pierce?"

Her head moved in a barely-there nod. "There's definitely two Pierces."

The doors to the elevator opened.

"Bout fuckin' time." Abe was on the other side of the doors. "Vincent's about to make me lose my mind."

"I think that's part of the skill set that earned him the position he has." Pierce caught Mona's hand with his, keeping her close as Abe led the way.

But not to his office.

"Why is Vincent down here?"

"Because he brought us a gift."

"A gift that goes in the basement?" Mona's hand tightened in his and she scooted a little closer as they walked.

"I would say it's only a temporary stop for this particular package." Abe turned toward the most isolated portion of the compound, his steps nearly silent as they went in spite of the weight of his boots. He stopped outside the door leading to the containment rooms. "Everyone in?"

Pierce glanced Mona's way. Her skin was a little paler than normal, but she stood as tall as her small frame would allow.

"Everyone in."

Abe dipped his head in a nod and swiped his badge before pulling the door open, holding it as Pierce and Mona went past. Vincent stood at the end of the hall with Shawn, Gentry, Seth, and Zeke. They all turned as Pierce came their way.

"Nice of you to finally show up."

"I would be happy to be available if I knew of your arrival in advance." Pierce ran his thumb over the smooth skin of Mona's hand. "In case you didn't realize, I have a number of things that need my attention."

Vincent's gaze shifted to Mona. "I'd noticed that."

Mona snorted.

"Better watch it, Vincent." The line of Zeke's mouth was less flat than normal. "She's got a wicked right hook."

"I didn't punch you." Mona's cool blue eyes fixed on Shadow's lead. "I slapped you. And you

175

deserved it." Her gaze eased to Vincent. "What did you bring?"

"Not a what, Ms. Ayers." Vincent turned toward the door to his right. "A who." He stepped to the small window cut high on the steel plane. "We were able to use one of our team as a decoy."

Mona's fingertips pressed into his skin. "Is she okay?"

"She's fine." Vincent's gaze moved to Pierce. "As I knew she would be."

"You're not using her, Vincent." Pierce held the head of GHOST's stare. "Not ever."

"There will be more where this one came from." Vincent stood tall. "And until we can find Sanders she's still at risk."

"She's safe here."

"You sure about that?" Vincent glanced at the men around him. "Seems to me I heard something about one of your men defecting."

"And he died for it." Pierce reached one hand into his pocket, searching for the bullet stashed there.

It was gone.

"Only because your little lady here can hold her own." Vincent crossed his arms. "Seems a shame to waste."

"She's not fucking going out there." Pierce stepped toward Vincent again, dropping Mona's hand. "Don't ask again."

Shawn slowly rounded Vincent, putting himself within striking distance.

Not that Shawn was planning to hit anyone or anything. He was preparing to run interference.

Stop the unraveling Pierce was barely keeping contained. The loose ends he was trying to tie up were more than anyone in his life knew.

Could know.

"Your entire company is on the line, Pierce. All of it. The men. The money." Vincent took a step closer to Pierce, closing the gap between them. "He wants to take it all from you."

That wasn't all Anthony wanted to take from him.

Suddenly Pierce's body shoved back.

Mona bumped him again, wedging her body between his and Vincent's. "How do you know that?"

Vincent's eyes dropped to Mona. His reaction to her words could have been missed behind a blink. "That's classified."

"Oh. My. God." Mona's eyes narrowed as she stared up at Vincent. "You knew." Her lip curled. "You knew this whole time what was happening." She let out a disgusted grunt. "And you did nothing."

Vincent squinted down at her in a look that would wilt most grown men.

But Mona only stood taller. "You're the reason I was kidnapped." She shook her head. "You're the reason I had to kill that man." The frown on her lips was deep and drawn. "You could have stopped this before it started."

"That's not my job, Ms. Ayers." Vincent's voice was less hard than before. "My job is to protect the security of the country. Not the security of a single business."

"But it's not just about us now, is it?" Mona's look of disgust held as she sized Vincent up. "Now it is about the security of GHOST. His mess is big enough it's getting on you. That's why you keep coming back here."

Vincent was silent.

"You need us, Vincent." Pierce pressed closer to Mona, breathing deep as he fought to find the calm he always struggled to keep. "And to be perfectly honest, we need you."

Vincent rocked back on his heels as he glanced at the handful of his men scattered around the space. "We are limited in our ability to draw him out since his interest isn't in us." His gaze leveled on Pierce. "It's on something else, isn't it, Pierce?"

There was no way for Vincent to know the truth of all Anthony was seeking.

"You're worried because he thinks you're a part of Alaskan Security." Zeke stepped in. "Because of Shadow."

Mona's eyes went from Zeke to Vincent. "How did he find out Shadow worked for us and GHOST?"

"A man with enough money can find anything." Vincent turned his attention to Pierce. "Isn't that right?"

"Even money has limits." It was what he clung to. The hope that there were limits to what Anthony could find.

Zeke turned to Pierce. "What did you do to piss him off so bad?"

The list was long between them. Too convoluted and twisted to lay into any sort of comprehensible timeline. "Anthony and I have known each other since we were children."

Vincent's focus sharpened in an instant.

"We've hated each other just as long."

It was a lifetime ago that they met. More.

He'd lived so many lives since then. All of them because of Anthony Sanders.

Because of his ability to bring out the worst in people.

"We will send additional men to you." Pierce glanced to Zeke. "Choose a team that will work well with the circumstances." He turned, walking toward the tunnel leading to his office.

"What's going to happen to him?" Mona stood at the door leading to the room holding the man who made the mistake of answering Anthony's posting.

"The same thing that happened to Howard and Chandler." Vincent turned her way, waiting as Mona stared through the glass at the man who most likely expected her to be an easy mark.

"You're going to kill him?"

"Ms. Ayers, I haven't had to kill anyone in this." Vincent glanced at one of his men, tipping his head toward the door. "And I won't have to kill him either."

Mona watched as the man from GHOST went toward the door. "You're going to let him go?"

Vincent tipped his head in a nod. "That's exactly what I'm going to do." He seemed happy with the ramifications of his plan. "Anthony will find him and it'll work itself out."

"You mean he'll be mad I'm not dead and kill him." Mona glanced at the door again.

"Exactly."

"But he kills everyone, no matter what." Mona's brows came together. "Or has them killed."

Pierce stepped back toward her. "Explain."

"He doesn't want any loose ends so as soon as someone doesn't serve his purpose, they die. Chris killed the men who tried to shoot Bess." Mona counted off on one finger. "Then Tod." Her eyes went to Vincent. "But you found him and brought him to us."

Pierce's blood went cold as the dots connected. "You were trying to catch him then. That's how you found Tod."

Vincent's jaw worked from one side to the other. "I don't have to explain anything to you."

Pierce shook his head, huffing out a laugh that was anything but amused. "You knew exactly what was happening and just let us walk around blind." He could barely look at Vincent. "Until they found you and you needed us."

"But why can't the government just get involved? I'm sure they could end this in an afternoon." Mona's brow was lined in confusion.

"We don't exist, Ms. Ayers. Not to the government. Not to the police. Not to anybody. Sending us aid would be admitting they know what we do, and there is no way the government is going to do that."

Pierce turned to his team leads. "Brief your men on the situation. Work with Zeke to choose who goes where."

"Got it." Shawn, Gentry, and Seth immediately left.

Pierce held his hand out toward Mona. "Come on, Love. Time to finish this."

It felt good to say and even better to imagine.

An end to decades of dissent.

Mona turned to look at the door to the vault holding her would-be killer.

"He's done. He won't do you any harm. I promise."

Mona turned back, her brow low. "I'm not worried about him hurting me."

Of course she wasn't. "What is the issue then?"

Mona glanced at the men remaining around her. "I have an idea."

"No." He didn't need to hear it to know it wasn't happening.

Zeke held one hand up Pierce's way as he turned to Mona. "What is it?"

Her eyes bounced to Zeke before going back to Pierce. "You're not gonna like it."

"I'm quite positive of that."

"Tell us anyway." Zeke's tone was softer than it usually was.

Mona rolled her lips together, eyes moving from Zeke to Vincent before finally finding his. "What if that man did kill me?"

CHAPTER 14

"I DON'T LIKE this." Pierce stared down at her as Eva and Harlow worked.

"I feel like I said you weren't going to like it."

Heidi stood off to one side, watching with Parker perched on her hip. "You really look dead."

"Don't say that." Pierce snapped it out, the sudden outburst making Parker jump a little.

Heidi pulled the toddler closer. "Tell Uncle Pierce to watch himself when you're around."

Pierce pinched the bridge of his nose as he turned to walk across the room. "I'm just not thrilled with this whole thing."

"No shhhhhh—" Eva's eyes rolled Parker's way. "Shoot."

"Nice catch." Harlow dabbed a makeup blender along the skin under Mona's eyes.

"I don't want to be the one who teaches him that word." Eva tilted her head as she stared at the center of Mona's forehead. "Does that look real enough?"

Heidi leaned in a little closer, peering at Mona. "Looks real to me, but I've never seen a dead person in real life."

"Tod was really dead when I saw him." Harlow tapped at Mona's cheek with the blender. "We're going for freshly dead."

Pierce turned back Mona's way. "Christ."

"Christ." Parker grinned at Pierce.

Pierce frowned back. "Where is his mother?"

"She's lying down. She doesn't feel good." Heidi smiled at Parker. "Mommy needed a break, didn't she?"

"Who'd of thought jelly was so useful?" Eva dipped a toothpick in the jelly she was using to recreate a bullet wound on Mona's forehead.

"I think we deserve a raise for this." Harlow leaned back. "Cause that's some movie-quality special effects shit."

Eva turned to Harlow, her eyes wide.

Harlow was unfazed. "Bess knows who's going to teach Parker all the bad words." She motioned to Mona. "Sit up so we can dribble this down your face."

They'd gone through the kitchen and every makeup box at Alaskan Security, looking for anything that might help make this happen.

Eva used the cleaned-out eye dropper from one of Parker's medication bottles to suck up some of the thinned-down jelly. "Everyone hold your breath." She tipped Mona's head back a little then dribbled some right at the fake wound. The warm, thick liquid slowly worked its way between her brows and down, making a path off to one side of her nose, over her cheek toward one ear.

"Does that look like the way blood would run if she fell on her back?"

All the women turned toward Pierce.

He frowned at Mona. "Unfortunately."

Eva smiled. "Great." She held one hand up toward Harlow.

Harlow immediately slapped it in a high-five. "Team work makes the dream work."

"If the dream is me being dead." Mona fought the urge to scrunch her face.

"It's someone's dream." Eva wiggled her brows at Pierce. "Right?"

Pierce's eyes stayed on Mona's forehead a second longer before he turned to the door. "Let's get this done."

"So, you might have to walk with your head back so the jelly doesn't run the wrong way." Eva stood up. "Come on. I'll help you."

"No need." Pierce came to the sofa where Mona was stretched out. He immediately scooped her up. "Someone grab a blanket." He marched from the room and out into the hall. "I don't like this."

"You keep saying that."

"I can't even look at you right now." He stared straight ahead. "I don't like not being able to look at you."

"It's stickier than I expected." Mona rolled her eyes to one side, trying to see where they were, but her view was limited unless she wanted to mess up all Eva and Harlow's hard work.

That meant she was stuck staring up at Pierce.

"I can feel you looking at me." His strides got a little bouncier as they went down the stairs.

"I can't really look at anything else." It was kind of nice to have an excuse to just stare at him. Especially since she'd worked so hard not to stare at him until recently. "At least you're nice to look at."

"I'll take that as a compliment." The line of his jaw was tight.

"You should." Mona studied the line of his mouth where it turned down into a distinct frown. He had so much already on his plate to worry about. The thought that she was currently adding to it bothered her. "I'll probably need a nice hot shower after this."

His eyes finally dipped her way. "You are most definitely washing that off the second this is over." His gaze lingered. "And you will most likely be cold after lying in the snow."

"Most likely."

She wasn't one to flirt. Never had been.

It felt awkward and strange.

Oddly stressful. Like a dance she didn't quite know the steps to.

"Then you should probably plan for a bath." The almost pained look Pierce wore earlier had softened.

The darkness in his gaze made her breath catch.

"Damn." Brock fell into step beside them, his face coming into view as he leaned into Pierce's side. "That looks pretty freaking real."

Shawn was at Pierce's other side. "Real enough." He shoved open the last door between them and the frigid air outside.

That was going to be the worst part of all this. Laying in the cold, trying not to shiver like a live person while they took the picture.

Pierce pulled her closer as the wind whipped around them, knocking her hair into her face, sticking it to all Eva and Harlow's hard work.

She reached up, ready to attempt to pull it free of the random things smeared onto her skin.

"Leave it." Pierce walked faster.

Shawn's face went slack when he looked her way. "He's right. Now it looks real as hell."

Pierce stopped, his blue eyes on hers through the line of hair snagged across her face. "Ready?"

Mona nodded.

He slowly went to one knee, carefully laying her across the pile of snow collected just for this purpose. It was dirty and clumped. Meant to look like she'd been dumped on the side of the road. Pierce carefully moved her hands, quickly positioning her in a way that felt unnatural and uncomfortable.

"Mess her hair up more." Shawn stood over her, a cell phone angled her way.

Pierce flipped her hair away from her head. His frown deepened. "I need to make your clothes match everything else, Love."

"It's fine." She closed her eyes. "Just do it."

He tugged one of her shoes off then grabbed the neck of her shirt with both hands, tugging until the knit fabric gave way, splitting along the shoulder seam.

"Brace yourself." Pierce pushed the bottom of her shirt up, baring her belly to the freezing temperature. He quickly stood. "Take the fucking picture."

"Eyes open, Mona." Shawn stepped in closer.

She picked a spot in the distance, unfocusing her eyes as the phone made shutter noises above her.

They'd set up in a spot where the teams loaded into vehicles. It was surrounded on all sides by the buildings, with only a narrow drive leading to it, which meant it was completely out of view of anyone outside the property, no matter how hard they tried to see.

"Hurry up. It's fucking freezing out here." Pierce leaned over Shawn's shoulder as the lead for Rogue continued to take pictures.

"You don't want to do this again, do you?" Shawn stepped to the side of her and took a few more photographs. Then he crouched down. "This is the money shot. Try to look the deadest you've ever been."

She held her breath, relaxing every muscle on her face.

"Perfect." Shawn reached out to pull her hair off her face. "We're done."

Her body seemed to take that as permission to begin shivering. Her teeth started to chatter as her skin tightened with goose bumps.

Pierce grabbed her immediately, pulling her up from the snow melting into her ruined clothes and matting her already tangled hair. "Inside."

He didn't have to tell her twice. "I can't believe you chose this place out of all the options in the world." Her teeth clanged together as she ran, Pierce's arm holding her close to him as he propelled her forward.

"There aren't as many options as you would think for a company like this, Love."

Zeke held the door open. They rushed past him into the heat of the building.

"Blanket." Pierce held a hand out to Eva. She passed over a thick chenille throw. He whipped it around Mona, pulling it tight to her body. "Come on. Let's go get you cleaned up."

"How'd they come out?" Eva leaned into Shawn's side as he flipped through the pictures. Her eyes widened. "You look good and dead, Monster." She grinned. "Good job."

Mona smiled back. "Thanks."

Life was funny. A year ago she was tiptoeing around the world, trying not to make waves.

Now she was pretending to be murdered by the man hired to kill her by a billionaire trying to piss off her boss.

"You can talk about this more later." Pierce held the front of the blanket, using it to drag her toward the hall leading to the rooming building. "Once that thing's off your forehead."

"It itches a little." Mona reached up to gingerly feel around the sticky pile of smoosh. "Did it look okay?"

"I'm not sure okay is a word I would use to describe how it looked." Pierce's eyes went to the splotch. "Looks."

"Is Heidi ready to send the photos out?" Mona went up the stairs beside Pierce.

"Vincent's team is working with Intel to decide when will be the best time to show proof of death."

"I'm part of Intel." Mona tried to slow down, but Pierce's hold on the blanket made it impossible. "Why am I not involved in that?"

Pierce punched the code into the pad on the door leading to the hall outside his rooms then pulled open the door, dragging her inside.

"Hey." Mona planted her feet, the still-shoed one grabbing the floor much better than the socked one. "Why am I not involved in deciding when's the best time to show proof of my death?"

Pierce stabbed his fingers into the keypad of the last door before swiping his badge and going in, yanking her along with him.

And he still wasn't answering her.

"Pierce." Mona used her arms to knock the blanket loose, stealing the grip he was using against her. "I should get to be a part of it. I'm the one who's dead."

He grabbed her, his hands rough as they pulled her close. His eyes were deadly and dark as they met hers. "Don't fucking say that again." He gripped her face with one hand, fingers holding it tight. "You are not dead and you will not be dead, understand?"

Mona lifted her eyes toward the sticky mass in the center of her forehead.

Pierce's hand held her face still as the thumb of the other hand rubbed across the false wound Eva and Harlow spent two hours creating. "It's gone."

It definitely wasn't gone. The concoction still stuck to her skin.

But Pierce wasn't talking to her anyway.

"You are not dead." He traced the tips of his fingers across her skin, his eyes taking on an odd look as they moved over her face. "You are fine."

"I'm a little sticky."

His gaze seemed to refocus as it met hers. He huffed out a breath that almost sounded like it could have turned to a laugh under different circumstances.

Then his mouth was on hers.

And this time she was ready for it. More than.

His kiss carried a desperation that hadn't been there before.

A need she never would have expected or been brave enough to hope for.

But now that it was hers, she wanted more of it.

More of him.

More of his need.

He backed her to the closest wall, pinning her in place as his hands went to her body, pushing up the sweater he destroyed for the greater good. Mona lifted her arms as he pulled it off. Pierce's fingers hooked in the straps of her bra, immediately tugging them down her arms, flipping the cups down to bare her breasts to his mouth.

Her head spun as his lips and teeth worked her flesh, his hands freeing her of the garment as his tongue flicked across one nipple, pulling it so tight it was almost painful.

As he moved to her other breast Pierce tugged down her snow-dampened pants, taking everything covering her lower half in one move, leaving her standing naked in his living room, covered in jelly and white eye-shadow. His mouth skimmed down her belly as he dropped to his knees.

The sight of a man as powerful as Pierce on his knees in front of her stole her breath. She couldn't look away from him. The angles of his face. The line of his jaw. Every move he made was graceful but filled with strength.

He was still the same man he was before. The one who intimidated her.

Filled her with panic and fear.

Pierce hadn't changed.

But she had.

Thank God, otherwise this moment wouldn't be hers.

And she planned to make the most of it.

His hands gripped her hips, the tips of his fingers digging into her flesh as his mouth pressed between her thighs, his tongue sliding along the seam of her pussy, pushing deeper to find a spot that made her ache with a need of her own.

Her head fell back against the wall even as her eyes stayed locked on the man in front of her. Without fear to lock her down, it was as if her whole world opened up.

A world Pierce currently owned.

His hold on her tightened as his tongue found a rhythm that made her knees weak. Mona fisted one hand in his hair, holding him as tightly as he held her.

Pierce shifted, wedging one of his shoulders between her thighs, spreading her legs farther apart, using his body and hands to keep her balanced. He made immediate use of the extra space, growling against her as his lips latched onto her clit, replacing the lap of his tongue with a gentle suck that immediately sent her over the edge, fingers tight against his scalp as her hips rolled, working her heated flesh against his face.

This woman was not the woman she knew. The woman she knew was bashful and hesitant in situations like this.

Not the kind of woman who rode a man's tongue like it belonged to her.

But there was something about knowing this man was at her mercy. A man who was at no one's mercy.

Only hers.

Mona grabbed the collar of his jacket, pulling Pierce up from the floor. He came easily, his lips running over her body as he stood. As soon as she could reach them her fingers went to his buttons, making it through the top two before his hands caught hers.

"I want to touch you." She pulled free and went back to work.

"Not yet, Love." Pierce snagged her hands again. "Later."

"No. Now." She twisted her hands, trying to work them loose.

"I promised you a bath." Pierce held her hands as he backed away, pulling her along. "I intend to deliver one."

And just like that calm Pierce was back. She could almost watch it happen. See it in the shift of his expression. The look in his eyes.

"Why do you do that?" Mona gave in and walked along with him, because honestly the jelly was starting to make her face itch.

"Do what?" Pierce backed into his room and continued on to the bathroom door.

"A minute ago you were different." Mona shivered as the hormonal heat in her body started to dissipate.

"A minute ago I was not thinking of what was important." He released one hand and lifted the dimmer, bathing the room in a soft light.

"What were you thinking of?"

Pierce twisted on the faucet above the free-standing tub. "Myself."

So when he thought of himself he did... that?

"I'm not sure I understand." Mona shivered again.

Pierce reached to another switch on the wall and flipped it on. "It will be warmer in here soon." His eyes dipped to where her nipples were puckered tight from her shiver. "Hopefully very soon." Pierce tipped his head to the filling tub. "In."

"You can't just tell me what to do."

"I'm sorry." His tone made it clear he was not. "Did you have other plans?"

He might be teasing her.

"Maybe." Mona reached up to run one finger through the dribble of jelly blood down her cheek before sticking it in her mouth.

Her intent was to suggest she was hungry.

But when Pierce's gaze immediately heated her plans changed.

If Pierce could think of himself and what he wanted then maybe she should do the same.

And what she wanted was to bring back the Pierce she craved.

CHAPTER 15

HE'D HAD YEARS to prepare for a moment like this. One that tested all the work he put into being a better man.

And this woman tested him like nothing else.

"I wouldn't be penciling those plans into your calendar just yet." He turned, knowing if he didn't walk away from her now something terrible would happen.

He half expected her to follow him, chase him with the determination that had the potential to ruin all of this.

So he walked faster, escaping to the bedroom he suffered in last night.

And, it appeared, would suffer in again this night.

Pierce went to his closet, peeling off the jacket of his second suit of the day and tossing it on top of the first. The sound of moving water threatened to pull him back to her, lure him in before he'd recovered his sanity.

His control over himself.

He took his time removing his cufflinks and unbuttoning his shirt, hoping the more minutes that ticked by, the better prepared he would be.

"Wow."

Pierce spun to find Mona at the door to his closet, wrapped in one of the thick towels from the bathroom. Her skin was pink from the heat of the water and her hair was slicked back away from her face, all traces of the mess they'd made of her washed away. "Do you feel better?"

"A little." She took a few steps into the closet, her eyes making their way down the front of his body, along the gap in the open front of his shirt. "It's strange to see you like this."

"I don't live my life in suits, Love."

"I know." She circled around him. "But sometimes it seems like you're two different people."

And that was the crux of the issue between them.

It wasn't that Mona was wrong.

She wasn't.

It was that she saw him well enough to realize the battle he fought every day.

"It made me mad at first." Her eyes came to his. "That you were pretending to be someone else." Mona's voice dropped, her tone soft. "But then I thought about it."

"And what did you decide?" He watched as she continued moving in a wide arc, circling him like a lioness hunting her next meal.

Mona's head tipped. "That we're all two different people."

"Are we?" He couldn't stop watching her. She was mesmerizing. A perfect dichotomy of unassuming yet commanding. She was quiet and graceful but carried a strength that was palpable.

A dark horse of epic proportions.

One even he never saw coming.

"We are." She moved behind him, her soft steps continuing on as she spoke. "You just don't want anyone to know."

Mona came around his side. "There's the man you show everyone. He's careful and contained." She looked around the large closet. "He wears suits and expensive watches and always tucks his hand into one pocket when he's upset."

Pierce held his breath. Her first assessment was alarmingly accurate and he was concerned her second would be the same.

And that it might possibly change what she thought of him.

How she felt around him.

"I like that man. He's consistent and calm and fair." She stopped in front of him, her eyes holding his. "But he's just who you try to be."

"A false front?"

Mona shook her head. "He's as real as the rest of you. He's what you wish you were."

"And what you wish I was."

Her lips barely curved into a smile. "Definitely not."

He stilled. "But you said you like him."

"I do." Mona's shoulder lifted. "But he intimidated me. Made me so nervous I wanted to throw up."

"But not now?"

She shook her head. "Not now." Her slow steps changed direction, moving her closer. "Because of the rest of you."

"The rest of me is what should make you nervous." It was what he'd tried so hard to keep hidden, smother away when she was close.

Mona reached out, resting one hand on the center of his chest as she closed the remaining distance between them. "He's like the me I try not to be." The warmth of her palm slid down the space between his ribs, the blue of her gaze following. "He struggles not to cave into his emotions. He fights the weaker parts of himself." Her eyes lifted to his. "He's imperfect."

"None of me is perfect, Love. None of it."

Her gaze dipped. "I'm going to disagree with you on that." Her fingers pushed at the fabric of his shirt, spreading it wider. "At least in the physical sense." She stepped a little closer, easing away more of his sanity as her hands trailed along his shoulders, dragging his shirt with them as they moved , sliding it off his arms. "You're so warm. Don't you get cold here?"

He smiled a little. "Not anymore."

"I'm not sure I'll make it to that point." Mona ran her fingers up the length of his arms. She traced along his shoulders, over the ridge of his collarbone and up to his chin, pausing at the scar tucked into the shadow of his jawline. "What happened?"

The pucker of white skin was a tiny glimpse into the part of him she saw in spite of his best efforts. "It was split open."

"By?"

"I don't think you really want to know that."

"You'd be surprised what I want to know." Mona slid her finger down the skin of his neck. "Was it Anthony?"

"It was."

"So you've hated each other forever?"

"Seems that way." It was a topic that would usually have him antsy. Worried he would say the wrong thing.

Expose the most important secret he kept.

But right now the fear wasn't there. All he felt was peace.

All he felt was her.

"Does he only hate you because of what happened with his brother?" The towel wrapped around her brushed his bare chest, teasing him with the reminder that it was all that kept them apart.

"No. He hates me for many reasons."

"Someday you'll have to give me a list." She spread her palms over his pecs, pressing gently.

"Not now?"

"No. Not now." Mona added a little more weight to her shove, managing to get his feet moving.

Something caught the back of his knees, taking him down. His butt hit the hard seat of the thin and aging wood chair he sat in every morning while tying his shoes. He'd had it since he was forced from home, sent to live in a place intended to break the rage he fought. It went everywhere he did. A reminder of what he used to be.

What he'd overcome.

The wood creaked under his weight as Mona leaned into him, the tuck of her towel teasing him. Making him regret purchasing anything with such staying power.

"What is it you're up to, Love?" He didn't hate the thought of her climbing atop him, sinking her sweet body over his as she took her pleasure in this damn chair. Changing the memories he tied to it.

"Whatever I want." Mona's hands came to his face, holding it as she brushed her lips over his. "Will you give me what I want?"

"Anything." He didn't even have to think about it. It was his goal from the beginning. To prove he had enough to offer in spite of his shortcomings.

Her lips curved into a smile that made him regret his immediate agreement. "That's very good to hear."

Her body slowly slid down his, instantly clarifying her intentions.

Pierce caught her, gripping her arms before she could go any farther. "Come here."

"No." Every time she said it the word came out faster. Bolder.

"Please?" He held her tight, refusing to let her gain any more distance.

"You said I could have what I want." Mona pulled against his hands, managing to get on her knees in front of him. "That you would give me anything."

Desperation pushed at him. "There are limits to what I can stand to offer you."

"You didn't say that." Her hands ran down his chest and over his stomach, the tips of her fingers hooking in the waistband of his pants.

She'd touched him before. A moment of weakness justified by his need to keep her safe. "I'm saying it now."

"Why is this a limit?" Mona worked the button of his slacks free. "I would think this is something you would be more than happy to endure."

"You are not my servant, Mona."

Her brows lifted. "I'm sorry, what?"

"I do not expect you to serve me in any way."

She blinked. Her mouth opened and closed, then opened again. "But you—" Her skin pinked in the perfect way that made his blood heat.

"That is different."

"It's not. Not even a little bit." Mona's fingers worked open his pants.

"I'm not letting you do that."

Now it was a single brow that moved, arching high on her forehead. "Fine." Her hands left his body and she stood, backing away. "Then we're done here."

"That's not what I said." Pierce stood, his desperation taking on an edge of frustration. He only wanted to make her happy.

Prove he wasn't like the men he was raised around.

The kind who take without giving.

Expect their money and power to offer certain liberties.

The kind of man who treats everyone as if they are beneath him.

Subservient.

"I will give you anything you want—"

"Obviously not."

He raked one hand through his hair. How could she not see what this was about? "I do not expect you to be on your knees for anyone, Love. Least of all me."

Mona's head tilted to one side. "That's not what that's about."

"I beg to differ."

"So when you were on your knees for me it meant I was above you?"

She was. In every way.

Mona stepped toward him. "Is that why you did it? To serve me?"

Pierce took a step back. Any answer he had seemed to work against him so he kept his mouth shut.

"No. It wasn't." Her eyes narrowed. "That's why you can't answer me."

Two more steps and he was back where he started, the chair creaking as he fell into it, a woman he was not prepared for advancing on him yet again.

"You did it because it pleased you as much as it pleased me." Mona leaned into him. "Didn't it?"

He swallowed down the answer that was a lie, once again choosing silence.

"Say you don't want to feel my mouth." Her eyes were on his. "Say you don't want it and I'll drop it."

"It's not a matter of not wanting, Love. It's a matter of doing what's right."

One finger came to trace a path down the center of his nose and over his lips. "Who's to say what's right between us?" Her finger slid over his mouth, moving from one corner to the other. "We're the only two here. I think we should lock everything else out."

Her lips replaced her finger and he couldn't stop himself from reaching for her, lacing his fingers in her hair and pulling her against him. Her mouth immediately opened to him, her tongue meeting his.

Her taste. Her smell. It was all more than he could handle.

"You are fucking perfect." Pierce yanked at the towel keeping her from him, ripping it away from the body he had only just begun to worship. "So damn perfect." He growled the words against her skin as he cupped one breast, pulling it to his mouth.

Mona grabbed his hair with one hand and yanked him from her. "No." Her gaze was defiant. "I don't expect you to serve me."

"Wha—" He scoffed. "But that's not—"

"Oh those aren't my rules." She gave him a sweet smile that belied the purely wicked thing she was doing. "They're yours."

Mona glanced around the space. "So we should probably just go find someplace more comfortable so we can get this over with."

Did she just suggest—

"What's wrong, Pierce? You look upset." The false rounding of her eyes feigned an innocence this woman hadn't an inch of.

"You are a wicked woman."

Her smile widened. "Thank you." The honesty in her response was telling.

He rolled his head from side to side, stretching the tension from his neck. "Fine." He leaned back in the chair. "Do your worst."

Mona eyed him for a second.

Then she stood.

An exhale of relief had just left his lungs when she snagged a tie from the line of hooks to his left.

Then she pulled another free.

He lifted a brow as she wrapped one around where his hand rested on the arm of the chair.

"I don't trust you." She deftly worked a knot into the silk, binding his arm in place.

"It would seem that way." Pierce watched as she repeated the process on the other arm. "I could point out that lack of trust is a major concern when developing a relationship." Mona finished the second knot. He flexed, testing the restraints. "And how did you learn to do this?"

"Zeke taught me."

"Of course he did." Pierce met Mona's cool gaze. "What was his reasoning for why you would need to know this?"

"He taught me to knock a man unconscious and then how to tie him up." Mona's smile was small and sly. "So you should be happy I skipped the first step."

Every minute they spent together she seemed to become more comfortable with him.

With herself.

But it was a double-edged sword.

"You don't have to do this, Mona." He had to try one last time to end this ridiculous idea that she had.

"Shut up, Pierce." Mona went to her knees in front of him. This time there was no towel to buffer the sight.

Pierce gritted his teeth against the image it evoked.

A woman pleasing the man above her as he sat on a throne.

It was not how he wanted this to be.

He gripped the chair, fisting the scrolled carve of the wood as she opened his pants, tugging them down to free his dick from the confines maintaining his sanity. Her palm was soft as it slid against him, her fingers gripping him with a perfect amount of pressure.

"Like that, Love." He pushed into her hand, trying to encourage her to continue, hoping she would lose interest in attempting more.

Her thumb brushed the tip of him, sliding through the slickness already collected there.

His lungs froze as she lifted the thumb to her lips and it disappeared between them.

Once again she was laying him low, knocking his feet out from under him, leaving him on shaky ground at best.

Sinking in quicksand at worst.

"Mona, please." He was begging but at this point there was no way to tell what for.

He no longer wanted her to stop.

But taking from her was wrong. He was the one who needed to give. He was the one who had to repent for the sins of his father.

For the sins of them all.

He closed his eyes, trying to block it out. All of it.

The past. The present.

The lies. The truth he hid.

But the heat of her mouth ripped him back, lifted his lids, fisted his hands, and tightened his balls. He shouldn't watch her. Shouldn't find pleasure in the sight of her lips wrapped around him. Of her tongue sliding across him.

Of her cheeks hollowing as she sucked him.

The ache he'd been fighting was almost a pain, one he tried to ignore as she stroked him with her hands and mouth, each move the sweetest torture he tried not to bear.

She was a queen. One who should bow to no man.

And yet she was.

"Stop." He tried to shove back but the chair was already against the wall, making it impossible to escape Mona or the painfully perfect act she was inflicting.

Her eyes lifted to him, the head of his dick sliding between her lips in a sight that snapped the thread of control he had.

Pierce pulled against the restraints, the old chair groaning as he did.

Mona leaned back a little, her eyes wide.

He lifted the chair, falling down against it with all the force he had, knocking the thin spindles of the arms loose and splitting the dried braces. He jerked one arm loose. Then the other, taking a few chunks of splintered wood with him as he stood, dragging Mona from the floor as he went.

"Enough." He wrapped one arm around her waist, lifting her up and against him as he backed her toward the bank of cabinets in the center of the room. "You've had your fun." He ran his nose along the side of hers as his hand went to the center of her thighs, finding her slick and hot. "I hope   it   was   worth   it."

CHAPTER 16

HER BUTT BUMPED the tray holding Pierce's cufflinks and cologne as he shoved her back, resting the cheeks of her ass on the smooth wood top as his fingers worked her clit. The height of the cabinets kept her feet off the floor, which meant Pierce's body was the only thing she had to use for any sort of leverage in the situation.

And she most certainly wanted to have some leverage whenever Pierce was concerned.

Mona wrapped her arms around his neck and her legs around his waist, pulling him closer in a move that dragged a groan from his lips where they rested on her skin.

It was impossible to stop fighting him now that she knew what it gained her. He'd seen the real her. More times than she cared to admit.

She wanted the real him. To know that side of him as much as she knew the rest.

"You are wicked." His free hand came to the back of her head, long fingers lacing in her damp hair before fisting tight. "A devil woman."

"It's your fault." She hooked her ankles together, struggling to bring him against her. "You did this to me."

It was the truth. He'd forced her hand in a way that she wasn't upset about. While he struggled to be real, she struggled to be better.

He made her better.

Made her stronger. More confident.

More what she wanted to be.

Pierce's thumb rested against the hardened nub he was intent on using against her as his fingers slid inside, stroking a spot that made her toes curl. It was an intolerable combination of sensations that almost immediately took her over the edge in a climax that stole her breath.

"That's right, Love. Take what I give you."

Her pussy clenched around his fingers at the rough sound of his voice. At the ragged sound of his breathing.

"More." She rolled her head into his shoulder as the room spun. It should be too much.

But it wasn't. Not even close.

She wanted all he promised her.

And he'd promised her everything.

Pierce's head dipped to her breast, lips locking onto a nipple as his fingers rolled the other, twisting with perfect pressure as he yanked a drawer to his right open. His mouth worked up her body, over her collarbone and along her neck as he sheathed his straining cock. "Tomorrow I will prove there's no need for this." He notched himself against her and immediately pressed in, not fast, but not slow. A steady thrust that gave her body time to adjust to the much wanted invasion. "And when you're ready I want nothing between us." He set a demanding pace immediately, each stroke of his body filling her completely. "I want to fuck you till you're so full of me there's no room for anything else."

Her thighs clenched at the thought. Of Pierce fucking her like that. His skin against hers.

Of Pierce filling her.

"I've never—" The words cut off as his pelvis ground into hers.

"Say it." His voice was almost feral. A growl that sounded more animal than man. "Say no man has fucked you bare. I want to hear it."

His reaction was confusingly arousing. "It's never happened."

"That's not what I asked for." Pierce leaned up, his hand coming to her face, holding it tight as he forced her eyes to his. "Say the words." His fingers dug into her skin as the shove of his body into hers became harder.

Faster.

Right now she'd give him anything not to stop. Even words that would normally make her blush. "No man has fucked me bare."

She'd asked for this. The unleashing of the man she sought.

And there wasn't a single regret to be had.

Pierce growled out a sound that shot straight to where his body ground against hers. "Only me." His hand holding her face pulled it to one side, stretching her neck as his lips went to the skin there.

"Yes." She was struggling to breathe from the intensity of all that was happening in her body.

In her mind.

"Tomorrow." Pierce's thumb once again went to her clit. "Tomorrow." The hand on her face went to her hair, using it to hold her in place as his lips covered hers, the taste of him anchoring her overwhelmed senses.

He leaned into her, the change of angle making his cock rub against the same spot his fingers found earlier. Her whole body clenched tight, riding the last seconds of pleasure before it all broke apart in a wave of sensation that froze her lungs and blurred her vision.

Pierce's body met hers, his cock impaling her completely with short, sharp thrusts that sent her higher, carrying her along until there was nothing left and her body went slack.

Her forehead fell to Pierce's shoulder.

He immediately pulled her close. "Damn it."

Her eyes opened. "What's wrong?"

Pierce wouldn't meet her gaze. "That's not how I intended for that to be." He rested his forehead against hers.

"How did you intend for it to be?"

He sighed. "Not in my closet." He pulled her against him, scooting her butt off the island as he turned toward the door leading to his room. "I should have been less—"

"I don't think you should have been less anything." No way did she want him thinking there was something wrong with what he just did.

Primarily because she absolutely wanted all of it to happen again.

Mona held tight as Pierce laid her on the bed, his body following hers. "You should always be exactly what you are."

His blue eyes were serious as they looked down into hers. "I don't like exactly what I am, Love."

"I do." Mona ran her fingers through his dark hair, smoothing it down into the style she was used to seeing it combed into. "I like all of you." She traced down the side of his face with the tips of her fingers. "I like when you're serious and buttoned up." She brushed across his lips. "And I very much like when you're not."

Pierce caught her hand, pressing a kiss to the fingers against his mouth before resting it against the side of his face and leaning into it. "I used to be only one man."

"You say that like it's a bad thing." Mona stroked her thumb against the barely-there stubble covering his cheek.

"It was a bad thing." Pierce rolled to the side, pulling her along so they stayed face-to-face. "I was out of control." His eyes darkened. "Dangerous."

"You're still dangerous." She smiled a little. "Otherwise Vincent wouldn't want to work with you."

"I used to be more dangerous."

She lifted a brow. "I don't believe you."

"My parents sent me away when I was thirteen." His touch was soft as it stroked over her hair.

212

"Where did they send you?" Mona shivered a little as the coolness of the air around her finally started to register.

Pierce shifted away. "A school meant to break me." He snagged a blanket from the pile on the floor as he pulled the spent condom from his cock, wrapping it in a tissue before depositing it in the trash can next to the bathroom door. He shoved down the pants and underwear barely hanging from his hips as he came her way, his full body finally on display.

She worked hard to pay attention to what he said as her eyes found their focus elsewhere, taking in the dips and planes of the muscle cut into his form. His suits didn't hide how well put together he was.

But they didn't do him full justice either.

"It's where I first met Anthony." He pulled the blanket over her body as he curled around her, his front to her back. "He was the most awful human I'd ever met." Pierce's voice lowered as his head tucked close to hers. "And that's saying something."

"How did you know so many bad people?" Mona cuddled back into him, his warmth a temptation she couldn't resist.

"Wealth can bring out the worst in men, Love." Pierce pressed a kiss to the back of her neck. "Makes them believe they are more than mortal."

"A God complex."

"Exactly." Pierce's arm wrapped around her waist, pulling her even closer. "It can make them believe everyone is lesser. Unworthy of anything but their presence."

A spot deep inside her chest ached. "You are not like them."

"I try not to be." There was regret in his voice. "Often I fail."

Mona twisted, fighting the weight of his arm and the blanket blocking out the constant chill she felt here. She faced him, pressing both hands to his face. "You don't have to try." Of all the things she expected to find in him, insecurity wasn't even a consideration. "You are the kind of man who lifts other people up." She shook her head a little. "You would never look down on someone."

"I look down on many men, Love."

"Men like Anthony Sanders?"

His eyes moved over her face, the line of his mouth softening. "I'm not sure how I waited for you to be ready for me, Love."

"You didn't." Mona pressed down on her lips as they tried to smile. "I think it had to be sort of a trial by fire."

"How flattering."

"I was terrified of you." She reached out to run the tip of her finger down his perfectly straight nose. "When you walked into a room I thought I was going to pass out." Mona smiled at the change in his expression. "Not because of you. Because of me. I knew I wanted to be better which meant I had to stand up to you and the thought made me want to throw up."

"I want you to stand up to me."

"I know that now, but it didn't occur to me then." She let her head fall to the single pillow they shared. "I was very sheltered growing up. I knew there were bad people in the world, I just never expected to find any of them." Mona curled closer to him. "When they found me I didn't know how to deal with it." She swallowed the regret tugging at her throat. "So I didn't."

"And you thought I was bad?"

"No." Clearly she wasn't explaining this well. "But if I can't stand up to someone who's not bad then how can I expect to deal with someone who is?"

"You shot a bad man to protect your friend. I would say you can deal with bad people just fine."

"I can't go around shooting everyone who's bad."

"It seems we have differing opinions on that."

Mona laughed a little. "Not everyone who's bad deserves to die." She closed her eyes as the lids grew heavy. "There are different degrees of bad."

Pierce's lips came to rest on her forehead as her limbs got heavy.

"Not here there aren't, Love."

****

MONA SET HER bag on her desk. "Let's find Anthony Sanders and kill him."

"You had sex with Pierce, didn't you?" Heidi sucked yogurt out of a tube at her own desk.

"What?" Mona looked around the room. She was the last one there. Even Bess beat her in, and considering she'd been sick for the past week that

215

was saying something. "What does that have to do with wanting to kill the guy who's trying to kill me?"

"Nothing." Heidi pointed to Mona's desk. "You just don't have breakfast waiting for you on a fancy tray."

Mona turned to her bag, pulling out her laptop. "I already had breakfast."

Pierce whipped up a homemade hash with sweet potatoes, chicken, spinach, and tomatoes before she was even out of bed.

She even got to eat it while he laid naked beside her.

And naked Pierce might be the best possible part of waking up. Way better than Folgers ever could be.

Heidi's mouth opened in a wide smile. "You dirty dog." She leaned forward, wiggling her brows. "And what did Pierce eat for breakfast?"

"Please stop talking about breakfast." Bess lifted one hand to cover her mouth.

Mona turned to the woman on her left. "Are you still sick?"

Bessie was pale and maybe a little green.

"I'm fine." Bess grabbed the ginger ale on her desk and took a little sip. "And we need to figure this out." She turned to the wall they'd been using to organize all the bizarre happenings. "So we figured out that Howard, Chandler, and Chris are connected. Now we need to figure out how they connect to Anthony."

"I can probably help with that." Eva flipped open a file on her desk.

"What's that?"

"It's all the stuff I collected on Anthony after Pierce gave me his name. I just didn't realize this was why." She pulled out a stack of papers and started reading. "He was born in Florida. His dad was the son of an oil tycoon who died when he was seventeen. The bulk of his estate was split between his two sons."

"One of his son's is dead."

"He is now, but he was alive when their dad died." Eva turned the page she was reading from around. A photo of an overweight man stared out at her, his eyes cold and hard. "That's the dad's obit."

Mona skimmed the text of the death announcement. "How big was the estate?"

Eva's eyes widened. "Big."

"What happened to the older son's portion when he died?" Heidi leaned in, looking toward the rest of the file on Eva's desk.

"Well, that's probably what has Tony all pissed off." Eva grabbed the next paper. "From what I can tell the son left all his assets to a trust for his only child. A daughter."

"Where's the daughter?" Bessie's tone was tight.

Eva shrugged. Her brow furrowed as she looked at the papers. "She's around seventeen now."

Mona fell back in her seat. "Holy shit."

"I thought my life was crazy." Harlow's brows lifted as she shook her head. "But some of this shit makes it seem boring as hell."

"So do you think the daughter is with her mom? Is she okay?" Bess rolled her chair Mona's way.

"Her mother's dead." Mona stood from her seat. "I'll be back."

"What? You can't just drop a bomb like that and then leave." Bessie turned to Eva. "Is his daughter okay?"

Eva shook her head. "I don't know. I can't find anything on her."

Mona hurried down the hall toward Pierce's office, the mess of information they'd been fighting working loose as she went. She marched through the door to find Pierce behind his desk. Zeke sat in the chair across from him.

He glanced Zeke's way. "I'll find you when I'm done here."

Zeke stood, tipping his head at Mona as he passed. She waited until the door was closed before speaking.

"Where is she?"

Pierce's eyes held hers. "She's safe."

"Is that why Anthony's here? Is he looking for her?"

"Partly."

"When you killed his brother all the money went to that little girl."

"All the money went to a trust she can't touch until she's eighteen.

That was the rest of why he was here now. "He wants the money."

"He wants everything, the same as every other man like him. He believes he deserves it." Pierce stood. "And he will get none of it."

She liked this man before, but as the pieces of his life fell into place around her she fell a little in love with him.

Because now she knew the real reason for Alaskan Security's existence.

"Is there any way for him to find her?"

Pierce rested the fingertips of one hand on his desk. "I hope not."

That wasn't good enough.

"If he finds her—"

"He will kill her the same way he would like to kill you." Pierce held her eyes. "To take everything from me the way he believes I took everything from him."

This was so much more than she thought. "Is there anything else? Is he going to try to hurt your parents too?"

Pierce's expression shifted. "No."

"Why not? He wants to take everything."

"They are already gone."

Mona blinked. "Your parents are already dead?"

"No." Pierce rounded the desk, leaning against the front with a cool calm she was struggling to feel. "My parents cut ties with me to save their reputations. My father spent the money required to make the death of Anthony's brother go away, but once that was done he made it clear I was no longer part of his life."

"Why?" It was unbelievable to think a parent would fault a child for seeking vengeance for another child's death.

"Because I made him seem human. My behavior made people think he was less than the perfect specimen he desired to be considered."

She was speechless.

"Don't be upset. It was the best thing that could have happened to me. I joined the military. Met men who made me better than I was." Pierce straightened, coming toward her. "Learned how to control the anger that I struggled with." His hands came to her face. "And it brought me you."

CHAPTER 17

"WE CANNOT MOVE her. Not now." Pierce sat in the theater room, six of the men who made up the invisible force no one else at Alaskan Security knew existed displayed across the screen in front of him. "It will risk bringing attention to her location."

"He may already know her location, Pierce." Henry crossed his arms, leaning back in the chair where he sat with the rest of the men Pierce entrusted to protect the niece no one else knew existed. "We can't be sure how long he was watching before we realized it."

Pierce raked a hand through his hair. He thought he could keep her safe.

He thought he could separate himself from her enough that even if Anthony found him he would never be able to find the niece they shared.

"Does Vincent know about Amelia?"

Just hearing her name made his chest tight. He'd been her guardian since he turned eighteen, taking the final reminder of his parent's failure with him when he left.

"I'm not sure." Pierce forced his eyes to the screen. "Have you seen any signs that GHOST might be on her trail?"

Henry looked at the men tucked into the small room around him. "Nothing."

Pierce let out a breath. If Vincent hadn't found her then chances were good Anthony hadn't either.

"Does she have any idea what's happening?" Cade, leaned forward in his seat. "Maybe if we told her—"

"That's not an option." He'd worked so hard to provide Amelia with a sense of normalcy. A life unlike the one she was born into. "Have you briefed Helen?"

"Helen is in the loop on everything." Henry crossed his arms. "She's got enough in that little house to take down half a small country if she has to."

"And she'll do it." Cade chuckled. "She might look like a sweet grandma, but that woman will take anyone out in a heartbeat if they get too close to Amelia."

Helen was the only other person who moved from his past to his future. She'd been Amelia's nanny when everything fell apart. Now she was her official guardian. The legal distance he used to ensure her connection to him would never be found.

"Helen's an angel."

"An angel of death if you cross her." Cade pointed to Henry. "Remember that time you got too close to Amelia and she thought you were going to fuck everything up?"

Henry's eyes went to his clipboard. "I remember."

Amelia was oblivious to who she was. What she'd been burdened with. Pierce wanted to carry that weight for her as long as possible. "How did she handle being let go from the flower shop?"

"About as well as you'd expect." Cade crossed his arms. "She gave the owner hell when he did it."

"I made it worth his while." Pierce turned to Henry. "What about school? Any issues keeping her safe there?"

"Only if he figures out where she is." Henry's jaw went tight.

They all cared about her. They'd followed her for years. Protected Amelia like she was their own.

And now she was at risk. Which meant he had to pull out every weapon he had. "I want to bring Shadow in."

Cade's head snapped up. "Fuck Shadow. There's no room for them to play fucking sides in this."

"They're not playing sides." He thought the same thing Cade did initially. Believed Zeke and the rest of Shadow's allegiance leaned to Vincent and the protections he could offer them.

"You willing to bet her life on it?" Cade's expression was hard. "Because that's what you're fucking doing if you bring Shadow into this."

"We have to do something." He should have done it before now, but the risk of exposing Amelia's location was too great.

Now he had no choice.

His options for keeping Amelia safe without taking all the innocence he tried to provide her were shrinking with each passing second. "I will come up with something."

"You better do it quick, because if he finds her then there's going to be a lot of death to deal with." Henry was serious as he stared through the screen.

Each man would willingly give his life for Amelia. There was no doubt in Pierce's mind.

"I'll be in touch." Pierce shut down the secured line and sat staring at the blank screen.

He'd created this mess. Every bit of it was done with the best of intentions.

But he'd been willfully blind. Purposely shut out the possibility that this could all come back to the one thing he always knew might happen.

But he'd been certain he'd done everything to keep her location from being tied to him in any way.

All in the mistaken belief he was powerful enough to protect her.

His phone buzzed in his pocket. He pulled it free and swiped across the screen, connecting the call from Dutch.

"Courtney just landed."

Pierce rubbed his eyes. "Who the fuck is Courtney?"

"She's Vasquez's daughter that you authorized to bring here. That ringing a bell?"

One more fucking thing. "Fine. Find her a place to stay and lock her down."

"You want me to lock her in a room?" Dutch didn't even try to hide his unhappiness with the plan. "I think you know how that's going to play out."

Pierce leaned forward, resting his head on one hand, squeezing his temples as he tried to work up the gumption to care about this girl.

He was unsuccessful. "Then you decide what we do with her."

Dutch was silent for a minute. "Something bothering you?"

Of course something was bothering him. Everything was falling apart. The framework he'd so carefully built was collapsing around him, putting everything he cared about at risk. "Just do something with Courtney." He disconnected the call and tossed his phone to the sofa beside him.

He'd called in every favor he had building this place. Taken advantage of every connection his family hadn't managed to take from him.

Borrowed begged and stolen to keep Amelia safe.

Now it could all be for nothing.

And Amelia's life wasn't the only one on the line.

Pierce stood, grabbing his phone from the sofa. He had only one choice. One way to end this without risking someone he cared about.

He pulled open the door of the theater room and nearly fell back.

Mona stared at him, her arms crossed tight to her chest.

"What's wrong?" He reached for her, disguising the touch as something she might need, instead of what it was.

A desperate man trying to meet his own needs.

"You come here every morning at the same time."

"I can't recall." Pierce ran his hands down her arms, focusing on the soft pile of her sweater. "It's possible."

"It's not just possible. It's a fact." Mona lifted a brow as she looked up at him. "I checked the security footage."

"I will take your word for it then." He smoothed back up her arms, stopping to let his hands rest under each side of her jaw. "Why does that upset you?"

"No one knows about her, do they?"

He traced along her skin with the pad of one thumb. "There are people who know about her."

"Shawn?"

Her tone was almost accusatory, but what she might be accusing him of was unclear. "No."

"Zeke?"

"No." Pierce stepped in closer, seeking the scent of her to calm the upset tearing through him.

"Who besides me then?"

Pierce rested his forehead to hers, closing his eyes. "Men you don't know."

"So there's an entire team here no one knows exists."

"They are not technically a part of Alaskan Security." Pierce opened his eyes. "They are not connected to me in any way."

Her brows came together. "You now that's not true, Pierce. Not anymore. Anything can be connected if someone knows where to look."

"Vincent hasn't made the connection."

"That's what you're going off of? If GHOST hasn't figured it out no one else has either?" Her hands came to his face. "Is that a risk you're willing to take?"

"What do I do, Love? If I bring her here she learns her whole life is a lie. She finds out what she came from and has to bear the weight of that knowledge."

"How does she not know what happened?" Mona's eyes were wide. "What in the world does she think happened?"

"She believes she lives with her grandmother. That her parents were killed in a car crash." It was what he and Helen came up with. An easy explanation that was a twist on the truth.

Her parents were in fact dead, and Helen loved her more than either of her grandparents ever did.

Mona leaned her head back. "That's fucked up, Pierce."

"How is protecting someone fucked up?"

"She doesn't even know who she is." Mona's hands squeezed his face, forcing his eyes to hers. "She deserves to know the truth."

"Then what? How am I supposed to protect her then?" It was his greatest fear that one day Amelia would begin to question the story she'd been told and seek out the real story of her past.

"What was your ultimate plan? She inherits an amount of wealth most people can't comprehend in under a year. How were you planning to handle that?"

Pierce pressed his lips together. It was an eventuality he always knew was coming. "I was going to ease her into it."

Mona blinked at him. "I don't even know what to say to you right now."

"I didn't want her to end up like the people we came from. I thought if I gave her a different start she would be able to handle what came after." He'd been too young when this all started to really understand what he was doing. The choices he'd made at eighteen were very different from the ones he would make today.

"She may not have an after if you don't do something drastic." Mona straightened, sucking in a deep breath. "You have to at least tell Rogue, Intel, and Shadow."

"No." It was an automatic reaction to a lesson he'd learned young in life. The fewer people who knew the truth the more hidden it remained.

"You have to." Mona sounded more sure of this than he was of anything. "And you have to do it now so we can decide what to do and get it done before Anthony finds her."

"And trust that none of them will turn against me again?"

"First of all, no one turned against you in the first place." Mona's chin lifted. "What Zeke did was stupid, but it was not because he chose GHOST over Alaskan Security and you know that." Mona held his gaze. "They are the reason I was willing to go out to lure Anthony from whatever hole he's hidden in. I knew no matter what I would be safe."

In his life he'd seen men twisted by money and all that came with it. Watched as it turned them to someone else. Something else. Believing there were men who would not succumb to the allure of a financial windfall was nearly impossible.

"He will offer anyone he thinks can gain him access more money than they can imagine."

"And they will all turn him down." Mona shook her head. "I can't speak for Alpha or Beta, but I would bet my life on Rogue and Shadow."

"If you are wrong—"

"I'm not wrong." Mona's jaw was set and her eyes were filled with a certainty he'd hoped to someday see.

He couldn't take that from her now.

"Fine." Pierce grabbed her hand in one of his as he dialed Dutch's number on his phone. Dutch answered on the second ring as Pierce led Mona through the halls toward the offices. "Call a meeting with Intel, Shadow, and Rogue."

"What time?"

"Now." Pierce squeezed Mona's hand a little tighter as the unwanted bite of fear twisted his gut. "It's an emergency."

"Got it."

He slid his phone into his jacket pocket. "Do I bring her here?"

"Definitely." Mona didn't hesitate. "And Helen."

"She is not going to be happy."

"Helen or Amelia?"

He was not looking forward to explaining the full situation to Helen. "Both."

"I'm sure she'll be happy when Amelia comes out of this alive." Mona stayed right at his side as he walked into the largest of the conference rooms. Intel was already there, lined up in their places at the front of the room. Brock, Dutch, Wade, and Shawn sat together, side by side in the row behind the women that loved them in a way that used to chafe.

The thought of having someone at his side he could trust seemed impossible given the secrets he held.

Until he met Mona.

Pierce tried to pull her along with him to the front of the room where his chair sat.

Instead she held fast, her fingers squeezing tight as she instead pulled him with her toward the chairs where his employees sat. She leaned into his ear. "Right now it's not you and them." Mona's pale blue eyes stayed on his. "It's all of us together." She went to the seat she usually occupied and pulled him down into the one next to her.

She scooted her chair around, angling it in his direction. The rest of Intel immediately did the same, with Heidi, Harlow, Eva, and the newer recruits circling. As the rest of the men from Rogue and Shadow filed in they joined the group, pulling chairs into empty pockets until everyone was in a tight circle with him at the center.

And Mona close at his side.

"What's going on?" Dutch leaned in from where he sat behind Harlow, resting his hands on her shoulders.

Pierce glanced Mona's way.

She barely dipped her head in a nod.

He looked over the faces surrounding him. Men he'd known since his days in the military. Men he'd trusted with the safety of others without blinking an eye.

"I've been keeping a secret from all of you." He cleared his throat. "I know what Anthony Sanders is here for."

"You're shitting me." Zeke snorted out a bitter breath. "Fucking figures."

Mona shoved a finger Zeke's way. "Shut it."

Zeke lifted a brow but went silent.

"I have a niece." Pierce started to reach one hand into his pocket but before he could Mona's hand slipped into his, holding tight. "I should say Anthony and I share a niece."

He laid out the good, the bad, the ugly, and the foolish of his life, avoiding the eyes around him as he spoke, knowing there would be judgment in their gazes.

The more he explained, the more clear his shortcomings became.

How foolish he'd been to think hiding Amelia away would work. How negligent he'd been by refusing to consider it was his past arriving in Alaska to wreak havoc.

"Where is she now?" Harlow was the first one to speak up when he finished.

"Close by." It's why Alaskan Security was where it was.

Because Alaska was the best place to disappear. It's where he sent Helen and Amelia and where he'd gone the second his time in the military was served.

When he thought he'd finally learned how to be a better man.

Shawn glanced around the room. "Who's watching her?"

"A team of six men who've been with her since she relocated." It was still painful, even after all these years, to acknowledge the full extent of his father's selfishness. "I was put in charge of her trust. It was one of the conditions of my willingness to disappear."

"So lemme get this straight." Heidi's brows were tight together. "Your parents were pissed that you killed the guy who killed your sister, so they basically paid to keep you from getting in trouble for it and then handed over your niece and her trust to make you both go away."

"You would be amazed what the wealthy do to protect their way of life, Ms. Rucker." He'd seen children with special needs disappear. Adults suffering from mental illness gone and never mentioned again. "Money fixes many perceived problems."

"Did they not want her money though? It had to be a shit ton."

"Shit ton is relative." Amelia's trust was sizable when she was young.

Now it was worth three times as much, even after years of private security and living expenses. It was one of his top priorities. Making sure she would be taken care of forever.

Have the world at her feet.

"So…" Zeke squinted at Pierce. "You're about to tell a teenager her whole life's been a lie and she's actually rich as shit." He snorted a little laugh. "That should go well."

CHAPTER 18

"I SAY WE go get her." Shawn looked at the men around him. "Right?"

"I think it's our only choice." Zeke scooted closer. "We sure as hell can't leave her out there. Even with a team following her. If they're not close enough to be there the second things get bad then they might as well not be there at all."

"They are in the house next door." Pierce pointed to the spot on the screen depicting a road map of Fairbanks. "They occupy it around the clock."

"Shit can get real ugly real fast." Zeke shook his head. "I wouldn't leave her out there if she was mine."

"Then what?" Pierce wiped his hands down his face. "I can't just keep her here indefinitely."

"Then we figure out how to get rid of Anthony and everyone's lives can go back to normal." Dutch looked to Harlow. "Right?"

Harlow gave him a half nod. "If all that's been happening ties back to him then it's possible that would be the end of it."

"You really think all of this goes back to him?" Brock was one of a handful of the men having a hard time wrapping their brains around everything.

If she hadn't seen the lengths people were willing to go to in order to have what they want she might be right there with him.

Mona pulled up a snapshot of the wall in Intel's office and set it to display on the screen at the front of the room. "We've been working to connect all the players we've identified and so far every single one of them can be tracked in some way."

Brock squinted at the screen. "That looks like a clusterfuck."

"It is a cluster fuck. That's why we couldn't figure it out." Heidi didn't look up from where she was working on her own laptop. "I mean maybe if Pierce spilled his guts a little earlier we might have been able to narrow some shit down." Heidi's eyes finally lifted to land on Pierce. "It's cool though. Not like it hurt our feelings or anything."

"This wasn't personal." Pierce was more agitated than normal. "I–"

Heidi lifted a hand, cutting him off. "It's too late now." She tilted her head at the screen of her laptop. "I think we should probably go get her sooner rather than later."

Pierce's spine went straight. "Why?"

"I'm not sure that information will help you right now." She turned to Shawn. "How fast can you be ready to go get her?"

"An hour?" Shawn glanced at Zeke. "Maybe less."

Zeke stood. "Less." He nodded at the men of his team. "At the doors in twenty."

Shawn and the rest of Rogue were out of their seats too, the entire atmosphere in the room shifting as they quickly made their way to the door.

Pierce started to follow them out.

Mona caught his arm. "Where are you going?"

His eyes were dark. "I'm going to get changed."

"No." She shook her head. "You can't go out with them."

"I most certainly can." He pulled at the tie around his neck, the sight of the pattern on it immediately catching her attention.

Pierce pulled her close. "I will be back, Love. If for no other reason than to watch your skin flush as I return last night's favor." He tugged the tie loose from his collar, her eyes following the fabric as it fell loose.

"The chair's broken."

His lips curved into a slow smile. "I would never tie you in such an uncomfortable position, Love." Pierce's lips brushed her ear. "I intend to stretch you across my bed."

"Pierce."

Shawn's voice made her jump.

"If you're coming then you better get moving."

Pierce brushed a kiss along her cheek. "I will see you soon."

He turned and walked toward where Shawn stood waiting.

"No." Mona looked around the room for back up. "There's twenty other guys going."

Pierce turned toward her. "I need to go with them. I created this mess. I need to at least help fix it."

"But he wants to kill you." She pointed at Shawn and Brock as she chased Pierce down. "He doesn't want to kill them."

"He wants to kill anyone who gets in his way." Pierce's tone was measured and calm. "I won't ask them to do something I won't do myself." He stepped in, resting his lips to her forehead. "I will come back. I promise."

And then he walked out. Left her staring after him, feeling like her old self.

Terrified and sick. Torn between chasing him down or throwing up.

"You can't argue with them." Bess came to her side, wrapping one arm around Mona's shoulders. Her lips twisted in a sly grin. "You can force them to make it up to you though."

Heidi walked across the room, chewing on the end of a gummy worm. "That what got you all knocked up again?"

Mona's eyes immediately dropped to Bessie's stomach before lifting to her unusually pale face.

Bess shrugged a little. "Can you blame me?"

"At least he'll be here to take care of you this time." Harlow walked past. "We should go get set up so we can be ready." She gave Bess a small smile. "Congratulations."

"I'm not sure it's congratulatory right now. I'm feeling a lot like I did something horrible to someone and karma has come for me." Bessie's nostrils flared and her mouth pressed into a grimace. "Speaking of." She darted toward the door.

Eva watched her go. "She's not really selling it, is she?"

"I'd still do it." Heidi chomped another worm in half. "I want a bunch of 'em."

"Oh God." Eva wrinkled her nose. "You better have sons. I can't even imagine Shawn with daughters."

Heidi smiled wide. "I think it'd be good for him."

Harlow made a rolling motion with one of her hands. "If everyone's going to be shitting out babies then we need to get this wrapped up. Let's go."

Dutch and Alec were already in their office, lining up everything they needed to be ready to help with the mission. Harlow took her spot next to Dutch and immediately went to work pulling up cameras along the route the teams would be taking to go collect Amelia and Helen.

Mona glanced up just as Isaac, the tech coordinator for Shadow walked through the door. She'd spent more time with the men from Shadow than probably anyone else in the room.

Now she knew why.

Knowing the people he cared about would be safe was an almost pathological need for Pierce.

"Hey." Mona rounded her desk as she headed for the giant man Zeke used as her training victim on more than one occasion. "Do you need desk space?"

Isaac glanced toward where Dutch, Alec, and Harlow sat. "I'll just grab a spot in the back."

"It's probably best for you to be up here with us." Dutch moved around some stuff on his desk, making space for Isaac's laptop. "That way we can all make decisions at the same time."

Mona grabbed Isaac a chair and pushed it across the room, the fist squeezing her chest relaxing a little as she helped get everything ready. The more prepared they were, the more likely there would be no issues.

And she wanted no issues.

Heidi, Eva, Bess and the rest of the girls crowded around Mona's center stage desk and watched as the screens across the wall lit up, each displaying the feed from a different traffic camera. The largest screen in the center stayed black as Dutch and Isaac went through the mission checklist with their respective teams. Alec sat silently, watching everything the two men did.

Suddenly the center screen flashed to life, the scene bouncing around in an erratic way.

Mona watched, catching bits and pieces of what was being recorded.

"It's Zeke's body camera." Isaac turned back to watch the feed. "I'd keep my eyes off it if you get motion sickness."

Bessie's hand went over her mouth.

Heidi lifted Bessie's can of ginger ale, holding it up without looking away from the screens.

"Thank you." Bess took the can and sipped at the bent straw sticking out of it.

Dutch tapped a few keys on his computer then straightened. The sound of an open line came from the speakers mounted next to the monitors. "Roll call."

One by one the men of Rogue called out their names.

Isaac pressed his earpiece. "Shadow call."

Again, each member of the team stated their name across the open line.

The feed in the center of the wall stilled, focusing on a single man.

"And Pierce." Zeke chuckled as Pierce glared at him.

"You online, Pierce?"

"I am." His voice made the twist in her gut and the ache in her chest tighten in tandem.

Bess passed over her trash can. "Need this?"

Heidi's head snapped Mona's way. "Are you pregnant too?"

"Definitely not." Mona swallowed down the familiar threat of a gag. "Just nervous."

"He'll be fine. Those guys will protect him."

"I am quite capable of protecting myself, Ms. Rucker."

Mona couldn't help but smile a little.

Dutch turned their way, pressing one finger to his lips.

It was a drill they were familiar with. In order to be a part of what was happening they had to stay quiet.

Heidi's lips clamped shut as they all watched and listened.

It took the teams thirty minutes to get to the street where Amelia and Helen lived. The weather had been particularly brutal lately, dropping piles of show in the span of a few hours. The roads were cold and slick and now was not the time to end up helpless in a ditch.

As the vans slowed in front of the single-story house Mona's attention bounced from the street view to Zeke's body camera. The second the vans stopped men poured out from the back of each, guns pulled as they ran toward the house.

Two men came out the front door of the house beside it, immediately falling in line with the rest.

She found Pierce almost immediately, his long strides easy to identify as he moved to the front door of Amelia's home. It opened and an older woman came out. A few of the men grabbed bags as she passed them out the door.

Mona's heart picked up speed as a smaller figure appeared. If you didn't know what you were looking at it would be difficult to know who it was.

Hopefully difficult enough this went off without a hitch.

Pierce was immediately at Amelia's side, tucking her close as Zeke flanked her other side, the men practically dragging her toward the waiting vans.

In under two minutes they had both Helen and Amelia, their bags, and both the men from the house next door loaded into the vans. They started to move even before the doors were closed.

Mona let out some of the air she'd been holding, the tension in her body relaxing a little.

They had her.

Now they just had to get home.

The vans turned out of the small housing development, making a right and falling in with the flow of traffic.

Dutch and Isaac took turns briefing the drivers on possible slow spots and alternative routes as they worked through the fastest and safest possible way to get them all back to headquarters.

The closer they got the more Mona was able to breathe.

Just a few more minutes and they would be back. Then they could come together and figure out how to find Anthony Sanders and—

Her lungs stopped working. "What's that?"

Dutch spun to look her way before following her line of sight to the screen still showing the exterior of Helen and Amelia's house.

A black Charger slowly eased down the street. The windows were blacked almost completely out, obscuring whoever was inside.

"We've got movement at the residence." Isaac stood from his chair, eyes glued to the screen. "Black Dodge Charger."

The sedan came to a stop between the two houses.

Her heart went to her throat as the doors of the sedan opened and four men spilled out. Two went to Helen and Amelia's house while the other two went to the house next door. Mona jumped a little as they kicked the doors in with a force that she could almost feel.

Minutes.

That's all that Amelia and Helen were saved by. Minutes.

"Looks like they got an ID on your girls." Isaac's tone was calm as he continued to watch the screen as the men disappeared into the houses. "They made entry."

In less than a minute they were back, rushing out the doors and to the Charger.

"Oh no." Both Mona's hands went to her mouth as the car raced away.

A second later an explosion rattled the camera pointed at the homes. A second later it happened again.

"Holy shit." Heidi's eyes were wide as she stared, open mouthed, at the screen. "They just blew that shit up."

Dutch and Isaac locked eyes.

Isaac eased down into his chair. "We're going to need you boys to get back here as fast as possible."

Dutch pointed to Alec. "Tell Gentry to get as many of his men as he can to the front gates." He picked up the phone, continuing to bark orders at Alec as he dialed. "Tell him fully-armed." Dutch turned away and started talking into the phone.

"Get a van to the front gate ready for a possible blockade."

"They're coming here?" Bess turned to Mona. "Are they coming here?"

Mona turned to the faces of the women around her. "They won't get in here." She shook her head, trying to be like Pierce. A calm in the face of a storm.

Even if she knew it was fake, they didn't.

"They'll never make it through the gates." Mona turned to Heidi. "Warn Vincent."

Heidi's eyes went wide. "Shit. I wouldn't have even thought about that."

Alpha and Beta were rotating men through, providing GHOST additional manpower to help secure their facility.

Otherwise there would only be a team of ten men trying to protect one of the government's most valuable assets.

Heidi danced in place as her phone rang over the speaker.

"How did you get this number?"

"Shut up." Heidi's eyes lifted to the screens. "You need to secure your location, like now."

"Any particular reason?" Vincent's tone was annoyingly calm.

"You should probably just trust me on this." Heidi lifted one shoulder. "Or don't and if that's what you're going to do you can just send our men back."

"I'm pretty sure you're not authorized to make that call."

244

"She's authorized to make any call she wishes." Pierce's voice was strong and loud as it boomed through the speaker.

Heidi gave her phone a smirk Vincent couldn't see.

"I'll be in touch." Vincent hung up.

"He's just a bucket full of fucking sunshine, isn't he?" Bess eased into her chair as her skin paled.

"He's not used to taking orders." Mona crossed her arms as she surveyed the situation spread across the bank of monitors.

The room was quiet except for Dutch and Isaac's occasional directions to Rico and Luca as they drove, the two vans moving together as smoothly as the men inside them did.

"Five minutes out." Alec dealt with the men at headquarters, organizing the chaos as they raced against the clock.

Zeke's body cam feed was replaced with the view from the camera overlooking the front gate. Mona held her breath as the seconds ticked by, watching as Gentry and the rest of the men moved into position, lining behind one of the vans used to transport teams.

"This is crazy." Lennie stood just behind Mona, Eva, and Bess, watching with the other two women from Investigative Resources. Willa's dark eyes were wide as one hand pressed to her mouth. Paige was a little pale, her lower lip pinched tight between her teeth.

Eva glanced back their way. "You'll probably get used to it." She eyed Paige's pallid face. "Probably."

"There they are." Harlow was on her feet, watching as the two vans moved to the main screen. "I don't see any sign of the Charger."

One of Alaska's biggest assets was also one of its biggest downfalls.

It was easy to disappear.

There were a decent number of traffic cameras in the more populated areas, but those were few and far between, which meant it was difficult to keep track of someone when you didn't know their path.

Two men ran to the gate, pulling it open manually while four more men stood around them, guns pulled. Both vans raced through the opening, bouncing on their shocks as they took the drive at a speed that tested the limits of control and safety.

The waiting van immediately pulled across the lane, blocking the path of anyone who might try to cut through the gate before it could be fully closed.

"I don't see anything." Harlow's head moved along with her eyes as she scanned the screens.

Mona's stomach finally unclenched, the twist of fear easing as she watched the vans make their way across the security cameras.

"We're going." Eva was the first one moving, making her way toward the door of the office. She paused looking at Mona over one shoulder. "Come on. They get butthurt if you don't go and tell them how big and strong and brave they are after a mission."

CHAPTER 19

"GET THEM TO a room." Pierce pointed toward the rooming building. "Suite six is set up and ready." He passed one of the bags Helen brought to Zeke. "I want a man on the room around the clock until this is resolved." He risked a glance at the young woman he'd only seen through the feed of the surveillance footage shared with him during their daily briefings. She looked so much like his sister.

So much like the mother who should have been the one to care for her instead of an inept young man who'd managed to make a mess of everything.

Amelia held his gaze, her deep blue eyes unwavering as fully-armed men ran around her, unloading the vans in case they needed to be taken out again.

In case Amelia's other uncle decided now was the time to make his move.

"Come on, Honey." Helen wrapped one arm around Amelia's shoulders, directing the young girl toward the doors leading into the building.

Amelia held his eyes as she went, until there was no choice but to look in front of her as they went inside.

"She doesn't seem too happy to not be dead." Shawn stood at his side, peeling up the mask covering his face, leaving it rolled to the center of his forehead.

"She's just scared." It was the most likely explanation. It didn't appear Helen gave Amelia any sort of a heads-up that they were going to be relocating. "She might also be in shock." He turned to catch Abe as he walked past. "Send Eli up to check on Amelia. Make sure she's okay."

Abe glanced to where Amelia and Helen went into the building. "She freaking out?"

"It seems like she's struggling." Pierce walked toward the entrance, Shawn and Abe falling into step with him. "I don't want this to be any more difficult on her than it has to be."

"She's seventeen. Everything's difficult when you're seventeen." Shawn eyed Pierce. "At least she's not about to end up responsible for the well-being of a toddler."

Shawn's words carried a hint of bitterness.

"I couldn't tell you." Pierce glanced at one of his oldest friends. "It's not personal."

"Not when we were eighteen it wasn't." Shawn's jaw set. "But it definitely became personal." Shawn's gaze was hard as it settled on him. "You were pissed as hell when you thought Zeke wasn't fully committed to you." Shawn snorted. "You wanted complete commitment even when you weren't willing to give it back."

"Zeke's potential defection put the entire company at risk."

Shawn's brows lifted. "Yeah?" He looked around. "And this isn't?"

"Why are you wearing your angry eyes?" Heidi bumped into Shawn's side. She immediately reached up to smooth one finger across the line of his brows. "You are all back in one piece. You should be smiling."

Shawn's full attention went to the woman at his side as he pulled her close, tucking his face into the crook of her neck.

"He'll get over it." Abe watched as Brock caught Eva, swinging her around as he walked down the hall, her laugh loud and easy. Abe's gaze shifted around the hall. "I'll go find Eli." He left, winding his way through the clog of men milling around the space.

Pierce watched as Bess smiled up at Wade, her dimples on full display as she beamed at the man she trusted implicitly.

Was he worthy of the same sort of trust? Maybe.

Maybe not.

"I don't think I'd expect to be Amelia's favorite uncle right now." Mona's voice was soft. "But I'm sure she'll rethink that once she realizes what her other uncle wanted to do to her."

Pierce turned his head to where Mona stood just behind him. "Are the houses gone?"

Her mouth pressed to a thin line as she nodded. "I mean, they're still burning, but I'm sure once that's done they're as good as gone."

Mona's pale blue eyes moved over him. "I forgot how different you look in your gear." Her lower lip went between her teeth.

"Should I wear it more often?"

"I guess that depends on your goals in life." Mona looked down the hall. "Are you going to go meet with Helen and Amelia?"

He gave her a single shake of his head. "I am not."

"Oh."

"I think she needs some time to wrap her head around what happened today before I add anymore to her plate." Pierce reached out to run the back of his fingers across the flush of her cheek. "I do need to check on Vincent though."

"Yeah." Mona let out a little breath that could almost be considered a sigh. "That would probably be good."

He stepped in close. "But once I'm sure there will be no immediate fallout I am at your disposal."

"Immediate?"

"There will most definitely be fallout, Love." Anthony would be furious he missed the opportunity to steal Amelia away. His retaliation would come, but whether it would be swift or calculated was anyone's guess. "And I have to make sure we're ready."

Mona's lips curved into a soft smile. "I know." Her hand found his, holding it tight. "Let's go then." She pulled him along, taking him down the hall to where the back garages met the main building.

He let her lead him, following Mona past his office to the end of the hall where Intel was already back to work. Bess stood at the wall he would happily repaint when this was all over, a Sharpie in one hand and a trash can in the other.

"Vincent just called." Heidi was at her laptop, eyes glued to the screen. "He's linking me into the cameras GHOST has set up."

"Fantastic. Give them what they need to link to ours."

"Got it." Heidi's fingers continued across her keyboard. "Seth and Roman are both at GHOST. Seth's been in contact with Dutch so everyone should be on the same page."

Pierce glanced around the room. For so long he'd felt the weight of carrying an entire company on his shoulders.

A company that served more purpose than anyone else knew.

"Seth has half of Alpha and half of Beta with him plus GHOST's security team." Dutch's eyes went to the screens on the wall as they began to change.

"I'm going to set them to rotate. Top screens are GHOST. Bottom screens are us. Center screen is the front gate." Heidi looked from her computer to the wall of monitors. "I think I got everything set up."

"I'm not sure he will be interested in the front gate at this point." Pierce scanned the feeds. "If he didn't take immediate advantage I would say the front gate is no longer going to be his primary target."

"What is his primary target?" Bess turned from the wall she'd been staring at. "You? Amelia? The money? Drugs?" She rested the hand holding the marker against one side of her head. "He's got a lot going on and it's making my head hurt."

"That's just pregnancy." Heidi spun to look at the wall, her eyes squinting. "Did you add another line on there?"

Bess glanced over her shoulder at the wall. "Yeah. I figured out how Chandler and Howard initially got involved with Chris." She pointed to a section of the map of names and lines. "My dad hired a private investigator to look into Chris right when he first started acting crazy, but the guy who eventually did the job was not who he tried to hire first." She poked the marker at a familiar name. "He spoke with someone from this company first but was told they couldn't find anything."

Investigative Resources

Mona's lips turned down at the edges. "I'd threaten to kill them if they weren't both already dead."

"We don't know for sure Chandler's dead." Eva crossed her arms. "We could still get to kill him."

"I wouldn't get your hopes up." Heidi leaned back to shoot Eva a regretful look. "If Vincent thinks he's dead he's probably good and dead." She smiled. "On the plus side he probably got killed because you started to figure out what was going on, so you kinda got to kill him after all."

Lennie sat at her desk, wide dark eyes moving around the room. "I think I changed my mind about all of this."

Heidi waved one hand Lennie's way. "You'll get used to it."

Mona took a few slow steps toward the organized, but still chaotic wall. "So Chris was working with Anthony first." She tilted her head. "How are they connected?"

"Chris had a falling out with his father right before we met. The private investigator my father ultimately hired thinks he was dating me in the hopes that marrying into a well-off family would help him get back into his father's good graces."

"Why did they have a falling out?" Pierce read across the names, each time hanging up at Chris Snyder Jr. It sounded so familiar.

And not in a recent way.

"His father is a conservative senator. Chris was part of a group of guys who ended up in trouble for the hazing death of another student when he was in college so his dad basically cut all ties to save his own skin." Bess glanced at Pierce. "I didn't know that about him when we were dating." Her skin paled a little. "I found it out from the PI."

"So much for Howard claiming he couldn't find anything." Mona grabbed a chair and scooted it toward Bess. "Sit down before you barf on the floor."

Bess fell into the chair, taking the trash can with her. Mona snagged away the marker and went to work filling in the blanks on the wall. "So for our purposes, the first contact Anthony made was with Chris. Then at some point after that, Bessie's father unknowingly pulled Chandler and Howard into the mix."

253

"Who then sent Eva here in the hopes it would ultimately give Anthony a way inside Alaskan Security." Harlow came to stand at the edge of the group. "Too bad for him Eva was hot for Brock Star's biscuits."

"I like his gravy too." Eva wiggled her brows. "And his—"

"We know." Harlow said it loud enough to stop Eva's continuing explanation. "Back to what we're here for."

"So once Anthony realized that plan wasn't going to work, he decided to try to take her and ended up with more than he bargained for." Mona started a list on a blank area of the wall.

"I'm happy to get you a whiteboard, Love."

"Too late now." Mona shot him a little smile over one shoulder before going back to her list of events. "That might be where he first found out about Harlow."

"And then decided to find a little hacker of his own." Harlow frowned. "Unfortunately he found Tod."

"Who had an agenda of his own and was only too happy to join Anthony's little party of psychopaths." Mona kept writing as the women continued working out the mess he'd made.

He knew a team of women could be unbeatable. History had shown the superiority of women warriors time and time again.

The Night Witches.

Shield-maidens.

The Mino.

They were smart. They were fearless.

They were the threat many men were too foolish to see coming.

And these women were no different.

"Then when it became clear Tod was a liability he was killed." Mona added it to the list. "While Howard is locked up in the basement here he manages to get Bobby to come to the dark side." Her expression sobered as she wrote the next line.

Bobby killed while trying to take Harlow.

"Then Howard is handed over to GHOST." Mona turned to him. "Did you authorize that?"

Pierce shook his head. "No." It was the beginning of his issues with Zeke. The first indication Shadow's lead was more committed to another team.

The sound of a phone ringing filled the room.

"Rucker, if you don't stop calling me—"

"Shut up, Vincent. I got a question." Heidi kicked her feet up on her desk. "You use Howard as bait?"

The line was silent.

"Come on, man. We're trying to figure this shit out and we can't do it if you're going to be a tight ass."

This was why these women were not someone you wanted against you. They were smart and fearless.

Willing to take on one of the most powerful men in the world and treat him like he was the one being difficult.

"If we had used Howard as a way to attempt to pull someone out it would have been unsuccessful."

"I mean, clearly. He's friggin' dead." Heidi smiled at her phone. "Thank you. Talk to ya later."

"Stop call—"

Heidi disconnected the call, pointing the hand holding the phone toward Mona's list. "Add GHOST used Howard as bait and got him dead to the list."

Mona finished in neat, clearly-written printing. "And then Chandler was probably killed." She turned to Pierce. "Has anyone checked that PO Box yet?"

"No." It was the least of his worries. "I'm not sure anything we would find useful will fit in a PO Box."

"Money fits in a PO Box." Heidi lifted her brows. "You could probably fit a bunch of money in a PO Box." Her eyes went to one side. "Or drugs." She straightened. "Aren't these guys supposed to be running drugs to Canada or some shit?"

Pierce stared at the wall. "I would say that's where it began." He pointed to the top of the map where Anthony's name was written in big bold letters. "It's what led to Anthony and I meeting. He was caught trafficking small amounts of heroin to people he knew to make money for a new Mercedes after he totaled the one his parents bought him."

"Rich people problems." Heidi dropped her feet to the floor as she turned back to her laptop. "So Anthony likes to make his money the dangerous way, and Chris thought being a drug dealer would make daddy love him again."

"I'm not sure how many politicians you know, Ms. Rucker, but they're not as concerned with the means as they are with the end result."

Heidi lifted her brows. "He's got a lot on his plate what with trying to establish drug domination and exact revenge all at the same time."

"Powerful men usually don't recognize their limits." Pierce turned toward Dutch. "Are you seeing anything concerning?"

"It's quiet as hell." Dutch turned to where Alec and Isaac sat. "Zeke and Gentry are working together to patrol the perimeter." He tipped his head to the screens. "We're keeping an ear to the ground and so's Vincent. If anything happens we'll know the second it starts."

Pierce tipped his head. "Very well." He turned to Mona. "Would you care to join me in my office, Ms. Ayers? I have a matter I wish to discuss with you."

"Now she's Ms. Ayers again." Heidi gave him a sly grin. "A second ago she was Love."

"Don't make me fire you, Ms. Rucker." Pierce turned to Mona, lifting his brows as Heidi snorted out a laugh.

He hadn't only created one monster. He'd filled a room with them.

And right now nothing made him happier.

Almost nothing.

Mona capped the marker in her hand and tossed it to Harlow. "Call us if anything happens." She followed him from the room, forcing him to slow until she was at his side.

He never wanted her to walk behind him. Only beside him.

Pierce pulled her in close, pressing a kiss to her temple as they made their way down the hall. "What do we do now, Love?"

"We should probably revisit trying to tempt Anthony to show his hand." Mona relaxed into his side, one hand coming to rest in the center of his chest. "Maybe it's time to put the pictures we took yesterday out there. Make him think I'm dead. Distract him a little."

Pierce quietly closed the door to his office, the automatic locks clicking into place. "I wasn't asking about that." He turned to her. "I mean what should we do now?" He let his eyes fall to her mouth. The one that tortured him so perfectly last night. "As in right now."

Her lips lifted into a smile that was an unbearable temptation. "I guess that depends on whether or not you're feeling less selfish than you were last night."

CHAPTER 20

"SELFISH?"

He prowled her way.

"That's what I said." Mona stood a little taller. "You were being selfish."

"I think I should show you what I'm like when I'm feeling selfish, Love." Pierce closed in on her, moving around her in a slow circle. "So next time you'll know the difference."

She shivered, not out of fear.

Not because she was cold.

This was a shiver of anticipation.

This man who used to make her shake in her shoes still managed to have the same effect.

Just now it was for an entirely different reason. One that was much more tolerable.

Tolerable seemed like the wrong word.

Pierce stopped at her back, the closeness of his body making every nerve in her body stand at attention. "There's nothing I want more than to be selfish with you."

Mona tipped her head to peek at him over one shoulder. "What about what I want?"

"Is that not what you want?" One wide, warm hand skimmed across her hip, the touch barely there as it moved over her belly. "For me to be selfish with you?"

"Maybe I want to be selfish sometimes too."

His lips brushed across the side of her neck, dragging down toward her shoulder as his fingers worked the button of her pants. "Then be selfish. Take all I offer and demand more."

Some secret part of her had done exactly that last night. Crawled free of its hiding spot and asked for things she'd never dreamed of.

Demanded. Just like he said.

Pierce's touch tucked into her pants, fingers immediately finding her clit as his other hand tugged down the cup of her bra, working the freed nipple as he stroked the most sensitive of spots with a perfect rhythm.

"I will make you come until you beg me to stop, Love." His voice was husky and rough. "Until you can take no more." The hand between her legs worked faster, taking her right to the edge of a climax. "And then you will take more."

Mona's legs went weak as she came, her head falling back against him.

"One."

His hands gripped her pants, tugging them down till they tangled at her ankles. Pierce turned her, pulling her body to his as he walked around the desk. The backs of her knees hit the chair and she went down, naked ass meeting smooth leather.

Pierce went to his knees, his eyes dark. "I will never look at this chair the same way again." He caught the hem of her shirt, pulling it up and off her arms, but leaving it looped around her neck. Mona reached for it, ready to toss it away, but he stopped her. "Everything stays within reach this time, Love."

The reminder of all that was swirling around them should have dampened the desire still spiraling through her.

But she needed this.

She needed him.

And maybe he needed her right now too.

A moment of their own in the midst of chaos.

His fingers dragged down her arms, taking the straps of her bra with them, flipping it down to expose her breasts. A low growl rumbled through his chest as he leaned in, hot open mouth meeting her skin. His tongue rolled across her nipple as his wide body pushed between her legs, spreading them as far as was possible with her pants around her ankles. The roughness of his gear as it rubbed her skin was as arousing as the sight of his fully-dressed body against the near nakedness of hers.

Pierce's mouth moved down her body, over her belly, and straight between her legs.

He gripped her thighs, pulling her toward the edge of the seat. The position left her spread wide for him and he took full advantage. He was ruthless as he lapped at her, tongue sliding against her clit as his fingers curved inside her, rocking in and out.

261

This time he didn't shove her to the edge, he carried her, bit by bit, until she was hanging by less than nothing.

And then he growled against her, mouth open, the vibrations of the rumble enough to send her over the edge once again, fingers in his hair as she prayed to whatever goddess made this possible.

Because it was certainly a woman.

"Two." He stood, wiping one arm across his face as he pulled her limp body up with the other.

"I can't." Her head was spinning and her legs no longer worked. There was no possible way she would ever be able to give him any more of what he was demanding.

"You can do anything you want to do, Love." Pierce turned her toward the desk. "And you should want to do this." He ran one hand down the center of her back, between the cleft of her ass to stroke against her overly-sensitive pussy before sliding it back up. He pressed between her shoulder blades. "Bend over for me, Love. Show me what I'll be taking."

The voice. The way he spoke.

The things he said.

The man didn't have to take anything. She'd offer it up on a platter if that's what he wanted.

The rake of his zipper twisted her stomach, the feeling one she was just beginning to associate with what Pierce stirred inside her.

Excitement.

Anticipation.

They were slowly taking the place of the emotions that used to tie up her insides.

His front blanketed her back, one arm stretching over the surface of the desk to grip the front edge. "This is the place I first saw you. Do you remember that day, Love?" The wide head of him pressed against her, easing in with the slowest of glides. "You walked past my door and never gave me a second look."

She'd been on her way to meet with Eva and Chandler. "I remember."

"I had to come find you. I hunted you for hours." Pierce's hips met her thighs as he seated himself fully. "Did you know that?"

She whimpered as he pulled away, stealing the gloriously full feeling. "No."

"And when I did find you, do you remember what you said to me?" His lips traced the shell of her ear as he pressed back into her, the drag of his dick across the spot only he seemed capable of finding making her eyes roll closed.

"No."

"You said you wouldn't stay here." His mouth moved down her neck. "That you would be leaving."

Pierce's hand moved across her belly, sliding down between her legs, fingers splitting to rest on either side of where his body impaled hers, the heel of his palm putting a divine sort of pressure on her clit. "Have you changed your mind, Love?"

"Maybe." It might be the bravest single word she'd ever uttered.

Because it was definitely going to be met with a certain amount of unhappiness.

And she didn't care even a little.

Welcomed it, actually.

"Maybe?" Pierce thrust into her a little harder. "You *maybe* have changed your mind?" His hand ground against her. "That's not good enough."

She cried out as his hips slapped against her, each stroke of his body into hers more forceful than the last.

More wild.

His hand released the desk and slid under her body, palm flattening against her chest as he lifted her off the desk, standing her against him as he continued to fuck her with abandon. "Is this not enough for you, Love? Should I give you more? Would that make you want to stay?"

Maybe she got a little ahead of herself here.

Pierce's fingers found her clit as his lips rested against her ear. "If I wake you every morning with my mouth between your legs, will that make you want to stay?"

Her pussy clenched around him at the thought. "It might help."

She should stop antagonizing him. Stop doing the one thing she'd worked so hard to avoid her whole life.

But what used to make her feel weak and afraid now filled her with something she'd had far too little of in her life.

Power.

"Done." His hand on her chest went to a breast, thumb and pointer pinching the nipple just to the point of pain. "Anything you want from me. Whatever it takes to make you stay."

The hand between her legs moved faster as his thrusts became short and sharp. "One more, Love. One more."

Pierce's length seemed to swell, filling her even more as he pressed deep, the combination of his hands and dick on and in her body making her climax once more.

One final thrust and Pierce held her tight to him, his cock twitching as he found his own release. His arms pulled her tight as he fell into the chair, taking her down with him.

Holding her close.

His breathing was rough as his lips came to rest against the side of her head.

"Three."

****

"NO WAY."

Mona stared Zeke down.

"I mean it." Shadow's lead shook his head like that would make a difference. "It's not happening."

"You know as well as I do that this needs to happen." Mona tried to stand a little taller, hoping it might make a difference. "Especially since Vincent's still sitting on those pictures we took."

All that work to be dead, wasted.

"I need you to convince Pierce we should do this."

At least she no longer had to fight the urge to vomit anytime she had to deal with Zeke. It made things simpler.

Helped her focus on the task at hand. Especially since Zeke was her best option right now.

Getting him to help her wrap this whole mess up was imperative. "You should be flattered I trust you to keep me safe."

"I don't trust me to keep you safe, Mona." Zeke leaned down, giving her the look that used to make her almost pass out. "It's not happening."

"I'll call Vincent and he'll make it happen." It was a threat she really didn't want to have to follow through on. Especially since she wasn't as confident in Vincent's protective abilities.

But he had to at least be decent at it, otherwise he wouldn't be in charge of GHOST.

Probably.

"I liked it better when you were less," Zeke's eyes went to the defiant stance she'd seen Eva do a hundred times, "self-aware."

"Thank you." Mona smiled. It was nice that he'd noticed how much work she'd put into being better.

"Oh." An older woman stepped into the training room where Mona found Zeke working with a few of the members of Alpha and Beta. "Look at this place." Her brown eyes came to Mona. "You must be the lovely Mona." She came at her suddenly, grabbing her in a tight hug. "I'm so glad Pierce finally found a nice girl." She patted Mona's cheek. "He's been on his own for so long."

She'd only seen Helen a handful of times and always from a distance through the lens of a surveillance camera. "How are you doing?"

"A hell of a lot better than I was yesterday, I can tell you that." Helen shook her head, eyes wide. "I thought I was gonna have a heart attack waiting for them to get there." She glanced at Zeke. "Then this one came rushing through my door and almost distracted me." She gave him a wink.

Mona stared at Zeke as his skin started to pink under the cover of the beard just starting to fill in across his jaw. She leaned into Helen's side. "I think you embarrassed him."

"I'm sure it takes more than an old woman having a hot flash to get him all wound up." Helen's gaze moved around the large gymnasium-style room. "What a thing he's built here." She smiled softly. "I always knew Pierce was cut from a different cloth than the rest of them."

"How's Amelia handling things?" It was impossible to imagine what it would be like to find out all you thought you knew was a lie at such a confusing time.

"Well," Helen sighed, "I'm not sure she's handling anything well at this point." The older woman turned toward the doors leading out of the room. "Could I get a tour?"

"Of course." Mona shot Zeke a look, hoping he knew it meant this wasn't over, then walked with Helen out into the hall of the building that housed the training spaces and the fully-filled bunk rooms. "Have you seen much yet?"

Helen glanced behind them. "Just whatever I saw on my way to find you." She turned back to Mona. "I was hoping you could help me out."

"Sure." Mona made sure the next words came out easily in spite of the unease brewing in her belly. "I'm sure Pierce will be happy to get whatever you need."

Helen's expression turned sad. "I'm afraid this isn't that sort of a thing." She sighed. "Amelia's been a handful lately. She's always been a strong-willed girl, but ever since she was let go from her job she's just been defiant as heck." Helen shrugged. "I know all kids are like that, but I just can't seem to find a way to help her through this."

Helen was definitely coming to the wrong person with this. "I'm afraid I might not be much help when it comes to that."

Mona spent her life being the quiet one. The agreeable one. The one no one noticed.

"Maybe you should talk to Heidi. She might be better equipped to offer advice." Mona turned toward the connecting hall leading to the main office building. "Actually, I know quite a few women who could probably help you when it comes to the defiant behavior department."

Intel's office was full when Mona and Helen walked in. All eyes immediately came their way.

"This is Helen. She has some questions about how to handle a defiant teenager."

Heidi grinned. "You brought her to the right place."

"That's Heidi." Mona pointed to where her best friend sat. "And that's Eva. She doesn't like being told what to do either."

Eva pointed at Harlow. "She's the one who steals shopping points she can't even use when someone pisses her off."

"Only his." Harlow tipped her head toward Dutch. "And now I get all his points anyway."

Helen turned toward the mess of writing on the wall. "Wow."

"Right?" Heidi shook her head. "Pierce needs to give us all raises."

"Pierce is giving everyone raises." Pierce's voice no longer made her panic.

It no longer made her want to shrink back.

There was no nauseous twist of her gut when he stepped into a room.

But her body's reaction to him was no less dramatic.

Or problematic.

His eyes caught hers immediately and the heat there only made everything worse.

He lifted a hand, curling a finger in her direction. "Come, Love. We need to have a chat."

CHAPTER 21

"THAT WAS QUICK." Mona glared at him as he closed the door. "At least now you don't have to worry whether or not Zeke has your back."

"I would argue that the primary back he has is yours." Pierce turned toward Mona. "I see you met Helen."

"She's worried about Amelia." Mona lifted a brow at him. "She's apparently acting like a normal teenager, and Helen wanted to know if I had any advice for her."

"What advice did you give her?" Pierce walked to Mona, stopping just in front of her.

"I told her I was the wrong person to come to for advice about how to handle a defiant personality."

"I'm not sure that's entirely true." Pierce eased a little closer. "You are the woman who keeps trying to offer herself up as a sacrifice, are you not?"

"It's only a sacrifice if I die, and I don't plan on dying." Mona's glare held as she looked up at him.

"Well, your persistence has paid off."

Her pale brows lifted. "Really?"

"After careful consideration, and much discussion with Vincent and the team leads, it would appear that the fastest way to conclude this mess is by forcing Anthony to make a move."

"And you're going to do that by letting me go out?" The hopeful edge of her voice made it clear Helen was not as off-base with her search for advice as Mona thought.

"I'm going to do that by letting *us* go out."

Mona's mouth opened, then clamped shut before opening again. "I don't like that idea."

"Too bad." He reached up to tip one finger under her chin. "Because the only way you're going out is if I'm right beside you when it happens."

"But he wants to kill you."

"In case you don't remember, there are two separate listings soliciting your murder, Love." He held up his pointer and middle fingers. "Two."

"But if you're there he won't want to kill me."

"That's the hope." Pierce leaned down, planning to brush a kiss across her lips.

Mona's head tipped back. "I'm not doing this."

"A second ago you were more than ready to run out the gates." His smile was easy in spite of the day in store.

Or maybe because of it.

For the first time in his life he didn't feel alone. Didn't feel isolated by a past that drove him from a world of wealth and power into a world of fear and control.

271

Mona's frown was deep and strong. "Stop smiling."

"I don't think I will." Pierce ran his finger along her jaw. "Not for a long time."

"Let's just dress Zeke up as you."

"While I appreciate the fact that you'd rather Zeke die than me, I'm going to have to pass."

She turned away from him, skin paling, one hand going over her mouth. "I feel like I'm going to throw up."

"Considering I'm sure you aren't yet pregnant I will try not to be offended by that."

Mona's eyes were wide when they came back his way. "Did you just say *yet*?"

Pierce moved in close to her again, unable to stay away from her now that he'd finally found the woman strong enough to stand at his side.

Meet him head on.

"You know exactly what I said." He tipped his head down, meeting his eyes to hers. "And it's the only reason I'm allowing this."

"Are you trying to argue that the only reason you're going out to potentially get killed is because you want to—"

"That's exactly what's happening." He finished closing the distance between them. "We will go out and do this. Finish it all." Pierce's easy smile slid back into place. "And then we will plan for our future."

Mona stared up at him. "I think the extra oxygen from all the plants in here has made you delirious."

His cell started to ring from the pocket of his jacket. "Put a pin in that." He answered, keeping his eyes on Mona. "Are we ready?"

"If she gets hurt you're getting hurt too." Zeke was not happy with the decision to venture out and was having no problem voicing his displeasure. "I will choke you to death with one of your fucking pocket squares."

"Understood." Pierce started to tuck one hand into his pocket, but stopped, reaching for one of Mona's hands instead. "Are we ready to suit her up?"

"I'm almost to your office."

"Excellent." Pierce opened the door to his office just as Zeke reached it.

"This is bullshit." Zeke immediately went for Mona, not even giving Pierce the option to be the one to fit on the vest that would limit the damage that could be done to her. "Arms in." Shadow's lead went to work strapping her into the too-big vest. "This is the smallest one I could find." His glare came Pierce's way. "If you could have fucking waited I might have been able to get one that would actually fit her."

"I need him to be in a reactive state." In all truth they should have done this yesterday, but taking Mona out like this was unthinkable until she threatened to once again drag Vincent into this, and considering the head of GHOST's current level of agitation, he wouldn't be as hesitant as he was last time.

Mona frowned down at the bulk of the vest. "Are they all this heavy?"

"It's worth it." Zeke finished buckling her in and stepped back. "How's it feel?"

"Uncomfortable." Mona shifted her shoulders around.

"It feels a hell of a lot better than getting shot." Shawn stood in the doorway. "This is a stupid idea."

Mona lifted her brows at him. "Do you have a better idea?"

"Yeah." Shawn took a step back. "How about we don't do this at all and just wait him out."

"Is that really what you want to do?" Pierce pulled off his jacket as Zeke passed him a vest. "Wait for him to make another move?" He fastened it into place before reaching for one of the two coats hanging on the rack next to the door. "The last move he made was to blow up two houses. Do you want to risk what he might do next?"

Especially now that he knew Amelia was on Alaskan Security property. There was no telling what Anthony might do to try to get to her.

Pierce turned to Mona, swinging the coat around her.

"I have coats of my own." She didn't try to stop him as he buttoned her up.

"This will make it more difficult for anyone attempting to take aim." He tried not to consider the possibility.

Mona was right. These men would keep her safe at any cost.

No matter what, she would be fine.

Pierce pulled on a tailored coat that hid the added bulk of the vest, but would still allow a

274

decent amount of movement should the need arise.

Zeke held out a pistol. He took it and tucked it into the back of his pants.

Mona held out her hand.

"Not today, Monster. Maybe next time."

Her eyes went wide. "Are you kidding me?" She turned to Pierce. "What was the point in training me if I can't carry?"

"The point was to make sure you could keep yourself safe when we weren't there to do it for you." He grabbed the front of her coat and pulled her close. "I adore you, but the last thing I need is you shooting Anthony the second he appears."

"Isn't that the whole point of this? To get rid of him?"

Not giving Mona a gun was clearly the correct decision. "We are going to be in a public area, Love. That means the rules are different and we have to play by them." He leaned in. "I will teach you the all the rules later and then you may carry whenever you wish."

"You're going to regret this if I'm the only one who has the chance to kill him."

"I don't doubt for a second that if you have the chance to kill him you will do anything it takes to make that happen, Love." He smiled. "And I will happily clean the mess up."

"Time to get moving." Shawn stood in the hall, arms crossed with a deep frown on his face. Heidi was at his side, a matching frown on her face as she eyed Mona.

Her gaze turned to Peirce. "I will literally murder you if she gets hurt."

"I'll allow it." Pierce moved right past them, Mona tucked tight into his side.

They went out the front where a single SUV sat idling.

"It's red." Mona's eyes skimmed down the side of the vehicle as he led her to the passenger's side. "Really red."

"There are times to hide and there are times to be seen." He opened the door and waited while she slid into place. "You wish to be seen, correct?"

"Seems like." Mona grabbed the belt.

Pierce caught her hand. "If you put that on, I need you to be prepared to immediately take it off, understand?"

Her gaze went to the buckle in her hand. Mona straightened a little in her seat, giving him a small nod as she pulled it across her body and clicked it into place.

The ways this day could go wrong were too many to count.

But the chance that it could go right outweighed them all.

He'd been living his life for someone else for so long.

Made every decision based on what it could provide another person.

And Amelia's safety was worth all of it.

But now that the chance to finally live for himself was within reach, the minutes couldn't pass fast enough.

Pierce climbed into the driver's seat and immediately backed out of the space.

"Aren't you going to buckle up?"

"If the need arises I will have other things to deal with, Love. When every second counts, none of them can be wasted releasing a seat belt."

"But what if we wreck?" Mona shifted a little in her seat. "What if your head hits the windshield?"

Pierce stopped the car at the gate and turned to face her. "Do you want me to turn around? We don't have to do this."

Now that he'd finally warmed to the idea it felt like the only option they had, but he would abandon it for her in a heartbeat.

Mona glared at him. "No, I don't want you to turn around." The indignation in her voice was fantastic. She turned to face out the front. "Let's go." Her eyes barely slid his way. "But if that face of yours gets messed up because you're not wearing your seatbelt—"

"You can remind me of it every day until I die." Pierce reached out the open window to punch in the code to open the gate. "Which I intend to be many, many days away."

He pulled through the gate and onto the road leading to headquarters. Alaskan Security sat at the back of a commercial section of Fairbanks, meaning the unlined roads around it were usually quiet and traffic-free.

Mona scanned their surroundings as he drove.

"I'm sorry you haven't been able to see much of my home." He reached for her hand, lacing his fingers with hers. "I promise to take you anywhere you wish to go when this is over."

"Even if that's tomorrow?" She dipped her head as she took in the buildings lining her side of the street.

"Absolutely." He would love nothing more than for this to all be over tomorrow.

His life finally free of the cloud that muffled out the sun for so long.

Pierce lifted their joined hands to his mouth, brushing a kiss over Mona's skin. "Where would you like to go first?"

"Hawaii." Her answer was immediate.

"Have you been to Hawaii?"

"No." She pulled her eyes from the window and finally looked his way. "Have you?"

"I have not." He rested their hands on his thigh as downtown Fairbanks came into view. "It will be one of many firsts we experience together."

Her gaze was wary as it lingered on the side of his face. "Where are we going now?"

"That is a surprise." He'd known immediately where he would take her. It was an easy decision, one that served their purpose of wanting to be seen, as well as offering him the chance to replace some of what she sacrificed to come here.

"As long as it's heated." Mona's face scrunched up as she eyed the thermostat display. "Does that say negative twelve?"

"Hawaii does sound nice about now, doesn't it?" He'd gotten used to Alaska over the years, but spending over half his life in Florida definitely gave him an affinity for warmer weather. He passed

Mona his phone. "What's the temperature there now?" He tipped his head her way as she woke it up. "The code is 1012."

Her thumb hovered over the screen a second before she typed it in and opened the weather app. "Eighty-three."

"Definitely not coat weather." He risked a glance her way. "I'm not averse to the idea of getting to see you in less clothing."

"Then you better hope your little friend comes out to play today." Mona switched his phone off and set it in the console between them. "Otherwise it might be a while before anyone gets to do anything."

"This can't drag on forever, Love. It has to end sometime."

"I would point out it's been thirteen years, but I'm pretty confident he's on a schedule now." Mona's gaze hung on a car sitting in the parking lot of a coffee shop.

"Don't look too long." Pierce avoided catching the car with his own eyes as he drove past the first of many sets of men watching them like hawks to ensure their safety. "You might show our hand."

Pierce pulled into the small lot in front of The Garden, the florist shop where Amelia worked until it was no longer safe for her to do. He immediately got out of the car, as if he had nothing to worry about.

Like he was any other man.

He opened Mona's door. She stared out at him with wide eyes and pale skin. "I think I'm going to throw up."

"Excellent." He held one hand out to her. "That will make this seem even more real."

She grabbed his hand in spite of her obvious fear.

It was what made her fearless.

Fearless didn't mean the absence of fear. It meant the ownership of it.

And Mona owned her fear. Stared it down while she pushed past it.

The shop was warm and humid when they walked in. Coolers lined with flowers of all shapes and sizes sat behind the counter where a young woman about Amelia's age stood with a smile. "Hi. Are you here to pick up an arrangement?"

"Not this time." Pierce offered her a polite smile. "We are here to look at your selection of indoor plants."

"That's cool." The girl pointed to a room off to one side. "They're all in there."

"Thank you." Pierce led Mona into the room. It immediately became clear where the moisture in the air originated. The windows of the space were streaked with condensation where the cold of the outside pulled the water free and collected it.

Mona stayed right with him as he wandered the rows of hanging baskets and potted foliage. Finally he turned to her. "Choose anything you'd like, Love. Whatever you want."

"Oh." She shook her head a little. "I'm fine. I pretty much kill anything green that comes within ten feet of me."

He looked from the plants surrounding them to the woman at his side. "But I thought you liked plants."

She shrugged. "I mean, they're fine. I don't hate them. I just can't really grow any of them."

"You don't love plants." He turned back to look at the row of snake plants. "Well then."

"Wait." Mona's lips hinted at a smile. "What made you think I liked plants?"

He rocked on his heels. "I thought I heard you mention being upset at having to give your plants away before moving here."

Mona snorted out a little laugh. "Eva bought me some fake plants as a joke." Mona pressed her lips together for a second, her eyes moving from one side to the other before coming back to him. "Um. Is that why there are suddenly five hundred plants in the offices?"

"It may be connected." He chuckled. "So do you prefer cut flowers then?"

Her head bobbed in a nod. "I do. Definitely."

"Then cut flowers it is." He wrapped one arm around her shoulders, savoring the final few moments of his first peek at what a normal life with Mona was going to be like.

Ten minutes later his peek was over.

Mona chose a beautiful arrangement of white roses, Peruvian lilies, spider mums, and button poms. She carried the packaged vase to the car, the blockage provided by the large arrangement making the squeeze in his chest relax a little.

The more difficult of a target she was to hit the better.

He tucked the flowers into the back floorboard before taking his seat and backing out of the lot.

"Now where?"

He met her eyes. "Now to the Post Office."

CHAPTER 22

SHE'D COME FULL-CIRCLE.

Started off considering barfing on Pierce's expensive coat.

And now she was right back where she began.

Considering barfing on Pierce's expensive coat.

"Do you think he's seen us?"

"Definitely." Pierce's posture was relaxed. He looked like they were simply out for an afternoon drive. Running errands before going home for a nice evening curled up on the couch watching television.

Instead they were potentially walking into an ambush.

"Do you think he'll be waiting for us?"

"I hope so." Pierce's dark eyes were constantly moving. Continuously scanning their surroundings as he drove.

Any other time she'd be enjoying the excursion. Her first trip off site since landing.

But even a pile of the most gorgeous flowers she'd ever seen couldn't make Mona feel any better.

This seemed like a good idea.

Probably still was.

The execution was the issue.

"I don't think I can act normal." Mona twisted her hands together, strangling the circulation from her fingers as she tried to find a way to make herself relax.

"Remember what you said?" Pierce's eyes came to hers for a short second. "We're all two people, Love. You just need to send in your other person."

She pursed her lips. "My other person hasn't been around as long as yours has."

"Then she should be primed and ready to make her first public appearance." He shot her a wink. "I would hate for Vincent to regret sending you out here."

She scoffed.

Pierce smiled. "I can assure you he will be watching."

Damn Vincent. He was probably sitting in his office hoping they would screw up so he could pretend he would have done better.

"And here we are." Pierce shifted the SUV into park.

Mona opened her door and immediately stepped out.

Screw Vincent. Screw GHOST.

They were the reason this was still happening. If they'd just come to Pierce when they first suspected what was going on it might have all been over by now.

"I wish you would wait for me to get your door." Pierce pulled her close, his mouth against her ear. "You need to stay at my side, Love. Anyone could have grabbed you just now and I'd hate to have to cover this lot with the blood of men too stupid to know who they're dealing with."

"Maybe you should have let me have a gun then." Mona kept her voice low. She leaned back to give him a smile. "Because I would be happy to do it.'

"Wicked woman." Pierce's arm stayed at her waist as he went to the door leading to the post office.

It was quiet, thank goodness. Only one person in line in front of them. An older woman shipping three packages. Mona tried her best not to look around, but it was strange to be somewhere she'd seen so many times on camera.

The line of PO Boxes was just to the right of the counter. There weren't a large number of them. Maybe a hundred tiny doors lined the small space.

And one of them was the box Chandler used her name and information to acquire.

"Our turn, Love." Pierce urged her forward.

Mona turned toward the man waiting for her to step up.

She'd never done anything like this. She'd never lied. Never tried to fake her way into or out of anything.

But was it really faking if her name was the one on the account?

No. Probably not.

Mona smiled. "Hello." She stepped up to the counter. "I'm hoping you can help me. I set up a PO Box when I first moved here and then as I unpacked I seem to have misplaced the keys. Is there a way I can possibly get another set?"

The man's expression was flat. "It's nine dollars for a new key."

"Not a problem." Pierce whipped out a credit card and held it between two fingers.

The man's eyes went to the card but he made no move to take it. "I'm gonna need to see your ID so I can look it up."

Well. Shit.

"Here you are, Love." Pierce reached into his inside pocket and pulled out her wallet.

They were going to have to have a conversation about personal boundaries.

And eavesdropping. But he might have already learned his lesson on that one. Especially considering he now had five hundred plants to water.

Mona pulled out her license and handed it over. The man didn't even glance up to check that she matched the photo.

That explained how Chandler was able to get the box in the first place. This guy didn't seem overly concerned with being the identity police.

He set her ID on the counter. "I'll be back."

Pierce picked her license up and handed it to her just as another person came into the small lobby. Mona kept her eyes on Pierce, which meant she was only able to see a little of the man as he walked up to take his place behind them.

He was big. Just as tall as Zeke, but definitely older. His short beard was peppered with grey.

Unfortunately that was all she could really make out since turning to get a better look wasn't an option.

"Here you go." The man slapped a key on the counter, immediately turning his attention to the man behind them. "Next."

Mona snagged the key. The number 67 was written on it in black sharpie.

Pierce pulled her close and started walking to the line of boxes. "Relax, Love. Everything's okay."

"Whatever." She went to the middle of the bank of metal doors, working her way to the right as the numbers went higher, stopping at the row containing box sixty-seven. She shoved the key in the lock and twisted, pulling the small door open.

She'd expected it to maybe be empty. Possibly contain a final envelope Chandler wasn't able to retrieve before his timely demise.

Instead it was completely full. A single taped box took up every bit of the small space.

Before she could reach for it, Pierce pulled the box free and snapped the door closed, twisting the lock back in place before turning and dragging her toward the door. As they walked by the large man who'd been in line behind them, Pierce passed off the box and kept going, moving faster with each passing second. By the time they went through the door he was almost at a run.

A van screeched to a stop just outside. The back door opened and two men jumped out and came running right at them.

Pierce tossed his keys at them as he continued running, hauling her along with him.

One of the men who jumped out was at her side. "Up and in."

Mona turned to Zeke just as he grabbed her and hefted her into the back of the van where another man was waiting to grab her and pull her in. Pierce jumped in behind her and the van started to move, doors still open as they raced out of the lot.

"What just happened?" Mona stared out the open doors as the man from the post office ran through the doors, ripping off his coat and the protective vest under it. He shoved the small box into the vest and threw it toward the empty lot next to the post office.

The explosion was barely audible over the roar of the engine as they raced away.

Zeke yanked the doors closed.

"Wait." Mona turned to Pierce. "What about him?" She pointed to the now-closed doors.

"Henry and Cade will come back in the SUV we took." Pierce glanced at Zeke. "Did anyone see him?"

"Nothing." Zeke's eyes went to one side, narrowing for a second before he turned toward the front. "Cade and Henry are moving."

"I'm not slowing down so they better move fast." Rico flew through a red light as they raced through town.

Mona fell against the side of the van. "He fucking tried to blow me up."

Zeke held his hands out. "You are the most confusing damn woman I've ever met."

Mona glared at him. "Then you haven't been paying attention."

"I pay attention." Zeke sounded a little defensive.

"Seems like you don't." She wanted to spar with someone. Take out the emotions clawing their way across her skin.

That mother fucker tried to explode her.

She turned to the man beside her. "Why aren't we going to go find him? We should blow all his shit up."

The man's brows lifted a little.

"Stop scaring the new guys." Zeke pointed at Mona. "They aren't used to you and your friends' bullshit."

"Bull—" Mona stood up. "I'll smack you again and then I'll let Heidi make you a dating profile that says you have a granny kink." She lifted a brow. "And I'll give them your real number."

The sound of laughing carried through the speaker on the dashboard.

"Wicked." Pierce sat across from her smiling.

A bump in the road sent her sailing, arms out as she tried to find something to stop her fall.

"Damn it." Zeke grabbed her, managing to roll her Pierce's way. "Thank God we didn't give her a gun."

She landed on Pierce's lap just as they crossed through the open gate and back onto Alaskan

Security property. He smiled down at her. "Did you enjoy your trip, Love?"

****

"I FOUND HIM." Harlow spun to face the screens at the front of the room.

Mona stared at the largest screen as the feed from the post office flashed across it. It was hard to breathe as she waited, watching for her first peek at Anthony Sanders.

After what felt like forever a man appeared on screen, carrying the same small box she watched explode in a vacant lot.

"He's skinny as hell." Heidi's lip curled, lifting one side of her nose up as she stared up at the video.

"What time was this?" Pierce sat on Mona's desk, watching along with them.

"This was yesterday." Harlow turned to her computer. "Around ten in the morning."

Bess chewed on the edge of a Saltine. "He could have killed people with that thing."

"I think that was the plan." Mona leaned forward, waiting for Anthony to return into the camera's view. "Right now he's putting the bomb in the PO Box."

"Was there a trigger connected to the door?" Heidi spent an hour researching homemade bombs, trying to narrow down what it was and where Anthony might have gotten it.

"There was a wire taped to the inside of the door. The box was wedged behind the door ledge so it pulled loose when Mona opened the door." Pierce reached back to find her hand with his.

290

A second later Anthony was back, slowly walking through the post office.

Like he hadn't just planted a bomb.

But he didn't simply walk out.

He paused, looking directly at the camera.

And then he smiled.

"Holy shit." Eva turned to Mona. "That dude's fucking crazy."

"I think that might be an understatement." Mona pressed her lips together as the cold reality of their situation hit her in the gut.

She'd seen the listings. She knew he wanted her dead.

Hell, she'd even played into it, covering herself in fake blood and bullet wounds.

For no reason, apparently.

But seeing his face. Witnessing the lengths Anthony was willing to go to in order to have all he wanted was disturbing.

It made her retroactively afraid. She shouldn't have gone out with Pierce. The only reason they were alive was because Pierce saw that little wire. It was something she would have missed on her own.

And would have been dead because of it.

"Are you able to find where he went after leaving the post office?" Pierce continued on with the conversation as if seeing the man who might take them all down wasn't a big deal.

"Can't we just make Vincent deal with this?" Her heart was racing. "I mean, he tried to blow up a government building." She pointed to the screen. "We have proof it was him. Can't we just give that to the government and let them handle it?"

Fear tightened Mona's throat and her chest, making it difficult to breathe.

To swallow.

Pierce slowly turned her way, his eyes focusing on her. In the blink of an eye he was up off her desk and pulling her from her seat. The walk down the hall was a blur as the potential of what might have happened spun through her mind.

She could be dead.

Pierce could be dead.

That personality-less man at the post office could be dead.

All because she thought making herself bait would be a great idea.

Pierce grabbed her around the waist and dropped her butt onto his desk. He leaned down to come eye-level with her, both his hands resting on the sides of her face.

"Breathe, Love."

She shook her head.

What in the hell was she thinking? She wasn't like Heidi and Eva and Harlow.

She couldn't be tough and confrontational and brave.

She was the girl who puked when someone was mad at her.

The girl who apologized for everything so no one would get upset with her.

The girl who tried to pacify everyone to avoid conflict.

Because conflict sucked.

"You must breathe." Pierce rested his head against hers. "It's okay to be afraid, Love. It doesn't change who you are."

"It is who I am." The truth almost hurt.

She'd tried so hard.

Thought she could do it.

His lips barely lifted. "You're right. It is who you are." His thumbs stroked over her skin. "But it's not all you are, remember? We're all two people. Who we are and who we want to be."

The soft slide of his touch relaxed her enough to finally get in a deep breath. "The person I want to be is in Hawaii."

Pierce laughed. "We can go find her as soon as this is all over." His expression sobered. "But we have to protect the people we love first."

She'd put Eva in danger by letting Chandler run wild. Let him ship her here where she was literally in the line of fire.

All because she wasn't strong enough to stand up to him. To tell him no.

Mona managed another deep breath. "Okay." She leaned into Pierce, resting her head on his shoulder as his arms came around her. "How do we do that?"

"I've got no fucking clue."

"Hey."

Mona lifted her head toward the open door where Heidi was practically bouncing in place.

"We found him."

Pierce turned, keeping one arm around Mona. "Where?"

"Not far from the townhouse Eva rented when she first came here." Heidi glanced down the hall as a few men ran past. "Rogue and Shadow are already gearing up."

Pierce's eyes came to hers.

She knew what he was going to say before he said it and it rolled her stomach.

"I have to go with them."

Mona reached out to run her hand down the vest he still wore over his dress shirt. "You should probably go get changed then."

It was not what she wanted to say. She wanted to knock him unconscious and tie him up and hide him away until all this was over.

"Go." She pointed to the door. "Get it over with."

He smiled at her. "I love you."

"I'm going to be so mad if that's the last thing you ever say to me."

He leaned into her ear as he unhooked his vest. "Then I will leave you with this." Pierce dropped the vest from his arms. "When I get back I plan to make good on my promise to stretch you across my bed." His voice went a little deeper. "And my intention to fill you until I can't fill you anymore."

He turned, pausing to pull the gun still tucked into his waistband free. He passed it to her. "Put this back in my top drawer."

And then he was gone, running down the hall with his vest hooked over one arm as he undid the buttons on his shirt.

"Damn it."

Mona stood up and rounded the desk, pulling open the drawer. It was padded with a spot specifically for the pistol in her hand.

She rolled her eyes.

Who had a drawer custom made for their gun?

Pierce did.

"Hey." Heidi was back at the door. "You ready?"

Mona shivered. "I'm going to run to my room and grab another sweater. I'll be back before they head out."

Mona closed the drawer and started toward the door. She stopped and glanced back at the bookcase leading to the hidden stairwell leading underground.

The tunnels hadn't worked well for her last time.

This time she was sticking with the halls.

CHAPTER 23

THE BUILDING WAS quiet as Mona hurried to her room on the second floor of the rooming house. As usual there were a couple of fully-geared men stationed in the hall outside her room.

She gave the men a wave. Both were from the team that was previously in charge of watching Amelia which meant she didn't know them, but they were men who Pierce trusted implicitly.

And that was good enough for her.

Mona swiped her badge and rushed into her suite, going straight for the bedroom. Something caught her eye as she went, slowing her pace.

The bowl of fruit from Pierce's kitchen was in the middle of her counter, fully stocked.

Including fresh bananas.

She couldn't help but laugh. The man bought out a flipping greenhouse thinking she liked plants.

Filled the building with them.

And now he brought down the fruit tray she perused every time she was in his kitchen.

Mona snagged a banana and hurried to her room, grabbing an oversized sweater, pulling it on over the clothes she already wore as an added layer.

Maybe it was nerves making her feel so cold.

Or maybe it was the fact that the temperature outside was well below zero.

Either way, she was much cozier in the added layer. Mona peeled the banana and tossed the skin in the trash on her way out the door.

She wanted to be back before they arrived at the address Heidi and Harlow found. Not that she could do anything but watch.

Her stomach turned as she swallowed down the bite of banana.

At least it wouldn't be terrible if it came back up.

Mona pulled open her door, forcing in another bite of banana just as the door next to hers opened. Helen jumped out, her eyes going up and down the hall.

"Is everything okay?" Mona glanced in the same direction.

"I can't find Amelia."

"What?" Mona turned to the men in the hall. "How could she have gotten past them?"

"I don't know." Helen pressed one hand to her head. "That girl's been testing the hell out of me lately."

"Maybe she just went to get something to eat." Mona was guilty of sneaking out of her room on a regular basis in search of snacks. No doubt a teenager would be just as bad about it.

"We would have seen her." One of the men shook his head. "No way did she get out."

"Well she's sure as hell not in there." Helen turned back to the room. "I've been through the whole damn thing and she's gone."

"I'll go check downstairs." The other man went to the stairs, disappearing down the well.

"Let's double check everything." The first man followed Helen inside her suite.

They had this, right?

Helen turned to Mona, her eyes pinched with worry.

Mona reluctantly followed her into the suite to help hunt down the missing teenager.

They went through the bedroom first, checking the closet, under the bed, and anywhere else a person might be able to hide away.

There weren't many options.

The man went out to the bathroom and tried to open the door.

It was locked.

He immediately put his shoulder into it, but the heavy door held tight to its steel frame.

"Use the key." Mona stepped in, going up on her toes to run one hand over the top of the frame.

She came up empty.

"She's probably got it in there with her." Helen banged on the door. "Amelia. Open this door right now."

"Hang on." Mona turned. "Let me go check the door on my room."

They were identical locks. The push button option that just needed a simple stab with a narrow key to pop the lock.

Her room had the exact same thing.

She rushed into her suite, going straight for the bathroom and retrieving her key before going back across the living room area and out to Helen's room. The other guard was back, holding the door open as she walked in, the key pinched between her fingers. The first guard popped the lock and shoved the door open. Helen went in, going straight to the shower and pulling back the curtain.

The room was empty.

"We'll find her." The first guard raced toward the door.

Suddenly they both froze, their eyes meeting. The first man turned to Mona and Helen. "Stay here. Keep looking."

"What?" Helen chased the men as they started to leave. "Where are you going?"

The men started to run, leaving Mona and Helen staring after them.

Helen turned to Mona. "What the fuck just happened?"

"I don't know. But we can go find out." She pointed into the room. "Grab your badge and let's go."

Helen hurried inside, immediately going to the small table just on the other side of the door. She leaned to look on the floor. "I swear it was right here." She turned to face Mona, her eyes wide. "Where all can that badge get you?"

"Probably almost anywhere." Mona turned to look toward the door leading to the tunnels.

Mother fucker. The damn tunnels.

"Come on." She ran toward the heavy steel door. "This is the only way she could have gone without being seen."

Even then, there should be some sign of her on camera. Hopefully someone from Intel was paying attention.

"Give me just a minute." Helen's voice carried out the open door. A second later she rushed out, running down the hall toward Mona.

Mona walked into the stairwell and immediately started down.

"Where does this go?" Helen stuck right with her, not even losing her breath as they took the stairs as fast as they could.

"To a set of underground tunnels that connect the buildings." Mona put her arm across Helen's chest the second they hit the bottom level.

A soft sound carried along the quiet concrete corridors.

Mona rested one finger against her lips and started to move, staying silent as she went so she could hear as much as possible.

Just like the night she snuck up on Harlow and Bobby.

Hopefully that was all the two instances had in common.

Helen was equally quiet as they moved along the tunnels, the older woman's movements making it clear Mona was not the only woman Pierce made sure was capable of handling herself.

The kachunk of a steel door sliding into place sent them moving faster down the corridor leading to the back garage area of the property.

Mona opened the door as quietly as possible, letting Helen go first before following her through and silently sliding the door into place. The lock at the top of the stairs beeped and a second later that door opened.

And closed.

"If this is her I'm going to kill her." Helen ran up the stairs, taking them two at a time.

Mona was panting by the time they reached the door. She swiped her badge and Helen busted through, clearly no longer worried about alerting Amelia to their pursuit.

Just as they stepped out the door at the end of the hall clicked closed.

"Shit." Mona started running toward it.

"Where does that go?" Helen ran along at her side.

"Outside." And outside was worse than the damn tunnels.

Mona swiped her badge across the lock.

The light stayed red.

She swiped it across the sensor again.

Still red.

"Why isn't it working?" Helen grabbed the card and tried it.

Red.

Mona turned to look back down the hall. It was silent. "The only reason would be if they locked the building down."

"Why would they lock the building down?" Helen's eyes snapped to Mona's before she could answer. "Shit." She shoved at the door. "We've got to get this open."

The exterior doors were solid steel in solid steel frames.

There was no way they were making it budge.

Mona glanced at the keypad.

She punched in one of Pierce's codes. If nothing else it might alert someone to this spot so they could get help.

Unless whatever led to the building being locked down was bad enough no one was paying attention to anything else.

The light flashed red.

Mona tried another.

Then another.

Finally she was out of door codes to try.

But she did have the code to his phone.

Mona held her breath as her finger moved over the buttons.

The light turned green.

She winced as she shoved the door open and the screaming cold immediately came for them. "He better fucking take me to Hawaii for this."

****

"IT PISSES ME off just fucking thinking about it." Brock eyed the townhouse where he and Eva first stayed when she came to Alaska. "Three fucking doors down the whole damn time."

"Probably not the whole time." Pierce moved along beside Brock, sticking close to the fence that ran along the back side of the property. "How

302

many damn addresses have we connected to him in all?"

"At least ten." Dutch's voice came through the piece in his ear.

"There you have it." Pierce leaned to peek around the edge of the planked privacy wood before moving again, closing in on the back door of the townhouse Intel was able to track Anthony's vehicle to by scouring the traffic feeds in the minutes after he planted the box at the post office.

"Any movement?" Dutch's words were tight.

"None at the front." Zeke and his team were positioned at the front of the building, slowly working their way in as Pierce and his team came in from the opposite direction.

"We've got nothing back here." Brock craned his neck from their most recent stopping point, scanning the back of the large building. "I can't tell if the lights are on inside or not."

"All our windows are covered." Zeke's words were hushed. "Seems like the one on the second level is a little brighter than the others."

The car Anthony drove from the post office was still parked in the driveway and there'd been no movement of anyone in or out since he'd walked in through the garage, closing the door behind him.

"Maybe we'll get lucky and he'll have done the hard work for us." Brock tipped his head and they were moving again, inching their way to the back sliding door.

"Wouldn't that be a happy discovery?" Abe tucked in tight to Brock's other side with Tyson right behind him.

The foursome moved again, ducking along as they pushed through the snow, not even trying to hide their tracks.

The plan was for Anthony to know they were there.

"We're in place." Zeke's team was set and ready to breach the front door.

Pierce scanned the last bit they had to cover. It was mid-day which meant many people were at work. "Clear."

They went quickly as they covered the final stretch. As they came to the backdoor it became obvious someone had been there recently.

"We've got prints." Brock cursed under his breath.

"They might not be his." Pierce scanned the multitude of prints in the snow for any sign they might have come from GHOST or possibly the local police. "We are most likely not the only people looking for him."

The four of them kept moving. Taking the time to inspect the prints wasn't an option until they were sure there wasn't someone waiting to pick them off from an upstairs window.

They split, two men backing against each side of the sliding door.

"Ready." Pierce held Brock's gaze as they listened to the sound of Zeke and the four men with him kicking down the front door and making entry before systematically clearing the townhouse.

With every 'clear' that came through the line his heart sank.

Abe huffed out a breath that clouded the air in front of him. "He's fucking gone."

"We don't know that yet." Pierce relaxed the hands gripping his pistol, forcing himself to focus. "He could still be here."

He had to be there. Had to be inside.

This had to end.

"Last room's locked." Zeke's voice was muffled as he directed one of the other men to kick it in.

Three solid thumps later the line went silent.

"Is he there?" Pierce looked at the men around him. "Zeke. Is he there?"

"I'm coming down to let you in."

Zeke's expression was grim as he looked out through the glass door, sliding it open. "He's not here."

"Fuck." Pierce shoved his way inside.

The place was a mess. Empty liquor bottles filled the sink and littered the counters. Bags of trash were lined along the kitchen wall.

"Not exactly how I expected a guy as rich as he is to live." Brock lifted the lid on a pizza box, grimacing at the molded contents.

"His whole world is unraveling." Zeke tipped his head to the back door. "It was unlocked."

"There's a ton of prints out there. It's impossible to tell who they might be from."

"He's probably been coming and going through the back to make it more difficult." Zeke leaned out the door to look around. "Doesn't look like there's any cameras back here."

"Son of a bitch." Pierce holstered his gun as he walked through the main floor.

"You are probably going to want to go upstairs." Zeke followed him through the open living room littered with trash and discarded clothing. "I think we've got a bigger problem than we initially thought."

"Bigger?" How the fuck could it be any bigger? They'd fucking lost Anthony again.

He'd burned down properties and planted bombs.

At the top of the steps Henry stood in an open doorway. The casing was splintered along the latch side. "This the one that was locked?"

Henry tipped his head in a nod, his eyes never leaving the room's interior.

Pierce stepped past him and into the small room and his stomach dropped.

"He's definitely been watching her." Zeke came in behind him, scanning the walls. "Looks like for a while."

"Jesus." Pierce wiped one hand down his face.

The walls of the room were plastered with photo after photo of Amelia. Some were clearly taken without her knowledge. Some were selfies.

"How did he get these?" Pierce walked to a picture that was much too grown up of a pose for a seventeen-year-old girl. He snatched it off the thumbtack holding it in place, ripping it down.

"Probably Instagram or something." Zeke pointed to a similar one. "He most likely just pulled them off the site and printed them out."

"She's not allowed to have social media." It was one of the rules he and Helen agreed to. A way to ensure Amelia's anonymity as long as possible.

Zeke snorted. "Have you ever met a seventeen-year-old girl?"

Pierce turned toward Zeke. "Shit."

"We've got an issue." Dutch was loud enough to catch everyone's attention at once.

"What's going on?" Pierce crumpled the photo and threw it to the floor as he walked back to the stairs.

"We just caught a suspicious-looking van on the traffic cam leading to headquarters."

"What's suspicious about it?" Pierce motioned to the rest of the men, sending them all out the front door to where their own van was waiting.

"You'd have to ask Harlow. She says it's suspicious. To me it looks like nothing."

"Then I'm asking Harlow. Why's it suspicious?"

"It just is." Harlow's explanation was technically lacking.

But it was more than enough for him.

It's why he started Intel in the first place. Men were black or white.

Women saw color.

"We're on our way back." Pierce jogged to the van, opening the back doors and making sure all his men were loaded before he climbed in after them.

"What the fuck is that?" Heidi's voice was higher pitched than usual. "Holy shit!"

All hell broke loose through the line in his ear.

"Dutch. What the fuck is happening?" Pierce grabbed the handle over his head as Rico floored the gas.

"Someone just came through the gate." Dutch's voice was tight, but still controlled as he barked out orders to the people around him.

He shouldn't have left. He should have stayed. Let Zeke handle this. "Get Mona someplace safe."

No one responded.

"Did you hear me? Get Mona someplace safe." He wasn't there to protect her. He needed someone else to make sure she was okay.

Dutch came back on the line, his words clipped. "Pierce, Mona's not in here."

CHAPTER 24

"GOD I HATE this place." Mona ran through the snow, following the footprints pressed into the perfect fall.

"You get used to it." Helen was definitely bionic.

The woman took stairs like she ran them daily and she wasn't acting even a little bothered by the snow and frigid air.

"I keep hearing that." Mona huffed along beside Helen, trying to keep up, hoping the exertion would at least keep her warm.

They were less than twenty yards from the building when the sound of an explosion came from the front of the property.

Mona reached for Helen just as Helen reached for her. They grabbed each other and fell to the ground, covering their heads as another explosion made the ground under them rumble.

"That's probably not good." Helen pushed to her feet. "Come on."

Mona lifted her head, watching Helen race toward the tree line.

"Shit." She couldn't just let Helen go on her own.

She fought her way up, dusting off the snow clinging to the thick weave of her sweater as she ran. Thank God she'd put on that second layer. Not that it stopped the cold, but it was better than nothing.

Mona scanned the space around her, trying to get her bearings. She was used to looking at the property through the security cameras, not in real life.

With the exception of the single time she'd ventured out here, and that wasn't of her own volition.

"I hope you ground the shit out of her when we find her." Mona managed to catch up to Helen, her breath coming in choppy bursts as the cold made her chest and lungs burn.

"You need to work out more." Helen was barely breathing hard as they reached the trees. "What's back here?"

"Trees and a fence." Mona stopped, grabbing Helen as a familiar sound carried through the air.

Helen's eyes widened. "It's a snowmobile."

Son of a bitch.

"Hurry." Mona pushed her numb legs to move faster. "They're trying to come get her."

"How do you know?"

"This isn't my first rodeo, Helen." Mona tried her best to use the trees around them for cover, but unfortunately the spindly branches didn't offer much in the way of camouflage. All they had were trunks, and there weren't nearly enough of those.

Probably by design.

At least the sun was dipping lower, offering a little more in the way of concealment.

Unfortunately that worked the same way for whoever they were following.

"This better be her." Mona clenched her teeth together to stop the chattering as she trudged on.

"It's her." Helen squinted in the dimming light. "She's trying to make me grey."

Mona glanced at her partner in crime. "You're already grey."

"What's that tell you?" Helen pointed toward the back of the property. "There. Come on."

Mona and Helen crept along, moving slower as they got closer to the fence peeking through the trees.

"Hurry." A feminine voice made them both stop.

Helen gave Mona a nod.

"I've almost got it." The deep voice of a man sent Helen moving again, leaving Mona to once again attempt to catch up with her.

"Helen's going to realize I'm gone and she's—"

Helen broke through the last of the trees. "She's going to come drag your ass back where it belongs."

Mona could only see Helen, the rest of the scene being blocked by a single large tree. Helen reached into the back of her pants and pulled out a pistol, pointing it at someone that Mona couldn't see. "Get away from her."

"I don't believe I will." The words were clear and concise. "I've done a lot to find her and keep her safe. You can believe I'm not stopping now."

Helen's brows lifted. "*You're* keeping her safe?" Helen snorted. "Come on, Mi-Mi. It's time to go back where you're supposed to be."

"I'm supposed to be with Anthony." Amelia's voice was that of every teenager who decided the life they had was unfair and stifling. "He's my uncle. He wants what's best for me."

"*I* want what's best for you."

"Is that why you never told me the truth about my parents? Why you let the man who killed my dad bring us here?" The pain in Amelia's words was palpable.

She'd been fed a diet of half-truths and all she wanted to hear from a man with a singular interest.

And it wasn't the safety of his niece.

The chances of Helen coaxing Amelia back were slim to none.

But so were the chances of Amelia leaving with Anthony. Pierce would never recover from it.

Which meant she had to do something.

Mona reached into the back of her pants, gripping the pistol she didn't put in its place like Pierce asked her to. Just as she was ready to step out, show Anthony he was outgunned, a shot made her jump back.

Helen's hand went to her chest as she staggered back a step.

Then another.

Then she fell to the snow.

"No!" Amelia's scream rang in Mona's ears as she stepped from behind the tree to kill the son of a bitch who was hell bent on ruining as many lives as possible.

All to feed his own need for power and vengeance.

Today vengeance belonged to one person and one person only.

Her.

Mona lifted her hand, eyes meeting Anthony's as Amelia fell to her knees beside Helen's unmoving body.

She gently squeezed the trigger as she exhaled, eyes open, stance tight.

Just like Zeke taught her.

She didn't hear either gun fire.

Hers.

Or Anthony's.

But this time when she hit the snow it didn't seem quite as cold.

****

"IT HIT THE building." Dutch's voice got louder. "I need everyone to the front of the building."

The sound of an explosion carried through the line as the van skidded through a turn and into the commercial area surrounding Alaskan Security's entrance.

"Victor's sending additional men." Heidi was all business. "They're on their way."

"They won't be here fast enough." Harlow was also shockingly calm. "I'm looking for her, Pierce."

He couldn't breathe. Couldn't think of anything besides Mona.

"She went to her room to get a sweater. Maybe she laid down or something and fell asleep."

"No way would she not be here." Eva said what he was thinking. "Something happened."

"Wait." Excitement edged Harlow's next words. "I just saw something on a back camera."

The van was silent as they closed in on the entrance, each man checking his gear, making sure they were ready for anything.

"It's prints. More than one set. In the snow leading to the back of the property just off the garage exit door.

The same place she'd been rescued from once before.

"I'll get us as close as I can." Rico didn't slow down as they passed the last crossroad.

The van was still burning where it was wedged into the front of the building as Rico raced through the destroyed gate. He flew around the building, tires spinning as the van skidded out, coming to a hard stop with the back end facing the back of the property.

The spot where Harlow caught sight of prints in the snow less than thirty seconds ago.

The doors opened and every man was out and running along the tracks in the snow. Pierce flew past them, his boots hitting the snow as fast as he could force them to go.

The sound of a single shot, narrowed his vision to a point as he ran.

Nothing else mattered. Not the business. Not the money. Nothing.

Mona was missing and he would move hell and earth to find her.

Bring her back to him whole and happy.

Give her all he promised.

All he had yet to promise.

A scream pierced the air followed by two, almost simultaneous shots.

One from a gun he recognized.

The screaming continued, the wail echoing through his head as he cut through the trees.

The shrieking wail dropped to a guttural cry.

The sight of three upright forms eased the squeeze in his chest.

He didn't realize he was yelling until they all turned his way, eyes wide. Helen was crouched down beside where Mona sat, the snow behind her tamped down and stained with blood.

Pierce fell to his knees in the snow. "What happened, Love?" He reached for her, needing to feel her against him.

To know she was safe.

Helen smacked his hands. "Don't you touch her." She twisted a bundle of fabric around Mona's upper arm, pulling it tight.

Mona's eyes were glassy as they met his. "There's a bullet in my arm." Her skin was pale.

Pierce pressed the button on his earpiece. "Call Eli. Tell him I'll be there in five minutes."

Zeke fell into the snow just beside Pierce. Mona's dilated pupils went to him. "I did what you said."

"I see that." Zeke took over for Helen, pulling what appeared to be a shirt loose from Mona's arm before ripping it into a smaller section and tying it back in place. "The twist will save your ass every time."

Mona's blue gaze went to a spot just beside the fence where a body laid in the snow. "He didn't twist."

"Good." Zeke stood up. "You carrying her or am I?"

"I can walk." Mona tried to stand.

"No walking until this bleeding is under control, Monster. We need to keep that heart rate down." Zeke picked up the pistol lying in the snow next to where Mona was sitting. He tipped his head toward the building, meeting Pierce's gaze. "Get her inside. I'll deal with this out here."

Pierce glanced up to where Amelia was crumpled next to Anthony, tears streaming down her face. "She's young. She doesn't understand what's happened. Don't give her a hard time."

Zeke scoffed. "What kind of asshole do you think I am?" He passed the pistol Pierce kept in his office to Abe as the rest of the men began taking over the scene.

"The kind who should probably be in charge of training every woman on staff." Pierce scooped Mona up, being careful not to bump her injured arm.

He turned to Helen. She was standing in nothing but a thin thermal shirt and a protective vest, working with the men around her as if she had been part of the team as long as they had.

He looked closer.

Her vest had a clear shot to the chest.

316

"He shot Helen." Mona's head fell to his shoulder and her eyes closed as her body started to shake. "I thought she was dead at first."

Pierce turned and began the slow trek to the building, trying to keep his steps as even as possible to avoid jostling Mona. "Helen doesn't strike me as the kind of woman who's easy to kill."

"She's a badass." Mona's voice was soft. "You should hire her."

"I technically already employ her." He skimmed his eyes down Mona's pallid face and walked a little faster, risking the rougher ride. "Stay with me, Love."

"I'm not going anywhere." Her eyes opened. "I probably should. I keep ending up in those damn woods." Her lips turned down. "And killing people."

"Some people need to be killed." Pierce finally reached the flatter snow of the paved drive.

"Amelia knew him."

"It would appear that way." He'd been so naïve to think he could keep Amelia under his thumb.

It was an unfair thing to do, even if it was for the best of reasons.

And now Mona was suffering because of the delusions of power he tried so hard to prove were not his.

And yet they were.

"I'm the one shot and you're the one frowning."

He glanced down to find her eyes were once again closed. "How do you know?"

"I just know."

"And I should point out that considering I intend for you to be the mother of my children, one would hope I'd frown under the circumstances."

The main door just beside the garages opened. "You dick." Heidi glared at him. "Did you not hear me yelling at you?" She went straight for Mona. "What in the hell happened, Monster?"

Mona's lips pressed together, her eyes starting to water.

"I'm here." Eva ran down the hall toward him, shoving a wheelchair in front of her. "Give her to us."

Pierce pulled Mona closer.

Eva's head tipped down. "I swear to God Pierce, I will do horrible things to you if you don't give me my best friend right now."

Harlow and Bess were right behind her with the rest of Intel hot on their heels.

He faced down the group of women.

All of them monsters.

"She's mine."

"I don't remember anyone telling you she wasn't." Eva pointed to the seat of the wheelchair. "Give her. Now."

"Put me down." Mona wiggled in his arms. "I want to go with them."

It was a blow to his ego. A stab to the part of him already aching from the events of the day.

But Pierce did as she asked, carefully setting Mona on her feet before helping her ease down in the chair. She was barely seated before Lennie dropped a thick blanket over her and the women whisked her away, leaving him standing alone.

"She's a hell of a girl."

His head snapped toward Helen. She stood right beside him, watching as the women disappeared around the corner leading to the main buildings. "She almost died today." His eyes dipped to the defect in Helen's vest. "*You* almost died today." He turned to look down the hall. "Because of me."

"How was this because of you?" Helen snorted out. "This all started because your sister had terrible taste in men and your parents would rather keep their place in the world than do what was best for their children."

She wasn't wrong. She also wasn't entirely correct. "It was my job to keep all of you safe."

"And you did." Helen started walking. "Mona and I were both ready as hell for today because of you." She turned toward him. "Are you coming? I want to go check on her. Make sure she's doing okay."

"She didn't want me." He tipped his head toward where Mona and the rest of Intel disappeared. "She wanted them."

Helen pointed his way. "She's got a safe place. A whole bunch of women who have her back no matter what." She smiled a little. "And I'm betting you had something to do with that too." She walked back his way, reaching out to pat his cheek. "You're a good boy, Pierce. Stop trying to convince yourself you're not."

Helen turned to walk away once more.

"Where's Amelia?"

Helen gave him a sad smile over one shoulder. "She's not real happy with me right now. I'm giving her a little space." She lifted her brows. "I think she likes your friend Vincent even less than me though, so at least there's that."

"Lovely." He could only imagine the delicacy Vincent would employ when dealing with a young girl. She was probably still sobbing.

Pierce turned and went back out into the cold. He needed to distract himself until Mona's kidnappers returned her.

Maybe he could pay a ransom.

Pierce pushed the button on his earpiece as he walked toward the edge of the lot. "Tell Intel I'll give them anything they want if they bring Mona back."

"I'm not telling them that. God only knows what they'll ask for." Dutch sounded slightly less agitated than he did earlier. "How you holding up?"

"Ask me in an hour." Pierce stopped as men started filtering through the trees. Vincent led the pack. Amelia was right behind him, her eyes narrowed in a scowl as she trudged through the snow in all white.

Vincent stopped as Amelia and the group of men who'd been tasked with protecting her for most of her life continued on. Her eyes stayed on the head of GHOST as she passed him, one hand lifting, middle finger high in the air as she walked toward the building.

Vincent didn't react. "Not sure if that was for you or me."

"I would guess both."

"My team is looking into the messages between them." Vincent crossed his arms. "Looks like she had a few secret social media accounts Anthony used to contact her."

"Thank you for looking into it."

"I'm not doing it out of the goodness of my heart, Pierce." Vincent smirked. "Don't want you to get the wrong idea about me."

A black SUV belonging to GHOST slowly came around the building toward them.

"It appears that Anthony was having a difficult time keeping the men he needed and his supply chain was falling apart." Vincent scanned the space as his men filtered in from the woods, two of them toting a body bag. "From what we can tell he was running low on cash and owed a number of people money." The SUV came to a stop right beside them and Vincent opened the passenger's door. "The kind of people you don't want to owe money."

"So he was planning to get his hands on her trust." It was what he thought all along.

"He had big goals, big balls, and a small brain." Vincent sat. "Not a good combination." He tipped his head at Pierce. "I'll be in touch."

Pierce watched Vincent drive away, the team from GHOST loading Anthony's body into a van before they followed the SUV out.

He turned back to the building.

It was over.

The driving force in his life was no longer the same.

And it was time to make good on all he promised.

CHAPTER 25

ELI STOOD IN the doorway to the small examination room. "I can't believe you all fit in here."

"Believe it." Eva pointed to Mona. "Fix her so we can get her back to Pierce before he burns the place down."

"I think he's got enough to occupy his time right now." Eli went to the bank of cabinets tucked in the corner and opened the top drawer, pulling out a pair of scissors before turning Mona's way. "They had to call the fire department to put the fire out."

"Is there a lot of damage?"

"Hard to tell." Eli perched on the edge of a rolling stool and came to her side. "Looks like the van was GPS controlled so at least there's only one body to deal with this time."

Mona frowned as Eli cut up the sleeve of one of her favorite sweaters.

Not because she was upset about the sweater, which she was.

But what kind of person killed a man and then mourned the loss of a favorite sweater?

"I think I'm a bad person." She turned away as Eli started to poke around at the wound still seeping blood.

Every face in the room scrunched up.

Heidi was the first to respond. "You are the least bad person I know."

"I don't feel bad for killing him." Mona's throat went tight. "Like last time."

Was she so afraid of confrontation that she was actually relieved when the situation was remedied?

Even if that was through the death of the person causing her the upset?

Eva moved in close, carefully wrapping one arm around her as she leaned her head against Mona's. "I wish I could have killed him for you."

Harlow was the next to pile on, her arms going around both Eva and Mona. "Me too."

Heidi and Lennie and the rest of the girls followed suit, crowding around Mona, working themselves into the lopsided group hug.

Heidi's face was right against hers. "You want me to call Vincent and have him bring Anthony back so we can all shoot him and not feel bad together?"

A laugh bubbled out, along with a single tear. "No." Mona sniffled, trying to wipe at her running eyes and nose. "Thanks though."

"So, while I appreciate the support you're giving her, I really need some space to work." Eli was crammed between Willa and Paige, his elbows tucked down as he tried to flush out her wound.

"Ugh." Heidi was the first to back away. She gave Mona's arm a once-over. "That definitely qualifies as shot though." She wiggled one finger in the direction of where Eli was now moving to the backside of her arm. "Bullet definitely went in."

Mona laughed a little as she turned toward Eli. "That's not going to scar is it?"

His eyes immediately jumped to hers and she laughed a little harder as Eva cackled beside her.

She relaxed her head back against the angled table, the clench in her belly easing. The girls all found places to stand or sit as Eli finished cleaning her out and stitching her up. Eva held her hand the whole time, sticking close.

Finally he finished and they loaded her back into the wheelchair.

"I really can walk."

"Yeah, but why?" Eva released the brakes and shoved her down the hall toward the hall that led to the main building. It was barely passable, but the fire was out and the remnants of the van were gone.

Shawn stood in the center of the space, directing men as they worked to get the damaged walls boarded up. Heidi grabbed his shirt, pulling him in for a quick kiss. "Where's Pierce?"

"I think he went to change." Shawn smiled softly at Mona. "How you feeling?"

"They won't let me walk."

"That sounds about right." He swatted Heidi on the butt. "Get her delivered and come back down here. I need you to make sure we can keep this place locked down."

She gave him a wink and a smile. "Kay."

Mona let them wheel her all the way to the stairs in the rooming building. Eva and Harlow actually discussed the possibility of carrying her, wheelchair and all up the steps.

"We're not doing that." Mona stood up. Her head was a little swimmy at first, but the feeling cleared as she went up the steps. "You guys should go check on Helen. Make sure she's okay." She turned to look back at the women who had as much to do with her finding a way to be better as she did. "I love you."

"Aw." Heidi's face crumpled a little. "We love you too, Monster."

She smiled. "I know."

Eva pointed up the stairs. "You better not fall. He'll kill us for letting you go on your own."

Mona turned and continued up the steps. "He'll get over himself."

Two of the men tasked with watching Amelia were parked outside her room as she passed. She took the final set of stairs to Pierce's back door, punching in the code she'd used to override the lockdown earlier to open it.

Someone had a secret skeleton key code.

Mona quietly opened the door. It was the way she'd entered and left every room for as long as she could remember, always trying to make sure no one was bothered by her arrival.

Pierce stood at the kitchen island, his dark eyes on her.

326

"Hello, Love." He lifted a glass from the top of the island and held it her way. "I thought maybe you could use this."

"I'm not going to turn it down."

He slowly came around the island, stopping in front of her.

She let her forehead fall to the center of his chest.

His arms were immediately around her, carefully avoiding her arm as he pulled her close.

She relaxed into him, letting him hold her weight. Letting him carry the load for just a minute.

Pierce held her, not saying a word, his head tucked close to hers.

Mona sniffed a little as she leaned back to look up at him. "My sweater's ruined."

****

THANK GOD SHE gave him something he could fix. A problem that had a simple solution.

"Come." He carefully tucked her into his side, grabbing the drink he made her on their way from the kitchen. He owed Shawn for giving him the heads-up Mona was on her way. It gave him a little time to prepare.

For her and for himself.

He led her down the hall and through his room to the bathroom. Classical music played softly through the speaker in the ceiling and a dozen candles bathed the room in a soft glow. The tub was filled with steaming water to warm any chill she might still be feeling.

It was all he could offer her.

Nowhere near enough.

327

Mona saved everything that mattered to him today. She saved Helen. She saved Amelia.

And she saved herself.

Pierce gently took the glass from her hand, setting it on the counter. "Let me help you." She watched him with soft eyes as he worked the mangled remnants of her still-damp sweater off her uninjured arm before slipping it over her head and carefully down the arm Eli bandaged.

Mona's eyes went to her next layer of clothing. "I ruined two sweaters."

"I will buy you all the sweaters you want, Love." He struggled with the second sweater. It was more fitted than the first, making the removal process a little trickier.

But eventually it was off.

He carefully helped her out of the rest of her clothes, tossing anything that might be salvaged into the hamper in the corner of the room, before helping Mona into the tub.

She lifted her bandaged arm, hooking it over one side to keep it from touching the water. Her body relaxed back against the slanted end, head going to rest against the towel he placed there. Her face rolled toward his. "Do you take many baths?"

He shook his head. "I do not."

Mona's eyes left his to roam the space. "You seem pretty versed in the best practices."

"I asked Helen."

Mona smiled. "I'm glad you'll get to be close to her again."

"Me too." Pierce took the washcloth he'd set out and dipped it below the water, wringing it out before squeezing on some body wash.

Mona's eyes went from the bottle in his hand to his face. "That's mine."

"It is." He passed her the cloth, tipping his head to the tray sitting on the corner ledge. "Everything you need should be there." Pierce watched as Mona carefully worked the soapy cloth over the blood-streaked skin of her arm and shoulder, being careful to avoid the bandage. "Is there anything else I can help you with?"

"I think I can manage."

He leaned in to press a kiss to her head. "Call if you need me."

"Is that an open-ended offer?" Mona leaned her head back as she ran the soap over her neck.

"Completely."

She smiled up at him. "Good."

Pierce went back to his bedroom, making sure the clothes he'd brought from Mona's room were clearly visible where they sat on the bed, before going out to the kitchen to finish their dinner.

He'd just pulled the chicken from the oven when Mona silently stepped into the room.

She was always so quiet.

But her presence was unmistakable.

"Do you feel better?"

"I'm warm." Mona's socked feet padded across the floor as she went to the box sitting in the center of the island. "What's this?"

"It's Amelia's. Things of hers from when she was young. Some of my sister's belongings." There were few things he'd brought from one life to the next, and most of them weren't his. "I should have given them to her long ago."

Mona pushed up on her toes to look inside. She reached in to pull out the single item that belonged to him, flipping open the front cover on the journal, her blue eyes skimming the page.

She turned to another page, this one halfway through the book.

Then another.

"You need to give her this now, Pierce." Her gaze met his. "She needs to know the truth and this is the best way to offer it to her."

"I'm not sure she has much interest in anything I have to say." He'd lost Amelia's trust before he ever had it, through wrong decisions and mistakes he never should have made.

"I don't disagree." Mona ran her hand down the front cover. "But this isn't coming from you. This is coming from a boy not so different from her."

The journal was his outlet over the years. All the times he wanted to tear down the world for what it made of him, what he hoped to keep it from making Amelia.

There were empty pages left. Many.

But he no longer needed them.

"I think we should take it to her now." Mona pressed her lips together as soon as the words were out, her eyes on him.

As if she almost regretted the offering of her thoughts.

It was an action that might have stung not too long ago. He would have thought she still struggled with her trust in him.

But that wasn't it.

Mona struggled with the same trust he did. Trust in herself.

"Then that's what we will do." He lifted the box from the counter. "Would you be so kind as to open the door?"

Mona punched in the code that overrode all others and followed him into the hall and down to the second floor where Amelia was alone in the suite next to Mona's.

Henry and Cade stood watch.

"Do you know how she got out earlier?" Mona held the journal tight to her chest.

"When you and Helen rushed in with Henry she was behind the door. The distraction of the van and the locked door of the bathroom created enough chaos for her to sneak away unnoticed." Pierce tipped his head at Henry. "How is she?"

He shrugged as he swiped his badge, unlocking the door. "It's hard to tell."

Pierce reached for the handle.

Mona immediately stepped in front of him. "You can't just barge into someone's room." She knocked on the door.

"What?" Amelia was definitely unhappy.

Mona quietly opened the door. "Amelia?" She waited. "May we come in?" She smiled softly. "Thank you."

He followed Mona into the suite. Amelia sat on the loveseat, knees tucked to her chest, face puffy and red, starting at them.

"We brought you something that might help you make sense of all that's happened." Mona pointed to the small peninsula between the kitchen and the living room. "Just set it there."

Pierce did as he was told, sliding the box into place.

Mona set the journal on the coffee table in front of Amelia. "Are you hungry?"

Amelia's eyes moved from the journal to Mona. She shook her head.

Mona nodded. "I can imagine." She gave Amelia another soft smile before turning, grabbing Pierce as she went.

"Wait." Amelia's voice was surprisingly strong.

They turned toward her.

She sniffed. "I'm a little hungry."

EPILOGUE

"ARE YOU HAPPY, Love?"

Mona squinted one eye open, peeking up at him. "If I'm unhappy right now then you should probably rethink your life choices."

"Never." Pierce ran his thumb across the set of rings on her hand. "And it's too late for you to rethink yours."

She laughed, stretching her legs so they reached a little more of the sun the umbrella over them was keeping at bay. "It's so warm."

"It is warm." Pierce laced his fingers with hers. "It's going to seem ten times colder when we go home."

"Maybe we should just stay here then." Mona's arm laced over the one he had wrapped across her chest.

"I'm positive we would end up on the less appealing end of a kidnapping if we attempted that." Pierce leaned to peek at where her head rested against his chest. "Your friends are quite partial to you."

It's why he couldn't marry her here, on the beach. There was no way all of Intel could leave Alaska at once, and there was also no way a single member of the team would be willing not to watch their friend get married.

But this honeymoon was the next best thing.

"I'm a little partial to them too." Her fingers stroked along the skin of his arm. "Thank you for being so good to them."

"They are good to me." Pierce owed the women of Intel not only his life, but the lives of everyone he loved.

Without them Mona would never have known she was the kind of woman who could handle anything.

She would never have known her strength.

All this time he believed he would be the one to show her. Build her up.

But it wasn't him.

Not by a long shot.

"They might like you a little." Mona smiled. "Just a little though."

"That's more than enough." Pierce ran his fingers across the pink scar still healing on her arm. "I have something for you."

Mona craned her neck to meet her eyes to his. "You didn't think Hawaii was enough?"

"Nothing is enough for you, Love." He reached into the pocket of his board shorts, pulling out the item that spent more time in his pocket than it did out of it.

But he no longer needed it. The reminder of the man he was smiled at him every morning and curled against him every night.

He was the kind of man who would do anything to deserve a woman like her.

And what she had in her hand was proof.

Pierce watched as Mona pulled the bow around it free and lifted the lid. One finger reached in to brush across the charm dangling from a gold chain. "I know what this is."

"Do you?" He thought he'd have to explain it.

He should have known better.

Mona pulled the jewelry from the box. "There aren't many men who would take a bullet for someone."

"I didn't take a bullet for someone, Love." He took the necklace and opened the latch, hooking it around her neck. "I took it for you."

"To be fair, I sort of took a bullet for you too." She glanced down at her arm. "And mine actually broke skin."

He laughed. "Hopefully I won't have the opportunity to return the favor."

Mona shifted around, easing up from where she was positioned between his legs on the two-person upholstered chaise. The fingers of one hand toyed with the gold-dipped bullet he pulled from the vest that saved both their lives. "I'm going to go see how Helen's doing."

"She's on the beach in Hawaii." Pierce reached for her, not quite ready to give up this moment. "She's fantastic."

"She's on the beach in Hawaii with a teenage girl who has more hormones than sense." Mona backed away. "A *beautiful* teenage girl with more hormones than sense." Mona curled one finger his way. "Come on, Mr. Pierce. Let's take a long walk on the beach together."

He pushed up from the chair they'd been on since breakfast. "Fine."

Mona's smile was wide as he caught up to her, taking her hand in his as they made their way down to the private bit of the ocean behind the duplex he'd reserved for the week. "I love it here." She leaned into him. "Don't you?"

"I love anywhere you are." The breeze was strong as they walked along the ocean's edge, heading toward the spot Amelia and Helen claimed as theirs the first day. Helen was in the water, flirting around with a group of men ten years younger than she was, having the time of her life.

Amelia was on a blanket, her dark hair tied up at the top of her head, the journal he gave her balanced on her lap as she wrote in it.

It turned out the empty pages weren't meant for him. They were meant for her.

She glanced up, her dark blue eyes meeting his. She lifted her hand in a little wave, offering a smile he hadn't seen as much of as he'd hoped.

"She'll be okay." Mona walked at his side. "Just like you are."

"I should have done so many things differently."

Mona's hand tightened in his. "Me too." She let out a long breath. "But all we can do is be better from now on."

"If you get any better I might not be able to handle it." Pierce kissed the side of her head as she laughed.

"Did I tell you I yelled at Vincent the other day?" She smiled, a wicked little gleam in her eye. "He was being an asshole to Heidi."

"He should watch himself. Shawn will peel all the skin from his body if he upsets her right now." Pierce stopped. "Speaking of Heidi and Shawn."

Mona lifted a brow at him.

"I hear these things happen in threes." Having Amelia and Helen with him gave him a taste of what it could be like.

To have a family. One that was happy and healthy and full of love and acceptance.

"Well if they happen in threes then you already missed your chance." Mona smiled up at him. "Maybe next time."

****